# THE
# SECRET AT
# NUMBER 7

# BECCA DAY

# THE SECRET AT NUMBER 7

bookouture

Published by Bookouture in 2025

An imprint of Storyfire Ltd.
Carmelite House
50 Victoria Embankment
London EC4Y 0DZ

www.bookouture.com

The authorised representative in the EEA is Hachette Ireland
8 Castlecourt Centre
Dublin 15 D15 XTP3
Ireland
(email: info@hbgi.ie)

Copyright © Becca Day, 2025

Becca Day has asserted her right to be identified as the author of this work.

All rights reserved. No part of this publication may be reproduced, stored in any retrieval system, or transmitted, in any form or by any means, electronic, mechanical, photocopying, recording or otherwise, without the prior written permission of the publishers.

ISBN: 978-1-80550-046-9
eBook ISBN: 978-1-80550-045-2

This book is a work of fiction. Names, characters, businesses, organizations, places and events other than those clearly in the public domain, are either the product of the author's imagination or are used fictitiously. Any resemblance to actual persons, living or dead, events or locales is entirely coincidental.

*For Dad, Debs, Isaac, and Molly,
who read every one of my books and are the reason I will never
write a steamy romance.*

# PROLOGUE
## MIRANDA

My house burned faster than I thought it would.

When the fire alarm first went off, when I realised what was happening, I thought I'd have longer. Longer to get out. Longer to call for help. Longer to rescue my belongings, the sentimental items that can never be replaced.

Now, I'm standing on the frigid grass, tiny pinpricks digging into the soles of my feet, watching my house burn, and all I can think about is how quickly everything happened. The flames spread with a hunger I wasn't prepared for. I can't move. I can't speak. My brain is completely void of anything other than the echo of the last thirty minutes looping in my mind.

I don't move when the neighbours flock onto our sleepy, quiet cul-de-sac, nor do I even flinch when the fire engines arrive in a blur of flashing blue and red. A door slams somewhere. Someone gasps. Someone else calls my name, but I can't react. I can only stare.

When a fireman rushes up to me and shouts over the roar and the commotion, 'Is everyone out of the house?' his words take too long to sink in. I'm frozen. Shut down. Non-responsive.

'Miss!' he shouts again. 'Is there anyone still inside?'

My lips part but no sound comes out. His question is too big. Too complicated.

My house burned faster than I thought it would.

The question is... did it burn fast enough?

# PART ONE

# ONE

One Month Earlier

Of all the houses on Herring Row, ours is the best.

That might sound like I'm bragging, but it's objectively true. It's on the very end of the cul-de-sac, which means it gets the least amount of traffic. No one comes this far down the curving lane unless they're visiting our house, which means it's blissfully quiet. And while the other honey-hued Cotswold stone houses all face each other, with their bay windows ensuring the residents either have to have their curtains closed, or accept the fact that the house opposite will always be able to see what they're watching on TV, our house faces the road. Nobody can see in, but we can see out.

I say we. My husband, Lee, is not the type to watch the neighbours out the window and snoop on what they're up to. I am. I can't help it. I find other people's lives fascinating. Always have. When I'm sitting on the train and everyone has their heads buried in their phones, I'm glancing at each of them individually, trying to guess where they're coming from, where they're headed, what might have happened to them earlier that day. Even when I was a teenager, I'd make up stories in my head about the people I'd met, probably giving them vastly more exciting existences than their realities. I am a people watcher, and there is nothing quite like getting up in the morning, sitting by my bay window with a cup of coffee, and getting a good look at what the other residents of Herring Row are up to. It's human nature, isn't it? Natural curiosity. No different to scrolling through someone's Instagram feed. Anyone who says they don't like a good nosy is lying to themselves.

Except now, of course, I don't even have to look out of the window. I have a new gadget, one that was not purchased for people-watching purposes, but that I have discovered does a marvellous job. When Lee first suggested getting a video doorbell, I wasn't sure. I'm not the best with technology, and I can only just about manage my laptop and the few apps I have on my phone, but once I realised I could watch what my neighbours are doing without risking being spotted snooping out of the window, I was an instant convert.

It's addictive. The motion alerts pop up on my phone at all hours, a tiny thrill each time. A delivery driver at number twelve. The dog from number nine slipping its lead again. I watch them all. And that's exactly what I'm doing when Lee approaches with a steaming cup of tea for me. He places it on the table next to me and peers over my shoulder at my phone.

'What are you doing?'

'What?'

I flinch like I'm a naughty child that's been caught by their parent. I tilt the screen slightly, as if that might somehow hide the evidence.

'Are you watching through the doorbell?'

'No.'

'Yes, you are. You're *spying* on them.'

'I'm not spying. I'm just... interested.'

Lee shakes his head and walks back to the kitchen. I fight

the urge to defend myself further. But there's no point. He's right, I am spying. But can he really blame me after everything we've been through?

I'm watching the newest residents of Herring Row as they unload boxes from their rented van, trying to get a sense of the kind of people that are going to be living next door to us at number seven. From what I can see from the somewhat grainy footage on the app, the wife is pretty and well dressed, with neat brunette hair pulled back into a bun. Her husband is well dressed, too.

I bet they're lawyers. They look like lawyers. The kind of people who drink red wine on weeknights and have a subscription to *The Times*. They have nice possessions, I can tell that much. She seems particularly nervous as the movers carry a marble-topped coffee table from the van to the front door. I wonder if it's an antique. She looks like the kind of person who would get her furniture from an antique store. There's not a hint of IKEA in that moving van.

'What does spying mean, Mummy?' my son, Mason, says, not taking his eyes off the weird toy unboxing video he's watching on the tablet.

I catch Lee's eye and he stifles a laugh. He finds it amusing when I have to navigate these little moral dilemmas.

'Um... it just means keeping an eye on someone. Like when I check on you at night to make sure you're not just *pretending* to be asleep.' I jab my fingers into his side and tickle him, and he lets out that belly laugh that he always does when he's being tickled. His little face goes bright red, and he wriggles under my hands. When he laughs and scrunches up his face it's the only time he looks a bit like me. He's the spitting image of Lee, all dark hair and dark eyes, while I'm blonde with eyes that are sometimes blue and sometimes green, depending on the light. My genes didn't even try.

When he's stopped chuckling, he looks back at his video and says, 'Who are you keeping an eye on now?'

'Our new neighbours.'

This is enough to bring his eyes away from the screen. He peers out of the window, leaning over the arm of the chair and very nearly knocking over my tea in the process.

See? Natural human curiosity.

'Maybe once they've finished getting all the boxes out of the van we can go over and say hi,' I suggest.

Mason frowns. 'Why?'

'Well, so we can meet them. Maybe we could give them something to say welcome. What do you think they'd like?'

'Um...' He screws his little face up as he thinks. His tongue pokes out, a sure sign he's taking the question very seriously. 'A Death Star Lego kit.'

I laugh. 'I think that's more what you'd like, mister. What about some tea and biscuits?'

'Can I have a biscuit?'

And just like that, all thoughts of our new neighbours are gone. He skips into the kitchen and it's not long before I hear 'but Mummy said I could have one!' followed by Lee's exasperated sigh.

The new neighbours have a lot of stuff, and it takes a while to unload everything. I finish my tea, then head up to the bedroom to pull out one of the gift baskets I have stashed away on the top shelf. Lee always mocks me for keeping them, so I'm thrilled each time I get to show him that they do come in handy sometimes. I deposit a box of teabags and two packs of biscuits into the basket, then pull my jacket and shoes on.

'Lee, I'm just popping across to say hello to the new neighbours!' I call. 'I won't be long.'

Lee appears in the doorway.

'Aren't you going to let them settle in first?'

I ponder this for a moment, thinking back to our first day on Herring Row. We hadn't even finished unloading our moving van when the wives and girlfriends of the road showed up with our welcome basket. It had been slightly overwhelming, their cheerful smiles and small talk. But I had appreciated the gesture. It had made this place feel like home faster than I'd expected. It was worlds away from what I had been used to when we lived in the city; I remember the first time I saw a neighbour knocking on our door just for a chat, I thought someone had died.

'One of the best things about this street is how friendly everybody is,' I say. 'Shouldn't their first day here reflect that?'

Lee knows it's a rhetorical question as he doesn't even try to respond. I get that he doesn't understand the way I am sometimes, but that's just where we're different people. He's content to just exist in a place. I need to belong.

I flash him a smile and make my way onto the street. Priya, the neighbour to the left of our house, the one who's directly opposite the new people, has clearly been watching like me, because she's outside in seconds. Her cardigan is barely on, as if she hadn't planned to come outside, but couldn't resist. Priya's in her mid-thirties but carries herself with the energy of someone who's never quite grown up, in the best possible way. Her wild curls are loose today, bouncing as she trots down her garden path in fluffy slippers that definitely weren't made for public appearances. She lives for moments like this. A new arrival, a fresh story to speculate over, and ideally a handsome man to bat her lashes at. She's warm, magnetic, and utterly unapologetic about her love of gossip and a good flirt.

'Hey,' she says, depositing a bottle of Prosecco into my basket. 'You're so predictable. If ever I receive anything from you that's not in a basket, I'll die of shock.'

'Gift baskets are good. They allow you to give a selection of items, you can tailor each one to each occasion, and they look—'

'It's fine. I'm glad you're predictable. Means I never have to worry about buying one anymore.'

I smirk at Priya and glance over her shoulder. Our neighbours Ellen and Beth are making their way over to us. I always think they look a bit like Tweedledee and Tweedledum when they walk together. They both have similar mousy hair, but Ellen is short and curvy while Beth is so tall and gangly she looks as if a puff of wind might blow her over. Ellen holds a small potted plant in her hand and Beth has what looks like a block of cheese. I'm not sure when I became the gift basket lady, but I'm not mad about it.

'Don't you go introducing yourselves without us!' Beth calls. They join us and place their items in the basket too, making it suddenly heavy and in danger of snapping at the handle. The lucky newcomers are going to have a welcome party of four. Of these women, Priya is the one I'm closest to. She's the most down to earth of the ladies of Herring Row. She doesn't try to pretend she's someone that she's not. If she doesn't like you, she won't fake it. If she does, she'll defend you to the death.

'Come on then,' I say, holding the basket from the bottom in an attempt to stop it breaking, and head towards number seven.

The front door is still wide open, no doubt to allow easy access to the moving van. Ellen presses the doorbell and it chimes through the house, but Priya being Priya sticks her head straight in through the open door.

'Woah,' she murmurs.

Before I can see what Priya is so fascinated by, Ellen and Beth bustle forward to crane their necks over Priya's shoulders, completely blocking my view.

And then they both gasp.

# TWO

'What? What is it?'

I stand on my tiptoes, trying to see over the wall of women, but before I can get a good look, they quickly retreat as a man comes to the door.

I blink.

He definitely did not look like this on the video doorbell. Sure, I could see he was good-looking. Tall, dark, and handsome vibes. But what the angle and distance and grainy footage didn't manage to pick up was his eyes. They're intense. Melt into a puddle intense. And now that he's standing right in front of me, close enough that I can see the faintest hint of stubble along his jaw, I suddenly forget how to speak.

I think the other women feel the same way because we all just stare at him for a moment, captivated. He raises an eyebrow and looks back at us, expectantly.

'Um, hi,' he says.

God, even his voice is sexy.

Ellen is the first to shake herself from her trance. She holds out her hand, pasting her signature red-lipped grin onto her face. 'Hi, welcome to Herring Row!'

'Thanks.'

He shakes her hand, and the rest of us take the opportunity to stop staring at him like he's a piece of meat. I tear my eyes away and focus instead on the basket.

'We brought you a little welcome gift,' I say, nodding at the basket just in case it wasn't totally obvious what gift I'm talking about.

'Thanks,' he says again.

A man of very few words, it would seem.

He doesn't take the basket so I continue to stand cradling it like a lemon, wondering whether I should just place it on the floor or not. There's an awkward silence.

'Whereabouts have you moved from?' Beth asks after a moment.

'Surrey.'

'Oh, lovely.'

Awkward silence.

We turn to Priya, hoping she might rescue this encounter.

After taking a second to consider her play, she says, 'Where's the Mrs? Maybe she'll appreciate the gift basket.'

Good job, Priya. If kindness isn't working, resort to shaming the handsome new guy.

'She's a bit busy at the...' he begins, but before he can say anything else, the woman I watched through the camera appears beside him.

If I thought the video doorbell did him a disservice, it's nothing compared to her. She looks like one of those women in fragrance adverts: a pure picture of elegance. Standing together, side by side, they are almost intimidating. She's wearing workout clothes with a couple of paint splodges on the knee, her hair tied back in a casual ponytail, and yet somehow, she looks ready to walk a runway. They belong on a yacht in the Maldives or something. I can feel Beth and Ellen straightening their postures beside me, as if standing a little taller might somehow close the attractiveness gap.

'Oh!' the woman says, clocking the welcome basket. 'That's so incredibly kind of you!'

Relieved to have someone to hand it to, I hold it out eagerly. 'Just a small something to say welcome.'

She takes the basket from my hands with effortless grace, her fingers barely grazing mine, but somehow even her touch feels elegant. 'Thank you so much.' She turns to her husband and grins. 'See, I told you what kind of street this would be.'

'We're very friendly here,' Beth says. 'It's safe, too. The kind of place where people still leave spare keys under their doormats.'

I let out a small laugh, though something about the comment irks me. I'm not sure sharing that little titbit with what are, essentially, two strangers, is the best idea. But this couple seem nice. I'm sure it's just my anxiety playing up.

'I'm Miranda,' I say. 'My family and I live right next door, in that house over there. And this is Priya, Ellen, and Beth.'

They all grin and wave as I say each of their names.

'So lovely to meet you all. I'm Anna, Anna Coles, and this is my husband, Fraser.'

Anna places a hand on Fraser's chest and rests her head on his shoulder. I kind of expect this to be the moment that Fraser also tells us how nice it is to meet us, but he doesn't.

'Would you like to come in?' Anna says, stepping to one side. 'It's a big old mess, I'm afraid, with moving and all. But I have the kettle set up for a cup of tea!'

I'm about to say that we wouldn't want to impose, but Priya has already barged her way inside. We follow, careful not to make eye contact with Fraser, and then I understand the girls' shocked reactions.

These guys are *rich*. Fancy, luxury, sofa-probably-cost-more-than-our-entire-house levels of rich. I also notice that there is very little sign of the 'big old mess' that Anna was referencing. The boxes that have yet to be unpacked are stacked neatly along one wall, and everything else looks tidy and orderly. I make the executive decision here and now that Anna is not coming round to my house any time soon. I may only have the one child, but with the mess he makes you'd think I have four sets of triplets running under my feet.

I shift awkwardly from foot to foot, taking it all in. There's a slight chill in the air, but it's hard to tell if it's because of the grandeur, or just the way these two carry themselves.

'So, what do you guys do?' Priya says, giving voice to what we're all thinking.

'I'm a doctor.' Anna moves over to one of the open boxes entitled 'Photographs' and pulls out a frame. She hands it to Priya and the rest of us crane over her shoulder to see. It's a photo of Anna in her uniform, holding up a certificate of accreditation for specialisation in sleep disorders from the Royal College of Physicians. She looks so poised, so effortlessly accomplished. It's the kind of photo you see framed on the wall of an expensive clinic.

'And Fraser,' Anna continues, 'is VP at Orbital Solutions Group.'

At this, Fraser shoots her a glare, like she's said something she absolutely shouldn't have done. Perhaps he doesn't want strangers knowing where he works. Not that he needs to worry. I haven't the faintest clue what Orbital Solutions Group is, or what Fraser actually does for a living, and I'm not about to ask him.

'What about you, Miranda?'

I quickly look away from Fraser to see Anna smiling at me.

'What about me?'

'What do you do?'

'Oh.' I blush, dropping my gaze. 'I'm not working right now. I used to be a hairdresser, but not so much since I had my son—'

'Except for me,' Ellen says. 'She does my hair.'

I nod, though I'm not sure dying Ellen's roots can count as working since she's never offered to pay me.

'Oh, wonderful! I said to Fraser one of the first things I need to do this weekend is scout out the best hairdressers and nail salons in the area.' Anna smiles. 'Maybe you could do mine?'

I nod again, words seemingly escaping me. I'm not quite sure how to react. Anna and Fraser seem like totally opposite people. She's warm and bubbly and hasn't stopped smiling since we arrived, and he's... I don't know. There's a weird air about him. Like he wants us out of his house right this second.

I nudge Priya with my elbow. Fraser is probably just not in the mood for this, I reason. Moving is stressful, tiring, and I'm sure he's eager to crack on and get unpacked without having to deal with three strange women in his house.

'Well, it's lovely to meet you,' I say. 'We should probably get back.'

Anna moves to escort us all to the door. 'Would you like to come round for dinner tomorrow evening? Fraser is a terrific cook.'

'Ah, I wish I could. I'm visiting my daughter at university. Sorry,' Beth says.

Ellen and Priya both shake their heads. 'And we're at a Taylor Swift concert. Another time, definitely.'

Anna looks momentarily stung. She turns to me. 'What about you, Miranda? Your husband and son are welcome too, of course.'

'Oh, I don't want to put you out. You've only just moved in...'

'Don't be silly. I adore company. Please come. The men can chat about whatever it is men talk about, and we can have a girly natter.'

She grins at me, as if she's already decided that this is what's happening.

'Okay, if you're sure…'

'Perfect. Let's say five o'clock? Thank you again so much for popping in, ladies. I'm looking forward to getting to know you all properly.'

She opens the door and we all bundle back out onto the driveway.

'Tea round mine then, girls?' Beth says. I know what that's code for. That's code for, 'let's go to my house and discuss the newcomers and agree whether we like them or not.' I consider this for a second: whether I think Anna and Fraser are going to fit as neatly into Herring Row as we did when we first arrived here. Anna will, definitely. She's extremely likeable and I can already tell the other women are keen to get her out for a couple of drinks. But Fraser, I'm not so sure about.

I shake my head, dismissing the thought for now. But as I glance back at their house to wave goodbye to Anna, I notice it. The way Fraser is looking at her.

He doesn't just look angry.

He looks furious.

# THREE

'Dinner?' Lee raises his eyebrows as he places a plate in the dishwasher. 'Already? Don't they want to get properly moved in, first?'

'I said that. But she seemed to really want us round there, though.' I peer through the window at the side of their house.

'What are they like?' Lee's words snap me out of my thoughts.

'Hm?'

'The new neighbours. What sort of people are they?'

'She seems really nice. She's a doctor. House-proud, by the looks of it. And friendly.' I glance back out the window.

'What's wrong?' Lee says.

'Nothing. I just get a weird vibe from him.'

'What kind of weird vibe?'

'I don't know, he just seemed to really not want us there.'

'Well, give the man a break, Miranda.' Lee resumes loading the dishwasher. 'He probably *didn't* want you there. I remember when everyone came over when we moved in here. God, I was so annoyed that you invited them in.'

'You didn't tell me you were annoyed!'

'Well, no, because it wasn't a big deal in the grand scheme of things, and I wasn't about to cause an argument over nothing. But it was the last thing we needed with an entire house worth of stuff needing to be unpacked.'

I pass Lee the final plate and he closes the door of the dishwasher. He's probably right. I'm sure on Saturday when we go round to dinner, Fraser will be in a much better mood. Yet, throughout the evening, I can't get the way Fraser looked at Anna out of my head. Lee may have gotten annoyed at me when I invited people in on our first day here, but I don't think he's *ever* looked at me quite like that. As soon as Anna had mentioned dinner, Fraser's entire body had tensed, shoulders rigid, hands balled into fists. His eyes, dark and unblinking, were fixed on her like he could pin her to the spot, and I could have sworn it made the air around us suddenly colder, sharper.

I'm still thinking about it come nighttime. Lee is already snoring beside me, but I'm lying awake, as I often do, staring at the ceiling. The insomnia still hasn't worn off since we moved here. I thought it would. I thought living on a safe, suburban street in the Cotswolds at the end of a sleepy cul-de-sac would help me to sleep better at night, safe in the knowledge that we're far less likely to have a break-in here than when we lived in London.

Our home in the city, our first home, was a basement. The front door was at the bottom of a set of stone steps, and the only window looked out at the brick wall of that stairwell. As such, we never had visitors. Even the postman struggled to find us sometimes. But that's what you get when you live in London on one salary and have a newborn to pay for. A whole lot of not much with an extra helping of mould.

We wouldn't have stayed there for long anyway. I was ready to move out the second I moved in. Lee would often come home from work to me insisting that I take him through the various houses I'd found on listing sites before he'd even had a chance to take off his shoes. I had Rightmove permanently open on my phone, refreshing it like someone waiting for a life-changing email. When the break-in happened, I think he knew he wouldn't be able to pacify me much longer.

I hope I never feel terror like it again. You always wonder, don't you? What you'd do in that kind of situation. I always thought I'd be one extreme or the other, either waking Lee up and cowering under the duvet while he goes to investigate, or picking up the guitar and swinging it ninja-like at whoever dares to enter my property. Turns out, I was neither of those people. I didn't do anything when I heard someone breaking into our home. I just froze. And listened.

I wanted to wake Lee up. I wanted to shake him and screech that there was someone in the flat. But my limbs wouldn't move. It was like I was locked in a straightjacket, arms pinned to my sides, body glued to the mattress. Even breathing became a struggle.

It was Lee who eventually woke up on his own to the sound of something being dropped in the kitchen. He thought I was asleep. I watched him as he flung himself out of the bed and raced out of the bedroom. I heard the commotion as he attacked the intruder, knocking him unconscious from behind. I listened as he went in to check on Mason before phoning the police.

And still I lay there. Frozen. Too afraid to move, too ashamed to scream. My body had betrayed me. I've since learned, in my years of attending therapy sessions in a vain attempt to recover from the incident, that it's actually a real thing.

'While fight or flight are the common responses to danger that you hear about,' my therapist said in one of our earliest sessions, 'there are more and more reports of what we call a freeze response. This is when a person feels a level of stress so strong that they become unable to flee or fight the threat, and instead, shut down.'

This never made me feel any better. The fact that it's becoming more common brings me no sense of comfort at all. In fact, it makes me feel worse, because it means that it might not be a one-off. The question rolls around in my head every single night. If something else happened, if some danger reared its ugly head and threatened my family, would I be as useless as I was that night? What kind of mother can't even protect her own family? Even having the video doorbell hasn't been enough to settle my anxious thoughts. I'll lie here, and I'll think that I can hear something, maybe a creak of a pipe or the clatter of something blowing over in the wind outside, but in my mind it's the front door opening.

That, beyond my general nosy tendencies, is why I watch. That's why I like to know exactly who is on this street at any one time. That is why the way that Fraser looked at Anna is troubling me so much.

It's then that I hear it. Voices coming from outside.

I turn my head on the pillow towards the open window and listen hard. At first, I think it might be people outside on the street. Perhaps a couple who've had one too many and got lost down our cul-de-sac. But as I listen, the voices get louder and angrier. I swallow, sucking in a slow breath, and swivel my body out of the bed. My toes touch the plush carpet and I focus on it, on how the pile feels against the soles of my feet. That's what my therapist told me to do, to concentrate on my senses as a way of helping to slow my heart rate and prevent the freeze response. My knees click as I stand and move over to the window. I push it open further and lean out, listening.

The voices are coming from Anna and Fraser's house. It's a warm summer evening, so their window is open a crack too. I squeeze my eyes shut, blocking out everything except their voices, trying to make out the words. But it's useless. The sound is too muffled. All I can tell is that they're arguing. My heart hammers. I have a nagging feeling that this isn't just a spat. Something is wrong.

I open my eyes and my breath catches. They're there. Both of them. In the window. I jolt to one side, hiding behind the wall, shaking. They didn't see me leaning out of the window trying to listen in on their argument. At least, I don't think they did. They were too busy shouting at each other. I desperately want to take another look but I don't dare look out of the window again. Instead, I drop to my knees and crawl across the carpet to retrieve my phone. The room lights up as I pick it up.

I rush to lower the brightness, glancing over at Lee. He's still snoring. I don't know how he does it. I turn back to my phone and navigate to the doorbell app. It's even more difficult to make out details on the feed when it's nighttime – the night vision makes everything grainier – but I can see enough. Anna and Fraser have moved. I can only see Anna's back now. I chew on my lip, willing them to take a step to the side so that I can see properly.

There's a sudden movement. It happens so fast I almost drop my phone.

'*Lee!*' I grab him by the shoulder. 'Lee, wake up!'

'What?'

He scrambles out of the bed so fast the duvet gets tangled around his legs. 'What's the matter?' He thinks there's another intruder.

'It's okay. It's nothing like that. I just...' I look back at my phone screen and squint. They're gone. 'You need to go check on Anna. Make sure she's okay.'

'Who's Anna?'

'The new neighbour. Next door. Just go and knock at the door, see if everything's okay.'

'What? Why?' He rubs his eyes, clearly experiencing a mixture of disorientation and annoyance at my having woken him up.

'I just want you to check that she's not hurt. She and Fraser were arguing and...' I trail off, not wanting to admit that I've been watching them through the doorbell. I replay what I saw in my mind, how Anna's arms flailed, how she stumbled back, and how Fraser slammed her against the wall.

How her head smashed so hard against the photo frame behind her that it smashed into pieces.

# FOUR

It's not ideal, is it? Going round to someone's house for dinner having sent your husband round at 1 a.m. the night before to knock on their door to check if the wife is okay after a big argument. I can't imagine how it must have looked to them. So paranoid. So intrusive.

I had expected the invitation to be recalled. I've been checking the doorbell app all day, thinking that at any moment Anna will knock and deliver some made-up excuse for why we're no longer welcome at dinner. But she never came. Nor did Fraser. The clock ticked on and now it's ten minutes before we're due round there. I want the ground to swallow me whole.

Lee is annoyed at me too. It took a fair bit of nagging last night for him to sleepily put his coat and shoes on and drag himself outside. I watched through the doorbell as he knocked at their door, as he waited, getting increasingly annoyed, as Fraser and Anna came to the door. I couldn't hear their conversation, I had to wait for Lee to come back to tell me what was said. Apparently, yes, they'd had an argument – the stress of moving had just gotten to them – and yes, they're both absolutely fine. They apologised wholeheartedly for waking us up, promising it won't happen again, and that was that. Apparently, I woke Lee up and embarrassed him, and myself, in front of our new neighbours for no reason.

I tilt my head sheepishly towards Lee as he faffs with the front of his hair in the mirror.

'You okay?' I ask.

'Mm-hmm.'

I look down at Mason and do the same with his hair. They look so alike, Mason and Lee, and they have the same dark hair. It's so thick you have to gel it, or it sticks up at all angles.

'No, you're not.'

'Just drop it, Miranda.'

'I just want to make sure you're okay.'

Lee slams one hand on the console table. 'Well, I'm *not*. I'm not okay. I'm tired from being woken up for no good reason and not being able to get back to sleep until 4 a.m., and I'm about to go to a dinner that I don't want to go to, sitting there in forced conversation with a couple who I barely know, save for rudely interrupting their argument, all because *you* just can't help yourself.'

Mason tenses underneath my hand. He hates it when we raise our voices at each other. Lee drops his gaze from me to his son, and his stern face softens.

'Come on,' he says, grabbing the house keys from the key box. 'Let's get this over with.'


I'm not sure what sort of welcome we're going to get as we wait for the door to be answered. The seconds stretch uncomfortably, and my stomach churns with the possibility that they're deliberately ignoring the doorbell.

The house looms quietly in front of us. It's weird. I've walked past this house so many times without even really noticing it, but tonight there's an odd air about it. The climbing rose that frames the bay window, usually charming in the summer daylight, makes everything a little darker, a little more closed off. The front door, sage green with a brass knocker in the shape of a deer, stays stubbornly shut. For a moment I think maybe they had just assumed we wouldn't show after last night, and we're about to have an awful moment where we realise that we are uninvited after all.

I glance at Lee, but he doesn't meet my eye, instead shifting his weight impatiently. His jaw is tight, his hands shoved deep into his pockets, his telltale signs of irritation. It's a shame. Under any other circumstance I'd be planning on jumping his bones tonight after Mason goes to bed. Lee doesn't often wear a shirt anymore, not since he changed jobs, and I'd forgotten how good he looks in one. His sleeves are rolled up, showing off his toned arms, my favourite thing about him. But it's safe to say that the frustration on his face is a bit of a mood killer.

'Maybe they're not home,' he mutters, ever hopeful that we can go back to our own house.

I sigh, fully expecting to never hear the end of this. What I don't expect, however, is for Anna to answer the door at that very moment, all smiles, as if nothing at all happened last night.

'I'm so glad you're here!' she says, stepping to one side to let us pass. Apparently, the casual ponytail and sportswear she wore yesterday did her an injustice. Tonight, all made up with straightened hair and a red lip, she looks even more incredible, if that's even possible.

I hesitate. 'Hi, Anna, are we still good to come over?'

'Of course! Fraser's in the kitchen. Dinner is nearly served. Please, come in.'

Lee and I exchange a glance, before nudging Mason into the house ahead of us – an unwilling sacrifice.

'Hi, little man.' Anna crouches down in front of him, perfectly manicured hands on her knees. 'My name's Anna. What's yours?'

He looks at me, asking for approval. I've always drilled into him the importance of not giving away personal details to people he doesn't know. Lee says I'm going to end up making him as scared of the world as I am, but it's just good parenting to ensure your kid knows not to talk to strangers, as far as I'm concerned.

I nod at him with a smile.

'Mason,' he says quietly.

'Well, Mason,' Anna says. 'Do you like football?'

Lee ruffles Mason's hair, and I resist the temptation to smooth it down. 'Taking you for tryouts next week, aren't I, bud?'

'Yeah. Dad says I'd make a good goalie.'

'Does he now?' Anna gestures towards the living room. 'Fraser set up his Xbox knowing you were coming. It's got the new football game on it if you fancy it?'

Once more Mason looks up at me, this time with pleading in his eyes.

'Can I, Mum?'

'Go on. Take your shoes off. And say thank you to Anna.'

'Thanks, Anna.'

Before I can say anything else his trainers are flung to one side and he's disappeared into the living room, all nervousness about being around new people abandoned. I pick up his shoes and place them neatly together, before taking off my own. The house is spotless and I'm not sure having my perpetually clumsy child loose amongst the expensive antiques is the best idea.

'Drink?' Anna says, leading us to the dining room.

I blink. It takes me a moment to absorb what I'm looking at. A lace runner lines the table, with tall candles dotted along the centre, and each seat has its own perfectly laid-out place setting, complete with linen napkins and crystal wine glasses. Even Mason's place has been thoughtfully set out, with kid-sized cutlery and a plastic cup. The effect is straight out of a magazine. Effortless, elegant, and completely at odds with the fact that they only moved in yesterday.

'When did you have time to do all of this?' I gape. My own dining table, by contrast, is currently buried under unopened post and random junk modelling that Mason insists on bringing home from school. I'm in utter disbelief that these people literally unpacked their things yesterday, and yet seem to have their lives more together than I ever have.

Anna at least has the decency to blush at her perfection.

'Last night. I'm a bit obsessive. I can't relax until I know the house is in order.'

I can only nod and smile. I can't relate in the slightest. I still have boxes from our last move shoved up in the loft, unopened.

We don't see Fraser at all in the lead-up to dinner. It's odd, really. This elaborate set-up, this big show of hospitality, and yet one half of the couple hosting us is nowhere to be seen. Anna fills up both our glasses and we lounge in the living room while Mason plays on the Xbox, and if you'd told me it was just the four of us in the house, I'd have believed it. I can tell Lee is feeling as awkward about it as I am, but Anna doesn't seem to have noticed at all.

'There are some bizarre sleep issues that people have come to me with in the past,' she says, after explaining exactly what kind of doctor she is. 'I had this one patient who lived alone but was convinced they could hear someone snoring in the room next door every night. They thought the place was haunted. The polysomnography revealed she was actually making the noises herself during her REM sleep phase.'

'Wow, that's... freaky,' I say. The hairs on my arms prickle, but not from the story. What I don't say is that it isn't half as freaky as her husband not even coming to say hello to the guests he's cooking dinner for, but I just think it. I glance over at Lee, who must sense what I'm thinking because he shakes his head, a warning look in his eyes.

The words spill out of me, nonetheless.

'Is Fraser okay in the kitchen?'

I might be imagining things, my paranoia kicking in as it often does, but I'm sure that at the mention of Fraser's name there is a physical shift in Anna. She seems to shrink slightly, like a balloon losing a bit of its air. It's only for a second, though. As quickly as it appears it's replaced with her usual cheerful self.

'Oh yes. He loves cooking. He'll be like a kid in a sweet shop in there.'

'Does he need a hand at all? I feel bad sitting out here while he slaves away for us...'

'He's fine. Really.'

After that there's another awkward pause. Lee shakes his head, silently telling me 'I told you so'. I pick at the skin around my fingernails, a nervous habit, and watch the flashing lights of Mason's football game, searching for something to say to break the tension. The room feels too still, too quiet, despite the digital roar of the crowds on the screen. But how do you know what to say to someone you barely know?

Thankfully, Lee says the perfect ice-breaker instead. 'Shall I get us some more drinks?'

Anna looks up at him with the same relief that I feel. 'Of course, I'll do it. Same again?'

She takes our glasses and disappears into the dining room. I give Lee's hand a squeeze and ruffle Mason's hair, ruining my gelling work, before getting up to follow her.

She has her back to me as I enter the dining room, busying herself with the drinks cabinet. I move slowly to stand by her so that I don't startle her.

'Thank you again for having us,' I say, marvelling at her booze collection and wondering if I can rearrange one of my kitchen cupboards to make room for this kind of stock. Expensive bottles, neatly arranged, like everything else in this house. A curated display of perfection.

'My pleasure.'

She hands me my glass and smiles at me, her cheeks pink, before returning to the cabinet to make Lee's drink. I stare at her for a moment, at her effortless, put-together appearance, and think about what I saw last night. I don't care what Lee says. An argument caused by the stress of a moving day should not result in someone being smashed into a photo frame.

'I'm sorry we disturbed you last night,' I say quietly.

Anna looks confused at first, but then realisation dawns on her features and the pinkness of her cheeks increases. A shadow flickers across her face, there and gone in an instant.

'Really, don't worry about it. It's us who should apologise to *you*. You must be wondering what kind of awful couple has moved onto your street.'

'Not at all,' I say, though, if I'm honest, Anna's assumption is not entirely inaccurate. I chew on my bottom lip, unsure of how to phrase what it is I want to say. In the end, I opt for something simple. 'Are you okay?'

Anna looks at me. Her eyes are shining. 'He's a good man.' Her voice is strong, earnest, no hint of uncertainty in what she's saying. 'I promise. I'm fine. I really appreciate you looking out for me, though. It's nice to know I have a friend on the street.'

Her words are warm, but for some reason they leave me cold. I smile, not convinced. 'Take my phone number, will you? Text me if you ever need anything.'

And I really mean that. I don't know this woman well, but I know that the way her husband treats her is not okay. Situations like this can escalate quickly, and Anna shouldn't be alone, on a strange new street, without anyone looking out for her.

So, I suppose, that person will have to be me.

# FIVE

When Fraser finally joins us for dinner, the tension in the air is palpable.

He comes out of the kitchen with large plates balanced along his arms and Lee is quick to help him lay them out on the table. It's an assortment of Japanese food: tempura, ramen, gyoza, plus a few dishes I don't actually know the name of. Everything looks restaurant worthy. There are even chopsticks.

Mason pulls a face and I give him a discreet squeeze on the arm under the table to remind him of his manners. He's not a particularly adventurous eater. For him, the perfect banquet consists of chicken nuggets and lashings of ketchup.

'This looks great,' Lee says, placing the final plate down in the centre of the table. 'Thanks for doing all this for us. I'm Lee, by the way.' He holds out his hand to shake Fraser's, and I wait for the rudeness, for the moment that Lee will discover exactly what I meant when I tried to explain the weird vibe I got from this man.

But it doesn't come.

Instead Fraser smiles at Lee – the first smile I've ever seen of his – and shakes his hand warmly. 'Fraser. No problem at all, glad you could make it.'

Then he actually chuckles. *Chuckles*. He nods towards the food like he's the ultimate proud host.

'Help yourself. Don't let it go cold.'

My jaw drops as I watch the two of them settle into their seats and begin helping themselves to food. Did I imagine it? The coldness? The way he's barely acknowledged me? I don't get it. Where is the lack of eye contact? Where are the short answers?

Confused, I start to serve up some of the plainer food onto Mason's plate, before sorting my own.

'Sorry you had to spend all evening in the kitchen,' I say, twirling noodles onto my fork, not wanting to embarrass myself with attempting the chopsticks.

There's no response.

I glance at Fraser. His face is completely neutral, unreadable. He shovels a bite into his mouth, eyes fixed firmly on his plate as if I haven't spoken at all. Like I don't even exist. What the hell?

Before I can repeat what I said, Lee lets out a satisfied groan. 'Mate, this is delicious. Where did you learn to cook like this?'

Fraser's whole demeanour shifts. He looks up immediately, lighting up. 'I lived in Japan for four years,' he says, his tone switching back to warm and conversational. 'Made a promise to myself that I wouldn't leave without learning to cook a few recipes.'

Lee leans forward. 'No way! That's amazing. What took you out there?'

'Work, originally.' Fraser pauses to sip his drink. 'But I ended up getting involved in a local community centre project. Stayed a lot longer than I expected to. Met some brilliant people.'

I blink, gobsmacked. My eyes travel to Anna's, who is watching me sheepishly. At least she's picked up on it. Lee is apparently completely oblivious.

Lee lets out a low whistle. 'That's seriously cool. I've always wanted to go.'

'You should.' Fraser smiles. 'But be warned, you'll never find sushi that good again once you've had it fresh off a street stall in Kyoto.'

They're off after that. Lee shares a story about ordering what he thought was a light lunch in Thailand and getting a plate of crickets instead, while Fraser laughs and counters with a tale about being roped into a village karaoke contest after three too many shots. Lee nearly spits out his drink. Fraser claps a hand on his shoulder like they're old uni mates catching up. The two of them sit there chatting away about life in Japan and I have to stop myself from asking Fraser if his issue is specifically with me, or with women in general. Because one thing is suddenly, glaringly obvious – he's got no problem talking to my husband.

After fifteen minutes of being treated like wallpaper, I place my cutlery down with a soft clink, my appetite sapped. I'm not even bothering to make conversation anymore. What's the point?

'Could I please use your bathroom?'

My question is directed at Fraser, but he doesn't look at me. Of course he doesn't. That would require acknowledging my existence. Instead, it's Anna who answers.

'Of course. It's just down the hall, that way.'

I don't need the bathroom. I just need to get away from that table. Once in front of the sink I stare at my reflection in the mirror, shaking my head in disbelief. I desperately want to splash water in my face but I daren't, in case my make-up runs. I spent an obscene amount of time on it today. I'm usually a throw-a-sweeping-of-mascara-on-and-hope-for-the-best kind of person, but I wanted to at least attempt to match Anna's flawless beauty tonight. What a waste of time that was.

My phone vibrates in my pocket, and I pull it out to see a message from Priya.

*How's dinner going? I want all the goss.*

I pause for a moment, wondering how to describe the evening I'm having.

*The husband is still as weird as last time. Actually, weirder.*

*Weirder? How? OMG is he trying it on with you?*

I laugh at that.

*No. Very much the opposite. Hard to explain over message. Coffee tomorrow?*

Priya sends back a crying emoji and then a thumbs up emoji. I exhale, some of the tension in my shoulders loosening. I slip my phone back into my pocket. At least she and the other women were with me when we first met Fraser. They know what he was like then. Lee, on the other hand, must think I'm making it all up with how friendly Fraser's been with him tonight.

I flush the toilet and wash my hands, despite having not gone, and take a deep breath before venturing out of the bathroom. I don't want to go back to the dining room. Honestly, every instinct is telling me to take Mason, who has spent most of dinner time picking at the edges of his tempura, and go home. Leave Lee and his new bro to it.

Before I get to the dining room, however, I'm stopped by the photos on the wall. There's one of Fraser and Anna on their wedding day. It's a beautiful shot. They both look beside themselves with happiness, as, I suppose, you would expect in a wedding photo. Anna looks radiant, beaming at the camera, but it's Fraser's face that makes my stomach twist. He's looking down at her with an expression of pure adoration. I can't quite connect the man in the photo with the man sitting in the dining room. How does one go from that – gazing at his bride as if she's his whole world – to giving her what can only be described as a death stare for inviting someone over for dinner? And worse, how did he go from looking at her like that, to smashing her against a wall?

As I look at the photos, my gaze is pulled to the door beside them, open just a fraction. It's the home office, by the looks of it. I can just about see the corner of a desk. A heavy, dark wood thing. Sturdy. Imposing. I wonder, as I peer through the crack, what I might find if I were to have a good old rummage in that desk. Who is Fraser Coles, really?

I shouldn't go snooping. I know I shouldn't. That would be an outrageous invasion of privacy. But still, my eyes linger. Because the truth is, I need to know what kind of man Fraser really is.

It's not just idle curiosity. It's not even nosiness. It's fear. Rooted deep and coiled like a snake in my gut. Because ever since the break-in all those years ago, since the moment I realised how utterly vulnerable we are, I haven't trusted the quiet moments. The ones where nothing is overtly wrong, but something feels off. That's how it started that night, too.

Now we've got a new neighbour. One who is capable of hurting his wife. Maybe it's nothing. Maybe I misunderstood. But then again, maybe I didn't. And I'm a mother. It's my job to know if there's a threat on my doorstep.

My fingers find the door and push ever so gently. The hinges creak.

'What are you doing?'

I spin around so quickly my head spins. Panic floods my veins like ice water. It's Fraser. Fraser is here. Standing too close, blocking the hallway. He caught me looking into his office. No, no, no.

'Oh, I'm sorry, I was just...' Just what? Admiring the craftsmanship of your door? Taking a self-guided tour of your home? Excuses fly around in my head.

I momentarily consider trying to convince him I got lost on the way back from the bathroom and that I was opening the door because I thought it was the way back to the dining room, but even Mason would see through that half-baked lie. Fraser's brow lowers and his eyes narrow just enough to make my stomach twist. He's looking at me as if I'm something he needs to scrape off the bottom of his shoe. Or worse, like he's picturing peeling the skin clean off my face. A shudder travels down my spine, and I stare at him for a moment, my mouth opening and closing like a helpless goldfish. My cheeks burn with shame – and something colder, something deeper.

*Fear.*

I decide that there is no good excuse for what I am doing. Instead, I duck my head and scurry past him, back to my son. As I go, the sense of his eyes burning into the back of my neck feels like millions of tiny, hot pokers.

I need to get the hell out of this house as quickly as possible.

# SIX

Monday mornings are reserved for a post-school-run coffee at Priya's house, and on this particular morning I practically sprint from the school gates. I've been desperate to talk to Priya about the dinner.

She was 'poorly' yesterday, which in Priya terms means so hungover she couldn't face sunlight, let alone guests, so I haven't had anyone to offload to. I very nearly told the postman about the weird dinner we had with the odd couple who just moved in. That's how desperate I've been.

Bouncing on the balls of my feet, I press her doorbell. She opens the door almost instantly, buzzing with anticipation.

'Come in! Come in!' she practically shrieks, dragging me over the threshold by my sleeve. 'Tell me everything!'

I laugh, shaking myself free, then make my way to the kitchen cupboard and pull out the teabags. The routine is second nature now. I'm not sure at what point I became so familiar in Priya's house. It's at the point, now, where if I came in and waited for her to make a cup of tea for me, she'd probably tell me to get off my lazy bum and do it myself.

She's only a year younger than me but shows absolutely no

sign of wanting to settle down any time soon. At this point, she's dated so many of the men in this town it's hard to nip to the shop without bumping into one of her exes. Her relationships never last long, and I've given up trying to remember their names. Still, she's happy. Plus, it gives us something to talk about each week. Which guy had the audacity to text her again after ghosting? Who turned out to be a secret fruitcake?

Except, this week, we're not going to be talking about one of Priya's fellas. Oh no. We're both dying to discuss a different man. One with an unsettling stare and a wife who tiptoes around him like he might detonate.

Cups of tea in hands, we make our way to the bay window seat, perfectly situated so that we can look over at Anna and Fraser's house while we talk.

'So,' Priya prompts, 'what happened?'

'I think he nearly killed me.'

She chokes on her tea. 'What?'

'Well, possibly a slight exaggeration, but he wasn't happy with me, that's for sure. He caught me trying to snoop into his office.'

'Oh my God! Did he hurt you?'

'No, no. Nothing like that. It was just…' I shudder, remembering the moment, the way his eyes bored into me. 'Seriously, Priya. The way he looked at me…'

Priya's face drops a little, disappointed that the gossip isn't quite as juicy as she'd originally thought.

'So he didn't actually lay a hand on you? What did he say when he caught you snooping?'

'That's just it. He didn't really say *anything* to me all night. He spent the entire time before dinner was served in the kitchen. Didn't even pop his head out to say hello. And then it got even weirder. He was being perfectly friendly to Lee, but *only* to Lee. It was like he had a split personality or something.

The second I tried to talk to him he turned cold again. And he was the same way with Anna, too.'

My phone buzzes in my pocket. I pull it out and frown at the unknown number flashing up on my screen.

'Hello?' I say, fully expecting it to be someone trying to tell me I can get compensation for the supposed accident I had last week.

'Hi, Miranda.'

My jaw drops. Priya cocks her head inquisitively.

*It's Anna*, I mouth. Priya's eyes widen. She puts her tea down so that she can shimmy closer to me and eavesdrop.

'Miranda? Are you there?'

'Sorry, yes. I'm here. What's up?'

'I was just wondering if, and sorry if this is too last minute, but I wondered if you'd be able to do a cut and blow dry at some point today? Fraser and I are going out tonight and with the move I haven't had a chance to get my hair done for weeks.'

'Oh, today? I'm actually at Priya's right now. We usually go into town on a Monday.'

Priya shakes her head manically and mouths the words, *What are you doing?*

'Not to worry. Sorry, I knew it was a long shot.'

Before I can say anything else, Priya has launched herself towards the phone. 'You can come round if you want, Anna. Miranda can do your hair in my kitchen.'

I slap my hand to my forehead. Fantastic. Now Anna knows that Priya was listening in. The poor woman must feel like a zoo animal being gaped at and studied. Subtlety has never been Priya's strong suit.

'Sorry about that,' I say, nudging Priya away with my foot. 'Yes, you're welcome to join us at Priya's house. We're just drinking tea, and I can sip and snip at the same time.'

Anna laughs, an infectious, unashamed chuckle. 'Sip and

snip. That's funny. Sure, if you're positive you don't mind. Give me fifteen minutes and I'll be there.'

By the time I've nipped home to grab my hairdressing supplies, Anna is already at Priya's.

She's perched elegantly at the kitchen table with a cup of tea. Her hair is down, the first time I've seen it as such, and she looks even more put together with it flowing in straight, sleek lines over her shoulders. I'm a little intimidated at the thought of cutting the hair of someone who clearly takes immense pride in her appearance. She really is quite beautiful. I tuck a strand of my own hair behind my ear, as if that might help to improve my appearance a tad.

'Thank you so much for fitting me in,' Anna says with a beaming smile.

'No problem. It's a much more productive use of my time than what I would have been doing.'

Priya recoils. 'Hey. I take offence at that.'

I ignore her and place my hairdressing box on the table next to Anna. I take her hair in my hands, allowing the strands to run through my fingers. Silky. Weightless.

'Just a trim, today, is it?'

'Yes, please. No more than a couple of inches off. Fraser likes my long hair.'

Priya raises her eyebrows so high I can see them out of my peripheral vision. I pull a face at her to let her know she's not being subtle at all. I get it. I'm interested, too. But the last thing we want to do is scare Anna, which I feel we are dangerously close to doing.

'How are you finding the village?' I say, reckoning that discussing the move is probably a safe topic of conversation.

'It's beautiful. Just like a little ornament I had when I was growing up.'

I know the ones she means. The china houses they sell in the gift shops in town. They always make me think of my grandma's house rather than a modern home, but then again, Anna's house is filled with old knick-knacks that she's somehow managed to piece together to look purposeful and cohesive. Like a still-life painting come to life.

'Do you have any friends or family nearby?'

'No.' She shifts in her chair. 'We've moved around a fair bit. I've always struggled to make friends. Ones that last anyway.'

I find that very hard to believe. She comes across as so easy to talk to. Everything about her is sweet and personable. If anything, I'd have expected her to be the type of person getting invited to parties every weekend. But then again, that's adulthood, isn't it? I don't speak to any of the people I went to school with anymore. I wouldn't be friends with Priya, Ellen, or Beth if they didn't live on my street. Once you reach a certain age, it seems you have three choices when it comes to making friends: the people living on your street, the people you work with, or the school mums. Friends by proximity. Friends by convenience.

'Well, we're a riot to hang out with.' Priya grins, and Anna laughs.

'Thank you for being so welcoming. Really, you're so kind.' There's a sincerity to her voice. She looks up at me as she says that, her eyes shining as if she really, truly means it. Something tells me the offer of friendship means more to this woman than a few boozy nights out. Like she's not just grateful for the company, but for the sense of belonging.

'So,' Priya says, while I unpack the hairdressing gown from my box. 'How did you and Fraser meet?'

'It's... a long story. A little embarrassing, actually.'

Well, that was the wrong thing to say to someone like Priya. I can practically hear her heart rate increasing with excitement from here.

She leans in, poised for gossip. 'We can keep a secret. Can't we, Miranda?'

'Oh yes.' I nod emphatically, even though the idea of Priya keeping a secret is about as ludicrous as the thought of her dating the same guy for more than a month.

'Erm... Well, he was married before me. Actually, his wife and I went to yoga together. We hung out a bit. Anyway, I met Fraser through her and one thing led to another and, well, you know...'

The room falls awkwardly silent. I'm not sure how to respond to that. Priya, for once, is quiet too. I don't know Anna well enough to crack a joke, which would be my usual fallback, so instead I just focus on what I'm supposed to be doing.

'I'm just going to take your cardigan off so that I can get the gown on. It's a bit chunky.'

Everything happens very quickly. No sooner have I slid Anna's cardigan off her shoulders than she snatches it out of my hands and pulls it so high her head nearly disappears behind it.

'No! I... sorry!' She lowers the cardigan back down to her shoulders. 'I'll put the gown on in the bathroom, if that's okay.'

I nod wordlessly, handing the gown to her, and watch as she takes it into the downstairs loo. But it's too late.

I already saw the finger-shaped bruises on her arms.

## SEVEN

The next day, all I can think about is Anna as I sit at the breakfast table, nibbling toast opposite Lee and Mason, who are both making a right mess with their cereal. Milk dribbles down Mason's chin, and Lee is absentmindedly flicking cornflakes back into his bowl.

'I've been thinking...' I begin, fingering my toast.

Lee snorts. 'Uh-oh, that's never good.'

I throw a corner of crust at him, and it bounces off his forehead. Mason giggles, delighted by the sudden food fight potential.

'Sorry, sorry!' Lee says, hands up in surrender. 'What have you been thinking about?'

'What did you think about Fraser? When we were at dinner?'

Lee stops eating, his spoon hovering between his mouth and the bowl. 'He was a nice guy. Why?'

'I don't know.' I shrug and pick at the edge of my toast, causing it to crumble under my fingertips.

Lee would say he was nice. He didn't have the experience that I did. I want to mention the bruises, but can't with Mason listening in. I didn't tell Priya – that would have been a sure-fire way to get the tongues of every woman on the street wagging – but Lee isn't a gossip. He'd be able to give an unbiased view on what I saw, and what I should do about it.

But before I can say anything else, a text message flashes up on my phone. It's from Anna. Speak of the devil.

*Do you fancy doing something today? I've joined the members' club nearby and can bring a guest. We can go to the spa, maybe grab some lunch?*

I stare at the message, fingers hovering over the reply box, though I have absolutely no idea what I'm going to say. Members' club? There's only one around here. I looked at it out of pure curiosity when we first moved to the Cotswolds. It's certainly not cheap. But then, this is antique-loving Dr Anna we're talking about. She's not cheap either.

I re-read the text. A spa at a members' club sounds exactly the sort of thing that would make me feel painfully inferior. But I can't say no. For all I know, this is Anna's way of reaching out for help. She might be looking to confide in me. A safe space. This woman is beginning to become a friend, and I have a responsibility to try and help her if I can. Even if that's not the reason for her invite, I might get the chance to ask her about the bruises. Surely if we're going to the spa, she'll have her arms uncovered? But how do you approach something like that? There's no polite way to say, 'Hey, I noticed those suspicious bruises. Who put them there?'

'I think I'm going to go out with Anna today,' I say, typing out a response to her.

'Yeah? Good, she seems nice.'

'She's super nice!' Mason pipes up, cereal spraying out of his mouth. A soggy chunk lands on the table, and I wrinkle my nose. Mason's enthusiasm for Anna is not surprising. Anyone who lets him play Xbox and gives him lots of sugar is going to be a winner in his book.

No sooner have I sent my reply than another message pops through.

*Amazing! I'll drive if you'd like? Shall we meet at 10?*

After the school run, I rush around the house tidying up a bit, just in case she comes inside for any reason.

Our home isn't awful. It has its moments – like when the cushions are actually on the sofa instead of being used as fort walls – but immaculate has never been part of its identity. It's almost constantly in a state of disarray. I'll tidy, and, like magic, there will be another mess right behind me. I'm not quite sure how the boys manage it, but they do. It's their superpower. That, and making an entire week's worth of clothes appear in the washing basket overnight.

Once I've tidied, I decide to direct my attention to tidying myself. A spa. That means swimming costumes. And *that* means bare legs. I glance down at my calves and grimace. Hurrying into the bathroom, I pull out my razor. I don't have time to have a full shower, so I attempt to shave my legs by simply splashing water at my skin. Safe to say, by the time the process is finished, a few small trickles of blood are running down my shins. Perfect.

I'm just getting myself dressed in what I hope is appropriate for a members' club – a long floral dress with long sleeves that I actually purchased for a spring wedding and haven't worn since – when I spot movement outside the window. It's Anna and Fraser. I rush back to my wardrobe and grab my phone, navigating to the doorbell app. The screen flickers to life, showing a grainy image of them standing by their car. I wonder if the residents of Herring Row realise I do this? Spy at any given opportunity. That's the wonderful, and slightly scary, thing about the doorbell. There's no way anyone would know.

Fraser is dressed in a suit. Not just any suit. Charcoal grey, perfectly tailored. The kind that means business. I assume he's heading off to work. He looks mouth-wateringly good in it. I mean, he looked good before in his casual clothes, but the suit adds an extra something. Like a final, unnecessary flourish on an already well-wrapped gift.

I shake my head, reminding myself what a creep he is. What's that well-known saying? The devil doesn't come dressed in horns and a pitchfork, he comes as everything you've ever wanted. As I watch through the app, Fraser lowers his head and kisses Anna. I frown. Anna turned her head as he did it, making it land on her cheek as opposed to her lips. That was not the kiss of a loving happy couple. It was forced. Stilted. Awkward. A kiss given out of obligation rather than desire.

The more I see of this couple – the loving photos, the angry stares he gives her, the argument and bruises – the weirder things are getting. There's something more going on between them. And I'm about to spend a morning totally alone with Anna.

If ever there's a chance to get answers, this is it.

# EIGHT

Ten minutes later Fraser is gone, I'm sliding into Anna's car, and we're on our way.

I'm relieved we're going in Anna's Range Rover as opposed to my desperately-in-need-of-a-clean Polo, where the back seat is littered with crumbs, forgotten toys, and the faint scent of spilled juice that no amount of scrubbing seems to fully remove. And it feels a little less like I'm intruding on a world I don't belong in when we arrive in Anna's car.

I have no idea what to expect from this place. I've never been inside a private members' club, never even come close. Unless you can count walking past the VIP section of a nightclub, gated off by a big red rope and a couple of scary-looking bouncers. I'm imagining something intimidating, something exclusive in the worst way, but as soon as we pull into the car park and I spy the classic Cotswold landscape of fields dotted with sheep and thick hedgerows, I know it's not that sort of place. There's no grand lobby. No imposing desk. Just a scattering of timber-clad cabins, a cluster of fire pits, and a gravel path leading to a selection of rustic barns. Effortlessly thrown together – except, of course, it's all been meticulously designed to feel that way.

We hit the pool first. When we emerge from the changing room, I eye Anna's arms as subtly as I can, but I can't see the bruises. For a moment I wonder if I imagined them. Or if, perhaps, they weren't quite as bad as I had led myself to believe. But no. The more I consider those two possibilities, the more I'm absolutely sure of what I saw. Some things you just can't unsee.

Anna doesn't seem in the least bit fazed, considering how much she reacted to me taking her cardigan off yesterday. She slides into the water oozing confidence, though I do note that she sticks to the shallow end and never puts her top half under the water. 'I'd rather not get my hair wet,' she says when she sees me looking, and I smile and nod, though I think she can tell what I'm thinking. Hair can be dried. Make-up, on the other hand, is another story. The only answer that makes sense is that she's covered the bruises, and she doesn't want whatever she's used rubbing off in the water, and that, to me, tells me she's got something to hide.

The pool is like no other pool I've ever been in. I'm used to big, tiled rooms with talking sea creatures painted on the walls and screaming kids splashing in water that's so freezing cold it causes everyone's lips to turn a little bit blue. This pool is long and inviting, a deep slate-blue that stretches out to an outdoor section, where the warmth of the water and the cool crispness of the air cause steam to rise in delicate swirls. We make our way to this section. A few swimmers move languidly through the water, their strokes slow, unhurried, as though they have nowhere else to be, and they exist in an entirely different rhythm of life.

'Do you come to this sort of place often?' I say, trying not to stare.

'Well, you have to come fairly regularly to justify spending the money. My membership allows me to visit any of the clubs in the chain. There are loads of them. I used to go to the one in London at least once a week.'

I resist the urge to ask how much it costs.

'So' – Anna places both arms on the stone edge of the pool and rests there, gazing out over the green landscape – 'how long have you been married?'

I'm not sure why the question takes me by surprise. Priya and I asked about her marriage yesterday, after all. It's an innocuous enough question.

'Just over five years now.' I can't believe it's been that long. It makes sense when I think about it. I was pregnant with Mason when we decided to tie the knot. We would have done anyway, so it made sense to make things official before Lee 2.0 turned up. But even though I know how old our son is, our wedding still feels like yesterday.

'Are you still in the early wedded bliss then?' Anna says with a smile. 'Or are things starting to get a little... stale?'

This question really does take me by surprise. Anna is far more forward than I'd have the guts to be.

'Um.' I search for the right words. 'Well, you know how it is. Peaks and troughs.'

I hope to God she does know what it's like and I'm not just admitting that our sex life is a bit bland to someone who probably rattles their headboard every single night. Except, does she? From what I've seen, I wouldn't say her and Fraser's marriage is quite as rosy as it would initially seem.

Anna runs her fingers through the water, tracing little ripples along the surface. 'Relationships don't have to follow traditional rules,' she says. Her voice is thoughtful, far away, as if she's saying it more to herself than to me.

I tilt my head. 'What do you mean?'

'Oh, nothing. Just that people can be happy in all sorts of

arrangements. As long as you're happy, that's all that matters, right?'

Her words linger in the air between us, weighty, like there's something she's not saying outright. I nod in agreement, though I'm still not quite sure what she's getting at. Is she saying that my acceptance of our peaks and troughs is an arrangement? Isn't that just what marriage is after a while? I wonder if this is her attempt at segueing into talking about her own marriage. I jump on the opportunity.

'You and Fraser seem really happy,' I say, trying not to wince at how fake my voice sounds.

My words have the desired effect. Anna seems to shrink a little. I knew it. They're definitely not happy.

'At times,' she says quietly.

The question is right there, on the tip of my tongue. I grind my teeth together. Just *ask* her. Ask her about the bruises. But I can't seem to force it out.

'Do you have anyone to talk to?' I say instead. 'You know, if you're ever having a hard time?'

'Nope. That sounds really sad, doesn't it? I'm an only child and my parents have both passed away. I have a few cousins, but I haven't seen them since I was a kid. For a long time, it's just been me and Fraser.'

My heart aches for her. She's clearly lonely, and if there's ever a woman at risk of being trapped in an abusive marriage, it's one without a support system.

'You can always talk to me,' I offer.

Anna looks at me then, eyes shining. The corners of her mouth turn up and her cheeks turn pink. 'Thank you. I'm so glad I've met you.'

I return her smile, hoping that this might be it, I may have said enough for her to open up. But she doesn't. She just looks back at the view, sunlight hitting her face and making her look almost goddess-like. After a while we decide to move to the sauna, a glass-walled sanctuary perched at just the right angle to overlook the lake. We sit quietly for some time with eyes half closed, wrapped in a kind of blissful stillness, our skin flushed from the heat. It's glorious. I allow my head to drop back and can literally feel my muscles loosening.

'This is the closest thing I'll get to a holiday this year,' I say.

'You're not going to go away with Lee and Mason?' Anna asks, a note of surprise in her voice.

I snort. 'Holidays aren't really holidays when you've got kids.'

'No. No, I suppose not.'

I peek at Anna out of the corner of one eye. I want to ask if her and Fraser are planning on having children, but I know better than to ask that sort of question. You never know what someone's situation is, and the last thing I want to do is put my foot in it. Before I can think of something more appropriate to say, she sits up straight, her eyes locked on something outside the sauna.

'I think I'm probably at my limit for the heat. You?'

'Oh, um, yeah. Me too.' Actually, I wish I could stay in here forever, melting into the bench, letting the warmth press all my worries into the background. But I don't want her feeling like she has to stay in here longer than she feels comfortable.

'Great! Come on.' She hops up and leads me out of the sauna, eyes lit up. I follow her gaze to the plunge pool outside that's waiting ominously for the brave.

'No, no, no.' I try to back away, but she grabs my wrist, already grinning.

'Oh, come on,' she says, dragging me toward the edge. 'You'll feel *amazing* after. It's like a total body reset.'

'It's ice,' I point out, digging my heels into the wet stone. 'It's literally designed to make you suffer.'

Anna ignores me, already shimmying out of her towel, standing there like some smug wellness guru who has experience in this sort of masochism. She looks completely unbothered by the prospect of plunging into what is essentially a torture bath. I, on the other hand, am still wrapped in my towel, clutching it like a security blanket.

'Just go to your knees. Or dunk your face. That's what the Scandinavians do.'

'I'm not Scandinavian,' I point out.

'You could be.' She winks. 'You've got the bone structure for it.'

Before I can say anything in response to that, she yanks my towel away and shoves me forward. I have two choices: trip and die, or stumble straight in with all the grace of a collapsing deck chair.

I stumble in.

Cold isn't the right word. It's an onslaught. A brutal, merciless attack on every nerve ending. My brain immediately goes into full survival mode: heart hammering, breath vanishing, every inch of me screaming get out, get out, GET OUT.

I manage to squeak out a sound somewhere between a gasp and a curse, my arms flailing. 'Anna, I swear to...'

'Breathe!' she calls cheerfully from the side. 'Deep breaths. It gets better after ten seconds.'

Lies. The longest ten seconds of my life drag on, my skin prickling, my legs threatening to give up on me entirely. My lungs refuse to cooperate, taking in tiny, useless sips of air. I can't even feel my toes. Are they still attached? Unclear.

But I'm in now. And it's not just Anna watching me. Two other women are spying from the pool. Gritting my teeth, I sink in up to my shoulders.

Anna claps like a proud mother. 'Yes! Look at you. Ice queen!'

I let out a half laugh. It's more a strangled wheeze, but the fact that I can force any kind of smile onto my face feels like a victory. Somewhere, somewhere deep in the madness of it, I'm starting to feel it. That tiny flicker of exhilaration, the way my blood is surging awake, the way my skin is becoming pure electric.

'Okay,' I admit through chattering teeth. 'It's not as bad once you get used to it.'

'Told you. Now dunk your head.'

I glare at her. 'Don't push me.' She laughs as I turn around and heave myself out of the water. I grip onto her outstretched hands, blissfully warm against my frozen skin, as I step out of the pool. It's only then, as the air rushes over my soaking skin, that I realise how alive I feel. It's intoxicating.

'I knew it,' she says, giving my hands a squeeze.

I wrap my towel back around me, burying myself in it. 'Knew what?'

'That you're the sort of person who takes risks. Who knows what life has to offer and is ready to jump.'

I'm not sure what to say to that. A lump catches in my throat, because if she properly knew me, if she knew how much I hesitate, how much I second-guess, how afraid of everything I am all the time, she wouldn't think so highly of me.

# NINE

By the time we head to the main barn to grab some lunch, our last stop before heading home and back to reality, my limbs have mostly forgiven me for the whole near-death experience in the cold plunge pool. They're still holding a bit of a grudge, sending little aftershocks through my muscles. And my skin is still tingling, my fingers are stiff, and I'm not entirely convinced my soul didn't leave my body for a brief moment. Anna, of course, is in her element. Rosy-cheeked, practically glowing from the whole ordeal.

'I feel *amazing*,' she says with a sigh, stretching her arms as we sit ourselves on one of the plush sofas. 'Like I've been reborn.'

I'm still not sure whether I enjoyed it or not, whether it was exhilarating or straight-up traumatic, so I focus on thawing my bones against the nearby fire. The warmth is heavenly, sinking deep into my muscles. I stretch out my legs with a groan.

When the waiter comes over, Anna doesn't hesitate. 'The full breakfast, please. Extra bacon. And a mimosa.'

My jaw drops. I was expecting her to choose a salad or something.

I hesitate. 'I'll have...' My brain is still defrosting, struggling to make decisions. My eyes flick to the table next to us, where a woman in a cable-knit jumper is cutting into something that looks like heaven. 'That. Whatever that is.'

'Eggs on sourdough with crispy kale and wild mushrooms?'

'Yes.' I nod. 'And a coffee. As large as you're legally allowed to serve.'

'She'll have a Bloody Mary,' Anna says.

I open my mouth to argue, but she just smirks. 'You survived the cold plunge, babe. You earned it.'

I sigh, surrendering. 'Fine. But if I die of hypothermia mid-meal, you have to tell my family I went out in style.'

She laughs and stretches out her arms behind her head.

'I love this place,' she says. 'It's even better than the one near our last home.'

'I bet you need a place like this with the hours you work.'

I try to picture Anna's life. I imagine her doing an early morning yoga class here before going to work in a sleek, modern clinic, wearing a figure-hugging white coat, then returning for a swim and some relaxation after her shift finishes. Not a bad life. Certainly less chaotic than mine.

'Too right. Although, I work a lot less hours than I used to when I was going through medical school.'

'Maybe I should visit your clinic at some point.' I say it without thinking.

Her head lifts and she peers at me expectantly. My cheeks redden. It was an off-hand remark, I hadn't even really thought about what I was saying, but now she's going to want more details.

'I have this... freezing thing,' I say with deliberate vagueness. 'My body kind of locks up when I'm scared. I'm surprised it didn't happen in the plunge pool.' I let out a forced laugh, trying to pass it off as a light-hearted issue, hoping she might forget I said anything.

She looks as if she might be about to push for more information, but before she can our drinks arrive. Anna clinks her mimosa glass against mine.

'To suffering,' she says with a grin.

'To terrible decisions,' I counter. But as I take my first sip of the spicy, perfectly balanced Bloody Mary, warmth finally flooding back into my limbs, I have to admit it's not a bad way to recover.

Today really has been more than I could ever have expected when Anna invited me out. It's weird. I'm different around Anna. Less inhibited. Looser. She's unlocked a version of me that most days I forget exists. The one who says yes instead of hesitating. The one who jumps into the freezing plunge pool instead of overthinking. I can already tell that when I get home, back to school runs and lunchboxes and endless piles of laundry, I'm going to be planning the next time we can hang out.

The sound of her phone ringing pulls me from this thought. The sharp trill feels out of place in our cozy little world of warmth and indulgence. Out of sheer habit I glance down at the phone on the table. Fraser's face stares back at me. Anna picks the phone up at lightning speed.

'Hi, darling,' she says, putting her finger up to her lips to signal that I should remain silent.

I strain my ears to see if I can make out what Fraser is saying on the other end of the line, but I can't without getting closer and making it blindingly obvious what I'm doing.

'Okay,' Anna continues, head bowed low as if she's talking on a crowded train. 'Yes, sounds good. Nothing much. I'm just sorting out a few bits at home.'

At this, she meets my eye sheepishly. I can tell she knows exactly what I'm thinking. Why did Anna just lie about where she is?

There are a few more 'Okay's and 'Yep's from Anna's side

of the conversation, and then she finishes off with a, 'I'll see you when you get home. I love you.'

The awkwardness when she hangs up is almost too much to bear. I can't not bring up the elephant in the room. Between doing her hair and my ice-bath experience, we've crossed some kind of invisible line into friendship territory. I think we're close enough at this point for me to ask.

'Sorting out a few bits at home, eh?' I keep my tone light, teasing, but I'm watching her carefully.

'Oh, that.' Anna looks down at her phone. 'Sorry. I know it's stupid. Fraser just...' She pauses and her cheeks flush. The first real crack in her usual easy confidence. 'He just hates spending money on material things like the membership here. I didn't even tell him about yesterday's haircut. He always says he'll cut my hair for me. Can you *imagine*? Don't get me wrong, I've met some wonderful male hairdressers in my time, but my husband is not one of them.'

She laughs, back to her usual self in a matter of seconds, as if there's nothing odd going on in the slightest. I, however, can't get her words out of my head. Not the phone call. Not the bruising. Not the weird behaviour or the searing looks from Fraser. Anna's excuse for why she lied about where she is makes no sense. Surely, he knows she has the membership? It's not like it's some kind of illicit secret. It will pop up on the bank statement, clear as day. And not telling him about the haircut? Even weirder still. The two of them are, quite clearly, well off. They don't exactly go to any trouble to hide their wealth. So why would he care about something as inconsequential as a £30 trim?

I haven't known this woman for long, but the more I get to know her, and the more I get to know about her husband, the more concerned I am for her safety.

# TEN

Fraser is coming at me with a knife.

He's got that look in his eyes again, twisted, evil, like the very thought of slicing through my flesh excites him. The blade gleams in the dim light. Sharp. Hungry. I scream and turn to run but he grabs me from behind. Panic explodes through me. No matter how much I writhe and kick and buck under his grasp, I can't break free from him.

This is it. This is how I die.

'*Miranda!*'

Lee is here. Lee will help me. Lee will save me.

My eyes scrunch shut and I want to call out to Lee, to let him know where I am so that he can get Fraser off me, but my throat is locked. The scream sits there, locked behind my gritted teeth.

'Miranda, wake up!'

Light floods into the room as the bedside light is switched on. My eyes dart around. My ceiling. My bedroom. Lee is beside me and I'm lying in bed, tangled in my duvet. The sheets are damp with sweat.

Fraser isn't here.

I look at Lee through a film of tears, trying to signal to him with the little movement I have available in my eye muscles. He understands immediately.

'It's okay,' he says, stroking my head. 'Just remember what Doctor Page said. Start by just moving a finger. Can you do that for me? Can you move your finger?'

I try. Nothing happens. My limbs remain pinned to the mattress, weighted by invisible chains. The pressure is unbearable, sitting heavy on my chest, squeezing my ribcage, squeezing the very light out of me. My breathing grows rapid. Short, desperate bursts. A mumbled cry escapes my lips.

'It's okay, I'm here with you. Just keep trying to wiggle your finger.'

My index finger moves slightly. My middle finger follows. Then a jolt courses through me as my body remembers how to be mine. I gasp, sucking in desperate breaths.

'Hey, hey. That's it. Breathe. You're awake. You're fine.'

I cling to Lee. Now that the sleep paralysis has worn off, I've succumbed to the trembling. My whole body shakes, sobs bursting from me in a wet, soggy mess onto his chest.

This is the first time I've woken up like this in a while. At least a few months. It has been getting better, or so I thought. Honestly, I feel sorry for Lee more than anything. His messed-up wife freezes when she's awake and freezes when she's sleeping, too. Imagine putting up with having to talk a grown adult down from a full-blown panic attack because they've randomly lost the ability to perform the most basic of human functions. It's pathetic.

'Are you okay?' Lee asks, still stroking my hair.

I nod, but I'm not okay. I'm nowhere near okay. I'm sick of this. I'm sick of being so scared all the time. I'm sick of my body deciding to just give up at the first sign of danger, real or imagined. It's exhausting and humiliating, and every time I think I'm moving past all this something else happens. Mason starts school, and I freak out at the thought of something happening to him while he's not with me. I hear about a car accident, and I convince myself that Lee was in the car.

A new neighbour moves in on our street...

We stay huddled up together for a few minutes. His warmth grounds me. Once my breathing regulates, I sit up, rubbing my tired eyes with my fists.

'I'm going to go and get a glass of water,' I say.

'Okay, I'll stay awake until you're back.'

He won't be awake when I'm back. He never is. But that's okay. I don't want him losing more sleep than he already has. No reason for him to be dragged into my sleepless hell. I slide my feet into my slippers, grab my dressing gown from the back of the door and pick my phone up off the bedside table, then make my way into the hallway. I pause outside Mason's room. He, like most kids, is afraid of the dark, so he sleeps with a night light that sends little R2-D2 characters floating around his room. Blue and white shapes dance across the walls, moving in hypnotic circles. That's another example of a time when Lee thought I was making him scared of the world. He said we shouldn't bother with a night light, that he needs to get used to sleeping in the dark, otherwise he'll never learn that there's nothing to fear.

But there *is* something to fear.

Already, in his short, short life, Mason's had an intruder break into his house. He was too young to understand, or even be aware, so I have to be scared for him. Who knows what that man's intentions were that night? What would he have done if we hadn't woken up? How many more terrifying events is my poor, sweet boy going to have to face over his lifetime?

The night light allows me to see his face. It looks babyish when he sleeps, like he's somehow back to being a toddler. My heart swells and I blink back tears. I love him so much it hurts. I wish I could tell him that he has nothing to fear, because I'm right down the hall and I'll never let anything bad happen to him. That's what mothers say. That's what I'm supposed to say.

The banister is cold on my palm as I descend the stairs, sending a small shiver up my arm. Our house is eerily silent at night. That's one of the only negatives I've found about living on Herring Row. Of course, the lack of footfall and traffic was one of the main reasons we moved here, a welcome change from the constant drone of the city. But at night, especially when my thoughts start to spiral the way they so often do, it can be unsettling. It leaves too much room for my mind to wander into dark places. You'd have thought the spa day would have been enough to relax me a bit. Apparently not.

I make my way to the kitchen and grab a glass from the cupboard, filling it with water. I pop one of my anxiety pills out of its packet. They were prescribed to me just after the break-in. I usually take a tablet with my breakfast, but now is as good a time as ever. I sit at our round kitchen table, and, downing the pill, I tap onto my phone. The room lights up blue, casting eerie shadows across the countertops. Blinking, I squint at the time. 3 a.m. An ungodly hour, if ever there was one. Late enough that I'm going to feel utterly wrecked come morning time, but too early to be up for the day.

I spend a few mindless minutes scrolling through Instagram, my thumb moving automatically, my brain barely processing the images flashing across the screen.

I'm watching a reel of yoga poses to try for an achy back, something I'll no doubt save to my bookmarks but never refer to again, when a notification pings up over the top of it from my doorbell.

*Movement detected.*

I frown. Movement detected at 3 a.m.? It's probably a leaf blowing in the wind, or something. As much as I love our doorbell for security (and, let's be honest, for spying), the damn thing is so sensitive it picks up the tiniest movement – squirrels, trees rustling, flies buzzing past – and makes me think there's someone outside our house. I open up the app.

As predicted, the front step is empty. There's no masked intruder. No one coming to break into our home and murder us at three o'clock in the morning. But...

My eyebrows draw together. I pinch the screen and slide my fingers apart, zooming in on Anna and Fraser's house. *There*. A flicker of movement. A shadowy figure by their front door.

My heartbeat thrums in my ears. My initial instinct is to call Anna, to warn her, but just as I'm about to do so the figure turns slightly towards my doorbell. There's a split second of overexposed brightness as the night vision tries to adjust itself. I breathe a sigh of relief.

It's Fraser. Not an intruder.

I watch, captivated. Why is Fraser outside at this time of the morning? What is he doing? He's lugging something with him. Something big. A suitcase, I realise. One of the huge ones that are always a bit questionable when you get to weighing your bags at flight check-ins. I have to assume that's what he's doing: preparing for a flight. That's the only conceivable reason to pack a suitcase and load it into the back of your car at this kind of hour like he's doing, right? He must have one of those painfully early morning flights.

Whatever's inside the suitcase, it's heavy. He struggles to lift it and once it's in the car he leans on it for a second, breathing heavily. His hands rake through his hair and he hangs his head. His body sags. He's not a happy man. I mean, he's never exactly seemed happy to me, but whereas before he came across as angry, now he looks different. Broken. Maybe Anna has kicked him out? If she has, good on her.

After a few seconds of looking sorry for himself he gets in the car and drives away, nearly clipping a Mini that's parked up on the pavement as he does so. I realise that might be the last time I ever see him, if he and Anna have broken up. Not that I'll miss him, exactly. I wonder if I should call her, see if she's okay. It's not exactly the best time to do so, but if he's only just left, I have to assume she's awake. Probably sitting alone and weeping with one of her expensive bottles of red wine in her hand. She might appreciate having someone to talk to.

I tap my nails on the table while I wait for her to pick up. It rings and rings, then goes to voicemail. I hesitate. Maybe she just didn't hear it. Maybe she's in the shower, or her phone is buried under a pile of blankets, or she's curled up in bed, staring at the ceiling, unwilling to speak to anyone. I try again and when it goes to voicemail a second time, I decide maybe she doesn't want to talk after all. Understandable. Even with our day out, we still haven't known each other for that long. I've probably overstepped by calling in the first place. I decide to leave her be and say a silent prayer that the other women of Herring Row won't make too much of a big deal out of it when they discover that Fraser is gone.

What an intense first week in your new home. Moving day. A big argument. Neighbours over for dinner. Then a break-up. I feel sorry for her. Anna is living, breathing proof that perfection isn't a guarantee of happiness. You can have the perfect looks, the perfect home, the perfect designer handbags, but if the foundation is rotten, everything crumbles eventually.

I spend another ten minutes sitting in the kitchen, scrolling on my phone, until the tension in my gut from my earlier episode starts to subside. I doubt I'll be able to go back to sleep now, but it's worth a try. Stretching, I heave myself up from the kitchen chair and make my way to the hall, wondering if Lee has miraculously kept his promise and is sitting up waiting for me.

As I place my foot on the first stair, a light travels across the wall, briefly highlighting the pictures of Lee, Mason, and me at

Disneyland that line the staircase, before plunging everything back into darkness. Car lights. I turn around, make my way over to the bay window and peer out.

Fraser is back. That's his car pulling into the driveway. I jump back behind the curtain and pull out my phone, navigating once more to the doorbell app. His obscured, grainy figure steps out of the car and he makes his way, perfectly casually, to the front door, lets himself in, and shuts it behind him. No suitcase.

I peek around the curtain at the house. For fifteen long seconds, nothing happens. Then the lights go out. The house sleeps. Like nothing ever happened.

A slow chill creeps up my spine. Because suddenly, I'm not so sure that what I witnessed earlier was Fraser being kicked out, after all.

And if it wasn't that, then what the hell was he doing?

# ELEVEN

'Lee! Lee, wake up.'

I shake his shoulder, gently at first, then, when he doesn't wake up, with more urgency. I know I'm not going to be popular for this. Waking him up twice in one night is not only questionable, it's savage. But I have to talk to someone, and Priya isn't answering her phone.

'What?'

Lee stirs, his voice thick with sleep. This time, when his eyes open, he doesn't have the freaked-out look of someone who thinks there might be a burglar in the house. He has the exasperated look of someone who has had just about enough of his wife's wild conspiracy theories about the new neighbours. Especially those that come to her in the middle of the night.

'I'm sorry. I'm so sorry. It's just... there's something weird going on next door.'

Lee doesn't even ask what. He just rolls over, burying his face in his pillow. I pick up mine from my side of the bed and whack him with it.

'I'm *serious*. You need to look at this.'

A muffled groan escapes him. He tilts his head so that a tiny corner of one eye is poking out, a sliver of reluctant attention.

'Look at what?'

I unlock my phone and place it in line with his barely opened eye. He recoils.

'Jesus Christ, Miranda. Are you trying to blind me?'

This time, I don't apologise. I just sit and wait for him to sort himself out, phone poised, ready to show him. He sits up and rubs his eyes, blinks a few times, then looks. I hit the play button and the recording of Fraser leaving the house with his heavy suitcase plays.

'What am I looking at, exactly?'

'Just watch.'

He does. His eyes follow Fraser as he hauls the suitcase into the car, slams the boot shut, and drives off, at which point I place my finger on the timeline and fast forward to Fraser returning. Once the clip finishes, I wait to see Lee's response.

He looks up at me. 'And?'

My jaw drops. 'What do you mean, "and"?' I stare at him, incredulous. 'Don't you think it's odd? He lugs what looks like an extremely heavy suitcase into his car at three in the morning, drives off, is gone for fifteen minutes and then comes back home without the suitcase?'

I wait for him to catch up. For his eyes to widen. For the shift in his posture, the sharp intake of breath. For him to *get it*. But he just rubs a hand down his face and says, 'Miranda, for the love of God. Go to sleep.'

I hit him again with the pillow.

'Why are you not freaking out?' I cry.

'Ow, quit it with that.' He bats it away with his elbow and it bounces onto the floor with a soft thump. 'What exactly do you think it is you've just witnessed?'

'I don't know. I'm not sure. But Anna isn't picking up her phone.'

Lee lets out a long-suffering sigh. 'It's the middle of the night. She's probably asleep. Just like I was before you woke me up with this nonsense.'

'Surely she'd have woken up to the sound of him opening the front door twice?'

'Not everyone wakes up to the tiniest sound like you, Miranda.'

'Lee, I'm serious. There were bruises on her arms. I saw them when I cut her hair. And she felt the need to lie about where she was when we went to the spa. Plus, there was the argument the other night. What if...' I hesitate, my voice catching and the hairs on my arms standing up on end. 'What if he *did* something to her?'

Coldness settles into my gut. The thought that Anna might be in serious danger has been circulating in the back of my mind since I saw the footage, but saying the words out loud has made it suddenly so much more real.

'*Did* something to her? Like what? Chopped her up into little pieces, stuffed her in a suitcase and dumped her body?'

We both fall silent at that.

I open my mouth, then close it. Because the truth is, I'm not sure what I think. I don't know if I'm being ridiculous, or grossly unfair to a man I've only known for a few days. I can't for the life of me figure out what he was doing going off with that suitcase at such a bizarre time only to return shortly afterwards without it. I just don't know. All I'm one hundred per cent certain of is my gut is telling me that something is off about him, and I will not just stand by and pretend I'm not noticing these things when I have a son to protect. I will not freeze up again.

'Who's been chopped up?' a little voice says from behind me.

Mortified, I spin around to see Mason standing in our bedroom doorway. His little face is screwed up with fear and confusion, his eyes darting between me and Lee.

'Nobody, sweetheart. What are you doing up?' I rush to his side and crouch down beside him. His hair is sticking up on one side. I reach out and smooth it down.

'I had a nightmare,' he says sleepily. 'And then I heard you arguing.'

'I'm so sorry. We weren't arguing. Mummy and Daddy were just having a silly grown-up conversation. Nothing for you to worry about. What was your nightmare about?'

'A monster in my room...'

'Mate, we've been over this,' Lee says from the bed. 'Monsters aren't real.'

I press my lips together, forcing myself to not comment. Monsters *are* real. Maybe not the furry, clawed, fanged kind that Mason pictures in his nightmares, but there are monsters, perfectly inconspicuous and unnoticeable, roaming our streets every day. They walk among us. They smile. They shake your hand. And if you're not careful, you don't see them for what they are until it's far too late. For all we know there's one living right across the street from us. My stomach hardens along with my resolve. Fear of what's lurking out there preparing to hurt you is nothing to be ashamed about.

'And even if there was,' I say, instead, 'they'd have a hard time getting past your daddy, wouldn't they?'

A small smile creeps onto Mason's lips. His shoulders relax a little. This is a conversation we've had before.

'What would Daddy do to that monster?' I ask.

'He'd whack 'em.'

'Where would he whack that monster?'

'Right on the head.'

'Yeah, I would!' Lee says.

Mason chuckles, his eyes shining as he pictures Lee jumping onto the shoulders of that big scary monster and giving him a good wallop. I take him by the hand. It's still so small in mine it breaks my heart a little. Five years old. Still, in so many ways, my baby boy and yet growing up so fast I can barely keep up. I lead him back to his bedroom, read him his favourite *Star Wars* book, and give him a kiss on the forehead. When I return to our bedroom, Lee is shaking his head.

'Are you happy now?' he says, though with less anger than before. 'You've probably scared the kid more than his nightmare did.'

'You're the one who was talking about chopping people up into tiny pieces,' I hiss.

I go to join Lee in the bed, shivering slightly as I slide under the covers, my body still tense. I pull the duvet right up under my chin. Lee puts his arm around my shoulder.

'Are you feeling less freaked out now?'

'A little bit,' I lie.

'Are you going to lie awake and think about it all night?'

I peek up at him. He knows me so well.

Allowing the corner of his mouth to turn up ever so slightly, he squeezes my shoulder. 'Why don't you go over in the morning? It will be a reasonable hour, so you won't look like quite as much of a psychopath as you are, and it will put your mind at rest when you see her.'

I nod, chewing on my lip. 'Okay, you're right. She's probably fine.'

'Now get some sleep and please, for the love of all that is holy, do not wake me up again.'

Smirking, I give him an affectionate kiss and we slide back down into the bed. It's not long before Lee's breathing turns heavy, and I can tell he's gone back to sleep. I try to do the same. I close my eyes. I take deep breaths. I tell myself to stop overthinking.

I don't sleep.

# TWELVE

When I sit at the bay window with a cup of coffee in my hands at 6 a.m., the world seems eerily quiet. The street is still, the pavement slick with last night's rain, the sky a murky grey that hasn't yet decided whether to brighten or stay gloomy.

I'm not one for getting up before Mason. I know some mothers do it. They like to rouse before their kids so that they can have some adult time to themselves to do yoga or meditate or go for runs or whatever else it is that we're apparently supposed to be doing for ourselves in the morning. Me? I like to stay tucked up in bed until the last possible moment. I always set my alarm for 7:30 on a weekday, which gives me just enough time to roll out of bed, get Mason ready and run a brush through my hair in an attempt to make myself look somewhat presentable for the school run, although Mason usually wakes me up at 7 on the dot. Even that is painful. But 6 a.m.? Unheard of.

Not today, though. I never managed to sleep after what happened last night, so instead I lay there, checking the time on my phone and counting down how few hours I had left before I needed to get up. Every glance at the screen made my stomach tighten a little more.

3:58.

4:32.

5:02.

I tried deep breaths, rolling over, shifting my pillow, pulling the blanket up over my head like I could block out my thoughts along with the light from the street lamp outside. Nothing worked. When I watched the minutes tick over to 5:45 I gave up, and now, here I am, hoping this coffee will be enough to at least see me through the school run, and wondering what would be an acceptable time to knock on Anna and Fraser's door.

Thankfully, I only have to sit in nervous anticipation for half an hour. At 6:30 the light in their living room turns on, which means they're up and awake and therefore I'm officially out of the potentially waking them up and entering deranged mad-woman territory. I wait another ten excruciating minutes, just to be sure, and then slip my coat and shoes on.

The air is crisp and cool when I step outside, and the birds are chirping away merrily. It's actually quite refreshing. I can sort of understand why people do the whole going for a morning run thing. I imagine it's a good way to wake yourself up. Though I can understand it, however, I won't be a morning person any time soon. I'd still trade this for an extra hour of sleep in a heartbeat. It's nice, but not nice enough.

Taking a deep breath, I step onto the pristine welcome mat, knock three times and wait, rocking back and forth onto the balls of my feet. I'm not a religious person, but I send up a prayer. *Please let it be Anna who answers the door.* Partly because I want to know she's alright, but mostly because I don't want to have to deal with talking to Fraser. There's a long silence as I wait. When a crow squawks, I duck, the sudden noise setting me on edge. I exhale sharply, feeling ridiculous.

No one answers. Shaking myself, I ring the doorbell instead.

I can hear the chime even from out here and it makes me wince. It's when I knock a third and final time that I notice the curtain in the window nearest to me twitch, as if someone has dropped it after holding it open slightly. I move over to the window, gingerly stepping around a small, slightly creepy-looking statue of a cherub as I do so. Its stone eyes seem to follow me.

My face presses to the glass and I peer in at the living room, where we had sat with my son playing video games just a couple of days ago. The light is still on, but there's no sign of life.

My knuckle raps against the glass.

'Anna?' I call, trying not to get frustrated. 'It's Miranda. Are you there?'

'What do you want?'

I'd been so busy trying to peer in through the window I hadn't noticed Fraser opening the front door. I whip around, my heart in my throat. I take a step back towards the door and, as I do, I accidentally kick the creepy cherub. It topples. A chunk of his nose flies off.

'I'm so, so sorry!' I pick the statue up and stand him up again, wondering if I should offer to replace it. Not that I'd know where to get something like that. But I don't get a chance.

'What do you want?' Fraser says again. When I finally reach the door, he eyes me warily, his mouth set in a tight line. My muscles tighten at the sight of him. I knew I'd have to face him again, of course, but standing in front of him is a lot more intimidating than it had been in my head when I first planned to come here. I roll my shoulders, attempting to loosen up.

'I'm so sorry to disturb you so early.' I force a smile onto my lips as I meet his blue gaze.

'I've been up for a while. What do you want?' he says, for the third time. Up for a while? Even though he was packing up a suitcase and driving off to who knows where at 3 a.m.? I wonder if he had as much on his mind as I did last night.

'Um...' I falter. Despite the fact I've been up for ages waiting to knock at this door, I realise I haven't actually planned out the words that would need to come out of my mouth. Now, under Fraser's stare, my brain seems to be short-circuiting.

Fraser watches me expectantly. I feel myself shrink a little under the intensity of it.

'I just wondered if Anna was around? I thought maybe I could take her to town, show her around, have a bit of a girls' day, you know?'

His eyes narrow and he looks me up and down, scrutinising me, as if he's trying to guess how much I weigh.

'A girls' day?'

'Yeah. I mean, you're welcome to join too if you don't mind standing outside the changing rooms and telling us which dresses you prefer.'

He grimaces slightly at that, as I had hoped he would. I figure if I can make him feel just uncomfortable enough, he might go and get Anna simply out of a desire to get rid of me. He crosses his arms, his biceps flexing slightly with the movement. The added bulk makes him look even more imposing.

'Anna's not here.'

'What?' The word slips out before I can stop it. Something lurches in my gut.

'She's gone to visit relatives.'

The air shifts. I hear the words, but my brain trips over them. *Gone.* Past tense. No warning. No explanation. Just... gone.

My mind reels. Was that what I saw last night? Was he driving Anna to her relatives? No, she definitely wasn't with him. He was alone when I watched him on the doorbell. Maybe she had already left and had forgotten her suitcase? Maybe he was just dropping it to her. But why at 3 a.m.? And why would she go away so soon after moving into a new house?

There's something else. Something Fraser has said that's

scratching at the back of my head, telling me it's wrong, but I can't place my finger on it.

'Oh, okay. Do you know when she'll be coming back?'

'I'm not sure.'

'Right.'

I want to say more but what else is there to say? It's really hard to hold a conversation when the answers are this short and curt.

'Well, I'll see you around,' I say, and he grimaces again, as if the idea of us seeing each other around physically pains him.

No *'thanks for stopping by'*. No *'I'll tell her you called'*.

Nothing.

I take a step back, away from the house. The second I move, he takes that as his cue to shut the door. Shaking my head in disbelief, I retreat down the driveway. I've half a mind to kick the cherub again, just out of spite, but I decide I'd better not. Once I'm safely off their land, I think back to what he said, and how he'd looked at me. There is something unsettling about him. He's rude, yes, but more than that. It felt as if he was hiding something.

As that thought settles upon me something else does too. A prickling in the back of my head. The unmistakable sensation of being watched.

I stop and turn back to face Anna and Fraser's house just in time to see it again.

The ripple of the curtain.

# THIRTEEN

Her phone is switched off. I tried ringing Anna the second I got home and it wouldn't connect. Wouldn't even ring.

After Lee went to work and I dropped Mason at school I tried again, with the same result. I'm trying desperately hard not to go there, to the deep, dark parts of my mind that I so often venture to. I know I have a tendency to see the worst-case scenario in everything. When the funfair was in town, Lee took Mason on a ride where you sit in a giant hippo and go up and down. It wasn't a particularly tall or fast ride, but all I could see in my mind's eye was the whole thing toppling over with my son inside it, his face disappearing beneath twisted metal. I've always been like this, even when I was in school. It got worse when I became a mum, and it became near unmanageable after the break-in happened. Sometimes I can't tell what's gut instinct and what's just overthinking.

Lee's words roll around in my head. *'Do you think he chopped her up into little pieces, stuffed her in a suitcase and dumped her body?'*

A shudder works its way down my spine as I go to the doorbell app, navigate to the page that stores all the recorded footage and find the clip from that night. I zoom in as it plays. It's grainy, difficult to see, but I can just about make out his features as he lugs the suitcase out of the house. He struggled with the weight of it. When he got it into the car, he puffed out his cheeks and wiped his brow.

A dead body would be heavy.

Trembling, I slide my finger along the timeline and watch the clip again. Then again, and again, and again. I'm being stupid. I'm letting my imagination get the better of me, allowing my bad experiences with Fraser to cloud my judgement. He's rude and he's apparently got some kind of grudge against me, but a killer? That's just absurd.

Except, what if it isn't?

What if there is a murderer living on this street, in the house next door, just two walls away from where my son sleeps every night?

I'm in the car before I can think about it anymore. It takes me a while to find the nearest police station on Google Maps. It's not exactly the sort of place I frequent. I type it in wrong twice, fingers fumbling against the screen, before the little blue dot finally starts guiding me to where I need to go. I had thought about phoning the non-emergency line, but that would involve police officers coming to my house, and the last thing I want is for Fraser to spot their cars parked on my driveway.

When I pull up outside the station, my fingers tap nervously on the steering wheel. I don't want to go in. Not really. I don't want the unnecessary drama, or for Lee to get annoyed at me for doing this without talking to him first, or to turn Fraser's life upside down if he is indeed completely innocent. But I know I won't be able to let it rest. That doorbell footage, the bruises and the way he smashed her against the wall just keep spinning around in my head. If there's even the slightest chance that someone dangerous is living on our street, I have to do something about it.

I'm not actually sure if you're supposed to just walk into a police station. I've seen people do it on TV shows, but that's about the extent of my knowledge with situations like this. Luckily, when I step through the double doors a friendly-looking officer sitting at a desk smiles at me. It's just enough to nudge me forward. I move to the desk.

'Are you alright there, miss?'

It occurs to me then how flustered I must look. Not to mention bedraggled. I threw my hair up in a top knot this morning for the school run, but it's started to fall down and is hanging off my head at an awkward angle. A limp, lopsided mess. This woman, however, has her blonde hair pulled back into a sleek, smart low bun. Not a strand out of place.

'Yes, I, um...' I glance around me, taking in my surroundings. There's a man sitting on one of the waiting chairs, but he's engrossed in something on his phone and doesn't seem to have taken any notice of me. I lean in and lower my voice, nonetheless. 'I'd like to talk to someone about some... suspicious activity.'

'Sorry, could you repeat that a little louder? Are you looking to file a report?'

'No. Well, maybe. I'm not sure.'

'Have you witnessed a crime?'

'That's what I mean. I'm not sure if I did or not.'

'Okay.' She gives me another smile, but it's different to the one she gave me when I first walked in. This one is more the kind of smile you give a kid when they tell you they know how to fly. 'What do you think you might have witnessed?'

I peer over my shoulder at the man again. He's still looking at his phone, but his eyes flick up to me for a split second. It's barely a glance, but enough to make my stomach tighten. He's definitely listening now. I turn back to the officer.

'I may have seen someone getting rid of...' I mouth the

words '*a body*' to her, and pray she won't ask me to repeat myself.

The expression on her face tells me she understands exactly what I said. She leans back in her chair, all traces of her smile gone, and pulls her computer keyboard towards her.

'I'm going to need to take a few details. One of my colleagues will be out to speak with you shortly.'

Well, I've done it now. There's no going back.

Sergeant Paul Hargreaves is a stocky man, with hair that I imagine used to be dark but is now mostly grey, and a much-less friendly face than the officer at the front desk. He has a weathered look about him. I'm not surprised. I can't imagine how police officers cope with the situations they have to deal with. I'd never sleep again.

He places a cup of tea in front of me and sits across the table with a notepad and pen. The tea is in a plastic cup and looks a bit like dishwater.

'Right, Mrs Jennings,' he says. 'Thanks for coming in. Let's have a proper chat. You said you've got some concerns about a neighbour?'

'Yes. I might be overreacting, but I thought it's better to say something than to say nothing.'

'That's okay. Why don't you start from the beginning? Take your time. There's no rush.'

'Alright.' I fidget in my chair. There's a faint hum coming from one of the air-conditioning units at the top of the wall that's just loud enough to be distracting. I shake my head, take a sip of the dishwater tea and try to focus on what I need to say. 'So, last night, at three a.m., I saw my neighbour dragging a suitcase out of his house. It was late, dark, but I have it all recorded on my doorbell app.'

I pull my phone out of my pocket and open the app. The

recording is there, ready, paused at the exact moment Fraser leaves his house. Sergeant Hargreaves leans forward to look at the screen. His brow furrows as he watches.

'And what do you think your neighbour is doing in this recording, Mrs Jennings?'

'Well, I thought he must have been catching a flight since it was at such a bizarre time. But then he came home after about ten minutes' – I skip forward on the video – 'without the suitcase. It was just really odd behaviour. And then I've not been able to get a hold of his wife all day. Her phone is switched off. I know it might not be anything, but if he's done something to her and this is a recording of him... well... you know.' The words knot in my throat. I can't bring myself to say any more. The thought is too gruesome.

Sergeant Hargreaves sits back in his chair, arms folded. 'Do you have any reason to suspect he may have hurt his wife?'

'She had bruises on the tops of her arms. They looked like fingerprints. Like someone had grabbed her. And they've been arguing a lot. They woke us up the other night.'

'What about last night? Did you hear any arguments or disturbances then? Before you saw him with the suitcase?'

'No, but they had their windows closed last night. When they woke us before they had them open. That's why we heard them.'

'You did wake up though, didn't you? You were watching the doorbell at three a.m.'

'Yes, but that was because of... a bad dream.'

A sickly feeling churns in my stomach as I remember last night's episode and the vision of Fraser advancing towards me wielding a knife.

For a long, long time Sergeant Hargreaves says nothing. He just looks at me thoughtfully, and I start to wonder if he's waiting for me to say more. Eventually, he leans forward again with his forearms on the table.

'We'll need you to file an official report. We'll then look into it and decide on next steps. If we need more details or clarification, we'll be in touch.'

I nod, relieved. 'Okay, thank you.'

'No problem.'

He stands, signalling that our time together is over. I stand too, and it's only when I do that I realise how shaky my legs are. My knees feel loose, like they're barely holding me up.

I take a step towards the door that Sergeant Hargreaves is holding open for me, but pause before I get there.

'Do you think I did the right thing? Coming here, I mean.'

He considers me for a moment, then smiles. 'You did the right thing coming in. Don't hesitate to reach out if you remember anything else, or if you notice anything unusual.'

I return his smile, feeling as though a weight has been lifted from my shoulders as I leave the room. This was the right move. I've done everything I can. The police will take it from here. That's their job. But as I walk away, a strange hollowness settles in my chest. I've told them what I know. I've done everything I can.

So why doesn't it feel like I've done enough? Why does it feel like this isn't anywhere near over?

Like it's only just beginning.

# FOURTEEN

'Ugh, he's so hot.'

I spin around to get a look at who Priya is talking about. This coffee shop is our favourite, and not just for the eye candy. It's family-owned, not one of the big brands, and the coffee is ten times better. Plus, it's got everything you'd want in a chill-out space. Big plush sofas. Cosy cushions and blankets. Shelves lined with books. I could quite happily lose an entire day in this place. The owner, Marjorie, takes great pride in her latte art and switches up the pictures she does each time. Today, my latte has a cat face on its surface.

'Who's hot?'

'*Shhhh!*' Priya turns in her chair and pretends to inspect the books next to us. The exaggerated casualness is a dead giveaway. It's then that I realise who she is fawning over. The guy Marjorie hired last month swoops past and picks up some dirty cups from a neighbouring table. I catch a whiff of his aftershave as he does so.

I roll my eyes at Priya. I mean, there's no denying he's good-looking, but he must be about ten years younger than us. Not that age stops her. 'How come men can date someone younger and it's applauded by his mates, but when women do it we're called cougars?' she always says when we question her choices in men.

I take a sip of my coffee, mutilating the cat's ears, and allow myself to sink into the cushions behind me. I'm so glad I decided to come out with Priya. It's the distraction I needed. If I was at home, waiting for three o'clock to roll around so that I could go and get Mason, I'd have ended up googling police procedure when a report of potential murder has been submitted. The whole point of going to the station this morning was so that I could wash my hands of it. I'll answer their questions and help with any investigation as much as they need me to, of course, but other than that, what happens with Fraser and Anna is none of my business. I don't know them well enough to feel as twisted up about this as I have been. I'm making an executive decision to stay out of it for the sake of my sanity.

While I'm internally congratulating myself for this new-found level of restraint, a notification pops up on my phone.

*Movement detected.*

Despite myself, I grab my phone and open the doorbell app.
'Oh my God!'
The words come out so loudly that the hot young waiter glances up from wiping a table and gives me a funny look.
'What's the matter?' Priya says, looking equally surprised at my outburst.
I've apparently forgotten what words are, my mouth hanging open idiotically, so instead I turn my phone to face Priya so that she can see for herself. Her brow crinkles.
'Is that... the police?'
I nod dumbly. There, on the screen, in real time, are two police officers stood on Fraser's doorstep. Fraser is there too, chatting to them over the threshold.

'What do you think they've done to have the police show up at their doorstep?'

I sigh, knowing that my plan to spend the day with Priya not thinking about what I saw last night is about to be well and truly foiled. The coffee that had felt warm and comforting just a few minutes ago now seems to sit like a stone in my stomach. Coughing to clear my throat, I take another sip and tell her the whole story. Her eyes grow wider as I talk, until it looks like they're about to pop clean out of their sockets.

'And *why* am I only hearing about this now?' Priya bursts out when I've finished. I love it. Her first response is not one of concern for Anna's safety or horror about the fact that there has potentially been a horrific crime committed on our street, it's of outrage that I didn't immediately come to her with the latest gossip.

'I didn't want to make a massive thing of it. I was hoping I could stay out of it. If it is nothing, if the guy has done nothing wrong, I don't want him knowing I'm the one who falsely accused him of offing his wife.'

'Are the police still there?'

'Oh, I'm not sure.' I'd gotten so wrapped up in telling Priya all about last night I've not been paying attention to the doorbell feed.

'I wonder if we'll see them take him away in handcuffs,' Priya says, with a hint of excitement that I choose to not point out is somewhat inappropriate given what might have happened to Anna.

I tap back into the app. The police have gone. The door is closed. Holding my breath, I slide my finger back along the timeline until the police appear again.

'They went inside the house,' I murmur, watching as Fraser holds the door open for them and they step in. 'Looks like they haven't come out yet.'

'God, I wish I was a fly on the wall. I bet they're asking him all about his relationship with her. Any recent arguments, that sort of thing. I bet he cheated on her and she went ballistic, and he did it to shut her up. He looks the kind who would do that. No, wait, *she* cheated on *him* and it was a revenge kill. Or maybe they both cheated on each other?'

'Priya!' I exclaim, my patience with her attitude to this whole situation well and truly fried. 'We're talking about a woman's *life* here. Have a little bit of compassion, won't you? And besides, we don't even know if that's what's happened. All I did was share my concerns. I might be barking up totally the wrong tree.'

Priya looks a little stung at my annoyance, but doesn't argue back. She takes a sip of her coffee and leans back in her chair.

'Just make sure you keep that camera feed on your phone,' she says. 'I definitely need to get me one of those doorbells.'

I keep the phone tilted upwards slightly, balancing on the sugar pot, so that we can see it out of our peripheral vision and be sure not to miss the police officers leaving. The screen flickers occasionally, the signal dropping in and out, and each time it does the tension in my muscles increases. When they eventually leave twenty minutes later, Fraser is, somewhat to my surprise, not in handcuffs.

'I told you,' I say, my voice sounding a lot less assured than my words as I come out of the app. 'I was wrong. If he'd done something to Anna, they'd have arrested him.'

'Maybe they don't have enough evidence yet...'

I can tell Priya is disappointed. She'd been hoping for an episode of a TV drama to play out on our street. I'm not sure how I feel. In one way, I'm relieved. The police not immediately arresting him means it probably was nothing. If their investigation even hinted at the possibility of murder, surely they'd have at least taken him in for questioning? Yes, this is the good outcome. Anna is fine, Fraser is not a killer, and all of this will be long forgotten once another whiff of gossip floats into Priya's ears. Fraser probably won't even know it was me who caused the police to go knocking on his door. It's all going to be fine.

But there's another feeling, one that's tugging at my gut and threatening to overwhelm that sense of relief.

*Dread.*

I close my eyes and press my knuckle to my temple, the beginnings of a migraine coming on. My phone vibrates in my hand, and I peek at the screen.

*Movement detected.*

I really need to disable these notifications.

I tap back into the app. The police have gone. Them driving away is probably what set off the movement detector. But Fraser is still there, standing on his doorstep. He turns to face my house. My heart leaps into my mouth.

He's staring straight at me.

Straight at the camera.

He knows it was me who went to the police.

## FIFTEEN

When I see 'Number Withheld' up on my phone screen, I freeze.

I had expected, after seeing the police leave yesterday without Fraser in handcuffs, that I might get a call to let me know the outcome of the investigation. But I haven't heard a thing. Priya even asked to come round for dinner so that she'd be with me when they rang, which I stubbornly refused, of course. That last thing I need is for Priya to tell Lee her overdramatised version of the story, and for him to get annoyed I told her before him.

But as it turned out, there was no need for her to stay with me after all. There was radio silence, which led to an evening of me staring mindlessly at the TV and trying to engage in conversation with Lee while internally screaming with anticipation.

The radio silence continued into this morning, and I toyed with the idea a few times of ringing the station myself to ask for an update, but couldn't quite bring myself to dial the number.

And now my phone is ringing and the fact that it's a withheld number means it's almost certainly the police. I'm too nervous to even answer the damn thing.

I manage to catch it just before it goes to a missed call.

'Hel—' I begin, but promptly choke on my own saliva. I cough and splutter a few times, holding the phone away from my face, then try again, hoping they haven't hung up. 'Hello?'

'Good morning. Is this Miranda Jennings?'

'Yes. This is me. I mean, this is I. This is she.'

My ears get hot and I'm glad this attempt at a conversation is happening over the phone, where my blushing can't be seen.

'This is Sergeant Paul Hargreaves from Banbury Police Station. I'm following up on the report you made yesterday about your neighbour. Do you have a moment to talk?'

'Oh, yes. Of course,' I say, as if I haven't been impatiently waiting nearly twenty-four hours for this call.

'Thank you for your patience while we looked into it. I want to assure you that we've thoroughly followed up on your concerns. We've spoken with your neighbour, Mr Coles, and verified that his wife is safe and well. She's currently visiting relatives, which explains why you haven't seen her around.'

My eyes shrink to slits. 'I see. That's... good to know.' There's that shiver of suspicion again. That niggling feeling that something is wrong. I wonder if he can hear how unconvinced I am across the phone line. 'So there's no issue?'

'None at all. Mr Coles explained the activity you noticed. He was moving some items into storage.'

'At three in the morning?'

I realise too late that I sound like I'm trying to insinuate that this man has not done his job properly. That's not what I'm trying to say. At least, I don't think it is.

'I understand it may have seemed unusual, but I can assure you, there's no need for concern.'

'Surely it's a concern that she's not answering her phone?'

'Mrs Jennings, Anna Coles is a grown adult. You reported her missing less than twenty-four hours after you last saw her.'

'I didn't report her *missing*,' I can't help but correct him.

He goes on as if I didn't say anything. 'And, in fact, she is not missing at all. As Mr Coles says he explained to you, she is visiting with relatives.'

'But is that actually true? Do you know for sure that she's okay?'

'There is nothing for you to worry about, Mrs Jennings. Now, if you know something you haven't yet told us that we should be aware of, please do share that information.'

'No, there's nothing else.' A lump forms in my throat. I don't quite know how else to respond. He's saying all the right things, everything I had hoped he would say, but it's not bringing me the comfort I had thought it would. There's still that annoyance scratching at the back of my mind, something that Fraser said that stood out to me as something to mention. I keep going over our conversation, but each time I try to reach whatever is tugging at me, it slips away like vapour.

'Is there anything else I can help with, Mrs Jennings?'

'I suppose not. I feel a bit silly now. I was just so worried. It looked strange, and I didn't want to ignore it if something was wrong.'

'Not at all, you did the right thing by bringing it to our attention. It's always better to report something if you're concerned. These things can often turn out to be nothing, but on the rare occasions they aren't, acting quickly can make all the difference.'

That makes me feel a little bit better. At least when Lee questions my rash decisions I can back them up with actual police advice.

'Thank you for saying that. I'm glad everything is okay.'

'We appreciate your vigilance. If you ever have any concerns in the future, don't hesitate to get in touch. Better safe than sorry, as they say.'

'Thanks, Sergeant Hargreaves. And, um...' The blush returns. 'Sorry if I caused any trouble.'

'No trouble at all. Have a good day.'

The line goes dead and I stare at my phone for a few seconds. A mixture of embarrassment and frustration curdles inside me. He spoke to me as if I were a child telling tales, and he didn't even answer my questions properly. He said that Fraser had explained that Anna was visiting relatives, but I already knew that's what Fraser would say because that's what he said to me. Do the police just take people's word for it? Unless they did speak to Anna and verify her whereabouts. But if they did, why didn't he say that?

And then it hits me, colder than a shard of ice slicing through my chest.

Holy crap.

*As Mr Coles explained to you, she is visiting relatives.*

Except when we were at the spa, when I asked Anna if she had anyone to talk to when things got rough with Fraser, she said no. She said she was an only child and that both her parents were dead.

She hasn't got any family to visit.

So that means Fraser is lying.

## SIXTEEN

Priya and I have gone through three bottles of wine.

Lee is visiting his mother. She's been poorly for a few months now, stage one lung cancer, and since her diagnosis he's gone to stay with her at least every couple of weeks. He asked both me and Mason if we wanted to come. Mason jumped at the chance; Nana Jennings always gives him way too many sweets and never listens to me when I tell her he's had enough. I, however, have to do Ellen's hair tomorrow morning. Typical. I practically never have work these days, but the one time I could really do with getting away from Herring Row for a couple of nights, I have to rid Ellen of her grey roots.

So, with no child or husband to take my mind off things, Priya and wine it is tonight.

I started off the evening declaring that I would explain what happened with the police phone call situation, and that once I was finished telling her we would discuss it no more, but with every glass I've become less tight-lipped about it all.

'Did you tell the police?' Priya says. 'About what Anna said about not having any relatives?'

'Immediately.' I sigh. 'I rang straight back as soon as I

realised. They just thanked me for the information and said they'd call me back if anything changed in the investigation.'

I shake my head, still in disbelief. The man that I'm accusing of hurting his wife has been caught out telling a barefaced lie to not only me, but to the police, and when I told them they seemed about as shocked as if I'd told them the sky was blue. I wonder if they already knew that Fraser was lying. Perhaps it wasn't news to them at all. But then why haven't they arrested him yet? My plan to spend tonight drinking and not thinking about all of this has spectacularly failed. The first part I have down to a tee.

'Have you tried ringing her again?' Priya asks.

I nod, solemnly. 'More times than I can count. Her phone is still switched off.'

A thought occurs to me then, one that I can't believe I hadn't considered before, and I pull my own phone out of my pocket and tap into Facebook.

'What are you doing?'

'Maybe she has a new phone or something. She may have posted on social media.'

I type in Anna's name, which doesn't help. There are thousands of results and none of them are her. I navigate to Instagram and try that instead. Still no luck. Finally, I go to Google and type in *Anna Coles, sleep*. This brings up a LinkedIn profile, which is definitely her, but doesn't look like it's been updated in a couple of years. Underneath that is an article on sleep paralysis that she was asked to comment on. My eyebrows fly up as I read.

*'Sleep paralysis feels like being buried alive,' Anna Coles commented. 'You're trapped in your own body, unable to move, sometimes unable to breathe properly. The patients I work with who suffer from it genuinely think they're dying. Sometimes sufferers will be convinced someone is in the room with them,*

*watching. We still don't really know what causes it or whether or not it's hereditary, but triggers like stress can increase symptoms.*

*'For some, cognitive behavioural therapy can help manage the anxiety that triggers it,' she continued. 'Others find medication useful – anything from antidepressants to muscle relaxants. In rare cases, sedatives and benzodiazepines such as Valium and Rohypnol have even been prescribed to help sufferers get into a deeper sleep cycle and bypass the paralysis altogether.'*

*Wow.* It's as if she wrote that about me. I mentioned my issues when we were at the spa, but it hadn't occurred to me that she might actually be able to help me. Probably not, considering no one has been able to fully solve my issue yet. But there's always a chance. I'll have to ask her when she gets back.

If she gets back.

I shake myself and continue scrolling through Google. Finally, I come across a Facebook profile that has her smiling face as the profile picture. I tap into it, and my heart sinks. The account is private. I can't see when she last posted, or even when she was last active.

Frustrated, I throw my phone down and turn my attention back to my wine.

'You'd have thought they'd at least ask to see what's in this *supposed* storage area,' I slur.

'Absolutely. They should be tearing that suitcase open.'

'We should break into the storage unit and look inside ourselves,' I joke dryly.

'Yes!' Priya lifts her glass as if to cheers to the idea, and her wine sloshes dangerously close to the edge. 'Let's do that!'

'Wait, no. We can't. We don't know where it is...'

'Oh, right.'

The two of us slump for a moment, dejected that our master

plan of somehow finding the storage unit and somehow breaking into it and somehow investigating what's inside the suitcase has been foiled.

'I bet there's something in that house,' Priya says after a moment, stroking her chin as if she's a cartoon villain. 'You said he got all funny about his office, didn't you?'

I think back to that evening, to the jolt of fear that went surging through me when he caught me attempting to snoop. I wonder if Anna ever felt as afraid of him as I did in that moment. Probably. Probably more so.

'If only my doorbell camera could see inside the house,' I murmur.

'Ooh! Let's break into there instead!' Priya's last word comes out more a burp than anything else, and she covers her mouth, giggling.

'We're not breaking in *anywhere*.'

Even drunk, I'm the more sensible of the two of us. Only slightly, but enough to keep us out of trouble for the most part. The amount of times I've had to pull her away from questionable-looking men or talk her out of getting into cabs with total strangers is laughable. One time, I physically dragged her away from a man who claimed he was a Hollywood producer, as if it's perfectly normal for them to be scouting for new talent in the middle of a sleepy little Cotswolds village. Whenever we go out drinking, she refers to me as her mum.

'Fine.' Priya throws her head back theatrically, then jolts it up again, eyes shining. 'We don't need to break in! I should just knock.'

'And say what?'

'Anything. It doesn't matter. Just something to keep him occupied while *you* sneak in and look around the house.'

I laugh so hard wine spurts out of my mouth. 'While I *what?*'

'Come on. The window at the side of the house is open. Look!'

She points dramatically, as if she's unveiling some great discovery. I follow her gaze over to Anna and Fraser's house. The window on the right-hand side of the house, which, if the layout is the same as mine, leads to the utility room, is indeed wide open. I look back at Priya, aghast.

'I'm not climbing in through the sodding window!'

'Why not?'

'Aside from the fact that I don't want to be arrested for trespassing, if he actually is a psycho killer I'd rather not be his next victim, thank you very much.'

'But that's exactly why you should do it.'

I shake my head at her, unsure of what point she's trying to make.

She sighs. 'What if Anna isn't his first victim? What if she's not his last? The police clearly aren't going to take this seriously, not until there's someone else that's gone missing or winds up dead. Do you want that to be one of us? Or Mason?'

I shoot Priya daggers at that. 'Don't say that. Don't even *think* it.' But she's right and she knows it. She's said exactly what I've been thinking since I first watched the doorbell footage.

I take another gulp of wine, a big one this time. 'Why can't you go shimmying through the window while I distract him?'

'He doesn't like you.' She flips her hair over her shoulder. 'And I have a certain way with men.'

There's no denying that.

I roll my eyes as I consider the absurdity of what we're talking about. 'There's probably nothing to even find in that house. He'll have cleaned up any evidence. Especially with the police poking around.'

'But they obviously didn't do a proper search. Maybe a

quick look around, but they won't have gone into his drawers or through his files or anything.'

'You're nuts,' I say, sitting back in my chair and downing the last of my wine. Priya promptly tops it back up.

'Come on, Miranda. Even if you don't find anything' – she grins in the way she always does when she's trying to talk me into doing something idiotic – 'think about what a great story it will make.'

I laugh a nervous laugh. I'm considering it, not because I'm at all interested in being able to tell a good story the next time we're catching up with Ellen and Beth, but because I know that something is wrong. I'm genuinely terrified for Anna. And for myself, and for my son, and for every person on this street. I had thought going to the police would calm my anxieties, but the way they've handled this investigation has just made it worse.

Maybe Priya is right. Maybe the police did do a rubbish job of searching. They've done a rubbish job of everything else, apparently.

And just like that, with my sensible voice washed away with the drink, I've agreed to commit my first crime.


My stomach churns as we walk across the road. I try to tell myself it's not nerves, that it's just the alcohol sloshing around inside me, but I can't kid myself into believing I'm brave enough to do something like this. My legs feel like they belong to someone else. This is Priya-level of drunken stupidity. I don't do things like this. I don't get off my face and do stupid stuff. I wasn't even brave enough to step into the plunge pool at the club without Anna physically pushing me in.

And yet, here I am.

As we approach the driveway, I glance back at my house. My doorbell is looking straight back at me. If I do this, it will be caught on camera. There will be video evidence of me breaking into my neighbours' house. But then, does it matter? Nobody except for me checks the doorbell footage. Lee thought it was cool for the first week, but soon got annoyed with the movement-detected notifications every time a bird flew past, and deleted the app from his phone. I'm pretty sure I can delete footage, too, on the off-chance someone wants to look at the archive as part of the investigation into Anna's disappearance.

The investigation that isn't happening.

My nerves shift to annoyance. This is the police's fault. The fact that I'm about to do this is down to them. Sergeant Hargreaves promised me they had done everything in their power to check all was okay, but they haven't. One short visit to talk to Fraser, that's it. No formal interview. No search of his property. No attempts to track his movements from that night or find the suitcase. They haven't even seemed to listen to what I've said about Anna's family situation. It's infuriating. The sheer laziness. The apathy. Like Anna's disappearance is a minor inconvenience rather than someone's life vanishing into thin air. They've been so useless, probably eager to avoid piles of paperwork, it's now down to me to do what they should have done.

With that annoyance comes the resolve to push forward. Priya nods at me, unable to hide her excitement as I disappear around the side of the house, and I hear her ring Fraser's doorbell. I peer at the other houses too, checking that no one happens to be looking out of their windows. Most of the curtains are drawn, thank God. Even though the other residents of Herring Row are my friends, I don't think anyone but Priya would understand what I'm about to do.

When I hear Fraser open the front door and Priya do her signature 'Hi!' that she always does when she's trying to attract male attention, I don't waste any time. I don't know how much of it I've got, and I don't want a chance to properly think about what I'm doing, or I won't do it.

Placing my palms on the outer window ledge, I jump a

couple of times to bring me up to the height I need to be at to swing my knee onto it. The rough brick scrapes against my hands, biting into the skin. It's harder than I thought it would be. Apparently, I'm not quite as sprightly as I used to be, and just the act of hauling my leg over sends cramp shooting down my calf. I make the executive decision, as I fall ungracefully through the window, not to watch the footage back on my doorbell.

Once into what is indeed the utility room, I make my way gingerly to the door. It's open a crack and I peer through it. I can just about see the shadow of Fraser at the front door. Crap. I can't believe I'm doing this. This was so stupid. So dangerous. If he were to get bored of Priya's story about how she's all alone in that big house of hers, and turn to go back to the kitchen right now, he'd spot me. I press myself against the wall, straining to hear Priya. What if she runs out of things to talk about? Nausea gurgles inside me. I clasp my hand to my mouth, willing my stomach to hold out for just a few moments longer.

I can't do this. I can't risk leaving this room and heading towards the office. I'd have to cross the path behind him. My muscles twitch with indecision, my mind spinning. My feet take a few tentative steps back of their own accord.

Priya will have to understand. I'm not like her. I'm not brave. I'm not reckless. I don't live my life without thinking about the consequences. I'm sobering up, fast, and it's making me realise how ridiculous this plan was in the first place.

As I turn to retreat the way I came out of the window, something catches my eye. I freeze, cocking my head towards the sink that's next to the washing machine. It's filled with soapy water and there's what looks like a white shirt soaking in it. I take a step towards it. My heart thuds in my chest. It's so loud now, I'm convinced Fraser must hear it.

The water is ice cold as I plunge my hands into it and pull out the shirt. The shirt that Fraser is soaking to get out the stain.

The *bloodstain*.

I retch.

The door opens.

I barely have time to register the creak of the hinges. There's a horrifying moment where my eyes meet Fraser's and realisation dawns on his face.

Then I proceed to throw up all over the utility room floor.

## SEVENTEEN

'What the hell are you doing?'

'I'm so sorry.' My words come out muffled by a concoction of the vile taste in my mouth and the tears now streaming down my face. 'I was... I was just...'

My mind races for something, anything that might explain this away. I could say that I thought I'd seen smoke, that I was checking to make sure everything was okay. But no, that's ridiculous. He wouldn't believe that for a second. The lie crumbles before I've even thought it. There are no excuses. No reason for me to be standing in this room. My palms are clammy, and my heart is thundering.

Unsure of what else to do, I grab the kitchen roll from next to the sink, fall to my knees, and start feebly mopping up my mess on the floor. The toes of Fraser's shoes are in my eyeline – polished, still, menacing. He doesn't move. He doesn't speak. The silence stretches, thick and unnatural. Even though sweat is gathering at the back of my neck, my skin is prickling as if it's freezing cold while I continue to soak sheets of kitchen roll. Unable to bear it, I dare to peek up through gross, sodden strands of hair plastered to my face.

And there it is. That look. The one that makes you want to shrink up inside of yourself. To vanish.

Another jolt of nausea rises in my throat. My legs scream to run but refuse to move. I feel like a mouse cornered by a cat that hasn't quite decided whether to kill or play. I have two options. Either I can make a run for it, pack our bags and inform Lee when he gets home that we're moving, or I can attempt to act braver than I feel. The alcohol that's still in my bloodstream and not sitting in a puddle on the floor chooses the latter. Priya won't have gone anywhere. She'll be lingering just outside, desperate to find out what's happened. If he tries anything, I'll scream and she'll hear me.

'Whose blood is that?'

'What?'

I nod at the shirt, now draped over the edge of the sink where I dropped it.

'The shirt that you're soaking. There's blood on it. Whose is it?'

His eyes flick between me and the shirt. I can almost see the cogs whirring in his brain, piecing it all together. First the visit from the police. Then the knock at the door from Priya. Now finding me here, in his house, questioning him. If he didn't know it was me who called the police before, he sure as heck does now.

Finally, his face sets once more, and his gaze falls again on me.

'*Get. Out.*' He says the words separately, punctuated by pure hatred.

'I saw you!' My voice raises. I'm hoping Priya will hear and at least come to the window so that I'm not totally alone in this room with him. 'I saw you lugging that suitcase into your car at three a.m. Anna's not responded to her messages ever since. And I saw the bruises on her arms, the way you pushed her into the wall that night, and the way she had to lie to you about where she was when we were at the spa. What have you done to her?'

For a moment, I don't think he's going to respond. I'm not sure what the usual response is for being accused of murder, but Fraser seems strangely cool and collected. Too calm. It's unsettling.

He considers me, his top lip sneering.

'You think I killed my wife?'

'I don't know. I just know that something isn't right here and you're trying to get blood out of your shirt.'

'That's my blood, you stupid, obsessive bitch.' He grabs the shirt out of the sink and holds it in front of my face, causing droplets of soapy water to land on my lap. They seep into the fabric of my leggings, chilling my skin and making me flinch. 'Anna is visiting relatives, which the police confirmed when they came to check up on an anonymous report. I assume that was you?'

My stomach turns and I silently beg it not to make me throw up again.

'They... they confirmed it? But she told me she didn't have any relatives.'

'They spoke to her themselves.'

I'm sure I can feel all the blood leaving my face. Why didn't they tell me that? Have I just broken into some poor man's house, having sent the police round to check him out, vomited over his floor, and accused him of the unthinkable, all for a misunderstanding?

'Now that we've cleared that up,' Fraser says, 'you can get out.'

'I'll clean this up for you,' I say, pulling more sheets of kitchen roll and trying to scoop the vomit into one pile. The stench hits me again, sharp and acidic, burning my throat. I want to get out of here. Desperately. There is literally no place

I'd less rather be right now than crouching on Fraser's utility room floor. But I can't leave him with this.

'Did you not hear me?' Fraser says. 'Get the hell out of my house!'

I don't have to be told a third time. I scramble up from my spot on the floor so quickly I nearly slip in the sick. My foot skids an inch and panic jolts through me. Steadying myself, I glance back at the window. My instinct is to climb back out the way I came in, but then I realise how utterly ridiculous that would be and so instead decide to shuffle past Fraser before legging it to the front door. As I burst out onto his driveway, I spot Priya. She's sat on the wall outside her house, nibbling at her thumbnail. She jumps up when she sees me, eyes wide, and sprints forwards.

'What happened?' she near shrieks. I shush her and gesture for us to retreat into her house. My chest heaves, my breath shallow and sharp. I'm not brave enough to turn back and see if Fraser is watching me.

Once I'm over the safety of her threshold, a realisation settles over me. Amongst everything that happened in that utility room and everything Fraser said, there's one thing he failed to do.

He didn't deny killing his wife.


I don't feel drunk anymore. Now that I've had a chance to reflect on what I just did in the relative safety of Priya's house, and downed three glasses of water and an espresso, I feel like I've got the hangover from hell. My head is pounding.

Priya places a cup of tea next to me and I cradle it. Not because I want to drink it. I don't think my stomach can handle any more fluids for a while. I just want the warmth of the cup. I want to feel cosy and snug and secure, and not like I've just gone head-to-head with a potential killer. The heat soaks into my fingers, grounding me.

'Maybe he's right,' Priya says as she sits down next to me with her own cup.

'About what?'

'Maybe you are being a bit obsessive about Anna...'

I gape at her, unable to believe the words that have just come out of her mouth.

'I'm sorry, wasn't it *you* who suggested I climb through the window?'

'Well, yeah.' Priya shrugs, as if this is a totally normal, everyday conversation to be having. Her calmness makes my skin prickle. 'But I wasn't expecting you to actually do it.'

I jump up from my spot, slamming my cup down on the table. Annoyed isn't the word. I want to slap her. I want to go back to every time I've ever rescued her from a dangerous situation and leave her to get on with it.

'Well, why the hell didn't you say that?' I shriek. 'Why did you let me go along with it?'

'I don't know... I guess I got caught up in it all. The adrenaline, you know? You've got to admit, it will make a funny story in a few years' time.'

'No, no it won't make a funny story. We're never going to speak of today again!'

I think she can tell how pissed off I am, because the smile that had been tugging at the corner of her lips drops off her face.

'No one forced you to do it,' she says.

I'm about to snap back at her but stop myself, because she's right. It may have been her idea, but I'm the one who did it. I could have said no.

Defeated, I slump back into the chair and bury my face in my hands. My chest feels tight, like I'm trying to swallow air through a straw.

'Do you really think I'm being obsessive?' My words come

out muffled from between my fingers. 'Do you reckon she's okay?'

'He said the police spoke to her, didn't he?'

'Well, yes. But that doesn't necessarily mean anything. He could have had someone posing as her for all we know. They didn't exactly look into it much. I highly doubt they checked the person they spoke to was who she said she was.'

Priya gives me an odd look at that, a sort of pitying smile.

'Why don't you speak to them again? Ask them to put your mind at rest?'

I shake my head, unsure of what to do. The sensible voice in my head is telling me to drop it. I've caused enough issues. I've already effectively decimated any chance at a good neighbourly relationship. Thinking back to the gift basket now, I want to laugh. What a joke.

Sighing, I pull out my phone and try Anna's number one more time. Perhaps she's switched it back on now. Surely she has, if the police have spoken to her?

But it's still switched off.

The sensible voice in my head is telling me to drop it. But there's another voice. One that's telling me I'm the only one who can see what's really going on here.

And that voice is louder.

# EIGHTEEN

'Mummy, I don't want to go to school.'

I'm sure my child is purposefully testing me sometimes. After a morning from hell, sleeping past my alarm, rushing around to iron a uniform and fill a lunchbox, forgetting to take said lunchbox with us and having to go back home to grab it, this is the moment Mason decides to tell me he doesn't want to go in.

'You love school, bub,' I say in my most forced cheery voice.

'But I'd rather spend the day with you.'

Yep, definitely testing me. He's a genius, I'll give him that. Knows exactly what to say to pull on my heartstrings. A master manipulator in the making.

I stop mid-stride and crouch beside him so that I'm at his eye level. 'I'd rather spend the day with you, too, but you've got to go to school to learn all the things you need to know. You want to be super smart, right?'

He shrugs. He couldn't care less.

'Besides, if you don't go in your friends will miss you. Who will Jamie play with at lunchtime?'

That was the correct thing to say. Mention of his friends has him considering it at least. I give him a few seconds, preparing myself to put my foot down and start telling rather than asking.

'Okay,' he says after a moment of deep contemplation, and immediately starts walking in the direction of the school. Crisis averted.

I breathe a sigh of relief at the avoided tantrum and take a step after him, then nearly trip over myself as we pass Marjorie's coffee shop window. There, sitting at one of the tables in the corner, is Sergeant Hargreaves. My eyes widen. Seeing a police officer out of uniform going about their day-to-day activities is like seeing a teacher outside of school. It's disconcerting. Unnatural. I shuffle from foot to foot, hoping he won't see me staring in at him as if he's a zoo animal. Is it wrong to approach an officer who is clearly not working and just attempting to drink a morning cup of coffee in peace and ask them about a case? The answer – yes, it's absolutely wrong – is clear in my head. Completely inappropriate. A terrible idea. But then breaking into my neighbours' house was also wrong, and I did that. Clearly my moral compass is a little off these days.

'I just need to pop in here for a moment,' I say, moving towards the door.

Mason's little face creases. 'I thought you wanted me to go to school?'

'I do. I'll just be a minute.'

When we enter the café, a few people, including the hot guy that Priya was fawning over the other day, glance up at me, but Sergeant Hargreaves keeps his head bowed, staring at his newspaper. I assume this is his way of looking as unapproachable as he possibly can. It's working, but not quite well enough.

'I'm sorry to disturb you,' I say, taking the empty seat across the table from him and perching Mason on my knee.

Sergeant Hargreaves visibly sighs. 'Mrs Jennings. Nice to see you again.'

The words don't quite match up to the tone in his voice, but I choose to ignore it.

'I know you said everything was okay and that I didn't need to worry—'

'You're right. I did say that.'

I pause, thrown off by his interruption. He's clearly not in the mood for this. I can't blame him, but I wasn't exactly in the mood to get dragged into this whole ridiculous situation either, and yet, here we are.

'Look, Mason,' I say, pointing at the kiddie table Marjorie has set up for her customers with children in the corner of the room. 'Colouring books. Why don't you go and do some drawing?'

Mason gives me a look, like I've just suggested he go and play with a bunch of baby rattles. He's not the colouring type. At five, he reckons he's far too grown up for things like that.

'If you're good I'll get you a biscuit and you can eat it on the way to school.'

He immediately perks up and heads to the colouring table. Bribery. The most effective parenting tool known to man.

When I return my gaze to Sergeant Hargreaves, he's looking at me expectantly with his eyebrows raised. I clear my throat.

'I wanted to ask what kind of investigation was done. How you know for sure that Anna is okay?'

It occurs to me that he might not be allowed to talk to me like this in a public place, especially when off duty, but he seems keen to get me away from him. He leans back in his chair and folds his paper in half.

'As I told you before, we spoke to Mrs Coles and verified Mr Coles's story. This really isn't appropriate.'

'Yes, but did you check that it was actually her?'

'Excuse me?'

'Well, it could have been someone pretending to be Anna, couldn't it? Did you actually *see* her, or did you just speak to her on the phone?'

'Do you make a habit of breaking into your neighbours' properties, Mrs Jennings?'

My next argument dies on my tongue. I pause, repeating his words in my head to make sure I heard them correctly.

'What?'

'We spoke to Mr Coles this morning to confirm that the case had been closed, and he mentioned that you broke into his house.'

My heart rate increases. Oh my God. The son of a bitch went to the police. Mind you, that's exactly what I'd do if this were the other way around, but still. It feels like some kind of betrayal.

'Luckily for you he has decided not to press charges,' Sergeant Hargreaves continues. My heart rate slows a tad, relief washing over me.

'Okay,' I say dumbly.

Sergeant Hargreaves takes a big gulp of his coffee to finish it off and stands. He leans forward, looking me dead in the eye.

'Let me give you some advice, Mrs Jennings. Stay away from Mr Coles and his wife.'

I want to argue back, but what could I even say? Not that I have a chance to argue. He gets up and leaves, and I'm left feeling like a scolded child sitting at the table. My cheeks are on fire. I take a moment to compose myself before collecting Mason from the colouring table, which, despite his initial protest, he seems reluctant to leave, and exit the coffee shop. I cross the road, pausing outside the park to text Priya. Really, I know I should be talking about this stuff with Lee, but he won't understand like Priya does. Or maybe it's just that he won't give me the validation that I know Priya will provide.

She phones me almost instantly.

'That's it. I'm taking you out tonight,' she says before I can even say hello.

I roll my eyes. That's always Priya's solution to everything. Had an argument with Lee? I'm taking you out. Spent the day dealing with kiddie tantrums? I'm taking you out. Been scolded by a police officer for breaking into your neighbours' house? Guess what. Shots on Priya.

'It's fine,' I say, signalling to Mason that we should walk and talk. 'Lee only came back from his mum's last night. I can't really go out as soon as he returns. I should probably spend some time with him.'

'I've already messaged Lee and told him it's happening. We can go to that cocktail bar that's just opened.'

'A cocktail bar? That sounds like a terrible idea.' The last thing I need is alcohol fuelling my already chaotic life.

'It sounds like an amazing idea.'

'I don't really feel up to...'

'Mummy!' I feel Mason's hand jolt against mine. Car horns blare. Tyres screech. I gasp, realising I've just stepped straight out into the road without looking, and stumble backwards. My heel catches on the kerb. I descend towards the pavement, arms flailing. I'm inches away from landing slap bang on top of Mason, but I manage to catch the pole of the traffic lights just in time. Pain shoots across my wrist as I grip it tight.

The driver of a silver Range Rover swears at me. Loudly. Aggressively. Like I haven't already realised how stupid I was.

'Sorry!' I throw my hand up by way of apology as the car accelerates off angrily.

I feel sick. My heart is in my throat. I turn to Mason, whose face has gone very pale.

'Are you okay?' I ask.

He nods, tears gathering in his eyes. Guilt floods me.

'Good boy for not following Mummy into the road,' I say,

pulling him to me. I'm cuddling him for my own sake as much as his. I can feel my body tightening, seizing up from the shock and the terror. I need to ground myself. I press my cheek into his hair, inhale the scent of him.

As we stand there, I realise people are looking at me. Other school mums from across the road. The teacher who stands out by the lights to ensure kids use the crossing instead of cutting across further up the road. All judging me. All probably thinking that I could have very easily pulled Mason out with me in front of a car had he not been sensible enough to stop. Their stares burn into my skin.

After a few moments, once my pulse has returned to a normal speed and people have decided I'm no longer entertaining to stare at, I release him and take his hand.

'Come on. Let's get you to school before Mummy does anything else silly.'

He grips my hand tightly and we cross the road, this time with my phone securely tucked away in my pocket. Stupid. The amount of times I've rolled my eyes at teenagers not paying attention to their surroundings because they're too absorbed with what's on their screen, and then I go and do exactly the same thing. This whole situation with Fraser and Anna is taking over, becoming all I can think about. It has to stop, I know that. I'm just not sure if I can.

It's as we reach the other side of the road and approach the school gates that I feel it. I glance around at the other people around me. Everyone has seemingly moved on from the near-miss accident. They're all focused on dropping their own kids to school. No one is looking at me anymore.

And yet, I'm being watched. I can sense it.

I spin around, scrutinise my surroundings, searching for any sign of someone not going about their daily business.

It's Fraser. I'm sure of it. I don't know how I know, but my gut is telling me that I'm not safe. The stark reality of my situation settles over me and I pull Mason closer to me. This is not a game. This isn't just something to get drunk and gossip about with Priya. Fraser is dangerous, and I've been stupid and reckless.

I've put a target on my back.

## NINETEEN

It is a plain fact that nobody seems to want to acknowledge: jeans suck. They dig in, they pinch, they make sitting an ordeal. As I perch on a bar stool, waiting for Priya to bring over my drink, I long to be back in my pyjama bottoms.

It's my fault, really. I should have put my foot down with Priya. She's a big girl. She could have handled it. But the people-pleaser in me didn't want to let her down. Plus, on a more selfish level, I'm hoping that sitting in a hipster vibes cocktail bar with music so loud I can barely hear myself think might help to get Anna and Fraser off my mind. I should embrace tonight as an opportunity to switch off entirely. Blur out reality. Muffle the worry.

It's with this thought that I take the gin and tonic Priya brings over to the table. It's stronger than I would normally have it, must be a double, and it makes my eyes water.

'Do you reckon she's wearing underwear?' Priya nods to the other side of the room and I turn to see the girl she means, who is either wearing extremely questionable knickers, or is indeed commando.

'Do you reckon he's wondering the same thing?' I say,

clocking the barman who is also staring in possibly-no-underwear-girl's general direction. Priya laughs. I do, too. A real one this time, not just a reflex.

I'll give Priya her due. I don't want to be here. I'm not a fan of the loud music and sticky floors at the best of times, but particularly not when I'm cycling through feeling terrified in my own home and feeling like I'm losing my marbles. But she makes me smile, which is a pretty big feat these days. This is good. This is what not thinking about Fraser looks like. Who's Fraser? Beats me.

I finish my gin and tonic and we head to the bar for another round. The room hums with chatter and the clinking of glasses. Priya points enthusiastically to the cocktail menu.

'Let's go for something a little more... adventurous.' Her face glows in the warm light, confidence bouncing off her like a second skin.

'No, no. That's when it gets dangerous. When it doesn't taste like alcohol.'

I pull out my phone and squint at it. I texted Lee when we arrived to check if Mason had gone to sleep okay without me. The two blue ticks that appear confirm that he's seen the message, but he hasn't replied.

'I'll be right back,' I say, shimmying through the crowd before Priya can stop me. Bodies press in, bass-heavy music vibrating through my chest. It's as if I've gone deaf when I emerge outside and my ears ring. The rush of cold air is a slap to my senses. I tap into my conversation with Lee and hit *call*. My foot taps on the pavement as I wait for him to pick up.

He doesn't.

Annoyed, I type another message.

*Please let me know all is okay?*

When I return, Priya is leaning over the bar, deep in conversation with the barman who had been checking out no-underwear-girl. She flicks her hair, laughing at something he said. I can't hear what she's saying, but I can imagine. Two vibrant orangey-pink concoctions in a tall glass stand next to her. I look at her incredulously, and it takes her a moment to notice I'm back.

'What's that look for?' she says.

'I said no cocktails.'

'Oh shush.' She laughs, winking at the barman. 'You're always so careful, Miranda. It's okay to let loose occasionally.'

The temptation to point out that the last time I 'let loose' I got caught breaking into someone's house is strong, but she and I both vowed that we wouldn't discuss Fraser tonight, so I bite my tongue and pay for the cocktails.

I sip the drink cautiously as we return to our table. It's sickeningly sweet and, as I had suspected, doesn't taste in the least bit alcoholic, though the menu tells me all the cocktails served here are strong. As the level of the drink goes down, I periodically check my phone. By the time I've finished, Lee still hasn't responded and I'm ready to demand we go home to check everything is okay. Why isn't he messaging back? Has something happened?

I swallow hard and my grip tightens around my empty glass. The taste of the cocktail is suddenly sour in my mouth. My head starts to swim. I stand up, making the table wobble as I do so.

'You okay?' Priya says.

'I'm fine. I just... I think I've had too much to drink.'

'Okay, well, let me down this and we'll get a taxi.'

I blink. Once. Twice.

'Miranda?' Priya's voice is sharper now, cutting through the haze.

'I...' My mouth feels thick, my words slurring before they even leave my tongue. The world tilts, and the bar's bright colours smear together. This isn't alcohol. I've drunk more and been far more intoxicated than this without feeling this way. Something is wrong.

I grip the edge of the table, the wood grounding me for a fleeting second. Priya's face changes, her teasing smile replaced by concern. She reaches out. My knees buckle.

'Miranda, are you okay?'

I try to answer, but my body doesn't feel like my own. My arms hang heavy at my sides, my legs refusing to hold me up. I must be on the floor because all I can see is the ceiling and the tops of people's heads.

And then... is that...?

But my vision narrows as the room dissolves into a pinhole of light.

When Priya shouts for help, her voice echoes as if it's coming from the other end of a tunnel.

## TWENTY

I wake to harsh fluorescent lights and the antiseptic sting of a hospital room. My head pounds.

'Nurse? Nurse, she's waking up...'

Lee's voice pulls me back, and I turn my head slowly. Everything feels sluggish. It's like when I wake from one of my sleep paralysis episodes, except the headache is a million times worse. Lee is standing by my bedside, gesturing for someone to come into the room. Sure enough, two people enter. A man and a woman, both wearing hospital uniforms. Their faces blur slightly before coming into focus.

The man stands at the end of my bed and smiles at me.

'How are you feeling?' he says.

'I...' My throat is dry and scratchy as if I've swallowed sandpaper. I wince at the effort of speaking. 'Like I've been hit by a bus.'

'You're going to feel rough for a few days, I'm afraid. Your drink was spiked. Toxicology shows it was laced with Rohypnol. You had a particularly severe reaction.'

I blink, trying to process what he's just said. I've never had my drink spiked. I used to go clubbing all the time when I was younger and, even then, naive as I was, I was always careful. I never left a drink where I couldn't see it. Not once. Yet, here I am.

'Am I going to be okay?'

'Yes. You're going to be just fine. You needed oxygen when you first came to us and we'll continue monitoring your heart rate, but you should be good to go home tomorrow. Your body just needs time to recover. There will be emotional support for you when that time comes, too, and the police will likely contact you so that you can make a formal statement, if you choose.'

I nod, trying not to let on how badly I don't want any more involvement with the police. Not only that, but I desperately don't want Lee knowing about the run-ins I've already had with them.

'Do you have any questions for me?' the doctor asks.

Yes. Loads. I want to ask why this happened, how this happened, what he would consider a 'severe' reaction to be, why I reacted so much worse than other people who get their drinks spiked, how long I've been here. I want every single detail about what put me in this bed. But instead, I just shake my head dumbly.

'Okay then, I'll be back round to see you in the morning.'

Once he leaves, the nurse who had accompanied him checks my blood pressure and temperature, offers me paracetamol, which I gladly accept, then scribbles on a report and leaves. My fingers twitch against the bedsheets. I glance over at Lee and realise for the first time just how heavy with tiredness his eyes are. He must have been here all night.

'You scared the hell out of me,' he says. 'You're lucky Priya was there.'

'Where is Priya?'

'She's in the waiting room with Mason. He's desperate to see his mum.'

I smile, though it hurts to do so. The muscles in my face feel like lead.

'Can you get her to bring him in?'

Lee nods his head and leaves the room, and I lie there with the doctor's words in my head. I try to pull my mind back to the cocktail bar. When did it happen? It must have been the pinky-orange cocktail. That's the only drink I left unattended, when I went out to call Lee. The night begins to return to me, and I picture the scene, how Priya was completely distracted by the barman, how she had her back turned to the cocktails. Anyone could have snuck up behind her and dropped something into our drinks. A faceless figure in the crowd. Blending in.

But if it was just a random attack, why was it just my drink? Why didn't we both end up in hospital?

My chest tightens as I picture the scene, but I don't have long to think about it because Mason comes bounding into the room. He throws his arms around me, and I wince.

'Slow down, bud,' Lee says, moving to pull him off me. 'Mummy's not well, remember?'

'It's okay.' I wave Lee away and squeeze Mason, not wanting to let him go.

'Are you feeling any better, Mummy?'

'I am now I've got my favourite person with me.'

As I hold Mason, my eyes travel over his shoulder to Priya, who looks surprisingly sombre. Her eyes are red-rimmed, as if she's been crying. A lump forms in my throat. I don't think I've ever seen her like that. Even when in the throes of heartbreak, she always just shrugs sadness off and distracts herself with something else. 'Life is too short,' she always says. It's unsettling to see her any other way.

'Did you see anything?' I ask her.

She shakes her head. 'I'm so sorry, Miranda. I should never have insisted we go out. I should never have taken my eyes off your drink.'

'It's not your fault,' I say, and it's true. It's not her fault. It's the fault of whoever put something in my drink.

My throat tightens as the thought rolls around in my head.

It could be just one of those things. I could be the unfortunate victim of a random attack. You hear about it all the time, don't you? Some creep at the bar, lurking, waiting for an opportunity.

Or, and this is what scares me the most, someone could have picked me. They may have done this to me deliberately.

At this thought, Fraser's face swims into my vision. The idea makes my stomach churn, and I fight the urge to retch.

Priya squeezes my hand, and I can tell she knows exactly what I'm thinking. 'We'll figure it out,' she promises. But I know that's probably not true. If there had been CCTV evidence of my drink being spiked, it would have been recovered as soon as I got taken away in the ambulance. The fact that we don't know who it was means it wasn't captured. Either it was a blind spot for the cameras, or the person who did this was so damn slick and inconspicuous amongst the thick crowds that it's impossible to tell who did it.

'You don't know it was him,' Priya says.

I stiffen. The blood drains from my face. I look at her with wide eyes. An unspoken plea. Not now. Not in front of Lee.

She shakes her head. 'I knew what you were thinking.'

'Wait, who are you talking about?' Lee looks inquisitively between me and Priya, and I close my eyes, holding Mason a little tighter. I don't want to do this. I don't want to have this conversation here, like this.

'We'll discuss it later.'

'You haven't told him?' Priya says. I shoot her a glare. It's too late, of course. She's already dropped me in it.

'Told me what?' I can hear the annoyance in Lee's voice growing.

'Mase, how about you go with Priya to get a chocolate bar

from the canteen?' I say, hoping that the thought of chocolate might distract him from the growing tension in the room.

It works like a charm. He jumps off my bed so fast he nearly elbows me in the stomach.

'Really? You're the best!'

As Priya leaves the room with Mason, she glances back at me and mouths the word, *sorry*. Too late for that.

'What's all this about?' Lee says once Priya and Mason are gone. I rub my forehead, unsure of where to start and just how many details I can leave out. Breaking into Fraser's house, I can definitely omit. But the rest? I take a deep breath.

'I went to the police,' I say eventually, not meeting Lee's eye. 'About Fraser.'

'What?' He sinks down into the chair next to me.

'Just in case there was really something wrong. After I saw what I did on the doorbell and Anna went missing. I haven't seen her since. Can't even get through to her as her phone is switched off. I thought it was better to let the police handle it. You would have told me to do it, if you knew how worried I was.'

Lee exhales sharply. 'Jesus Christ, Miranda. I don't care that you went to the police. I care that you didn't tell me.'

My mouth snaps shut at that. I'd been so anticipating him going off at me for overreacting about the doorbell footage that it hadn't occurred to me he might be more upset about my not telling him. I consider how I'd feel about it if it were the other way around, and decide he's entirely justified in his reaction.

'Sorry,' I say, rather sheepishly. The word feels small and inadequate. 'I just didn't want to worry you. I was hoping that by going to the police it would all be taken care of by them and I wouldn't have to be involved anymore.'

'And has it been?'

'Has it been what?'

'Taken care of? I mean, if you think he's the one who spiked your drink then...'

I place a hand on his thigh, willing him not to jump to conclusions. One of us doing that is bad enough. I rely on Lee to be my voice of reason when I go into one of my panics.

'I don't know who spiked my drink. It could be completely unrelated. But I...' I falter. I'm about to tell him what I saw just before I blacked out. How, among the blurring sea of faces I was convinced I saw Fraser, but now, in the daytime and looking back on it, there's a level of uncertainty that stops me. 'It just seems like a weird coincidence, is all.'

Lee scratches his head. The flood of information seems to have made the tired rings under his eyes even deeper.

'What have the police said about it all?'

This is the bit I don't want to get into. The bit where I admit the police think I'm off my rocker.

'They said they looked into it, but they're not concerned.' I blush slightly, hoping by some miracle Lee might choose to leave it there. Of course he doesn't.

'What does that mean? Not concerned?'

I sigh, resting my head back against my pillow. 'They reckon they've spoken to her. Checked she's okay and confirmed that she's visiting relatives.'

'Right, so... so he hasn't hurt her?'

'We don't know that for sure! She told me she didn't have any relatives. We have no idea how thorough their investigation was.' My voice is sharper than intended.

Lee stands up very suddenly and paces the room. 'So, you're telling me you saw the man pack a suitcase into his car, convinced yourself so much that he was hiding a body that you went to the police, and when they confirmed that they'd spoken to Anna and that she's fine you still continued down this theory that we're living next to a psycho killer?'

The words sting, slicing through my resolve like a blade.

'What about the spiking? I didn't imagine that, did I?'

'But you said yourself you don't know it was him!' Lee cries. 'In fact, you have absolutely no reason to think it was him other than this insane notion that he's chopped up his wife!'

'Sorry to interrupt,' a voice cuts in. We both turn our heads to the door, completely thrown by the addition of a third party into our argument.

It's two police officers. Neither of them are Sergeant Hargreaves. It's a young woman and man with dark hair that I've never seen before.

'We need to take your statement, if you're feeling up to it?' the man says.

I glance over at Lee. He meets my gaze for a moment, then shakes his head. 'I'm going to take Mason home to get some sleep. I'm sure Priya will stay with you. We'll be back in the morning.' With that he leaves the room, shuffling past the two officers as he does so.

What he said is true. When you lay out all the facts of what's happened, I sound like I'm mad. I sound like I'm making all of this up.

But despite that, deep in my gut, a cold certainty has taken root. I've never been so sure of Fraser's guilt as right now. I know he did this to me.

And I know he killed Anna.

## TWENTY-ONE

Apparently, I'm a bit of a special case. It's not normal for someone whose drink has been spiked to end up comatose in hospital as I did. Because I had such a spectacularly bad reaction, I slept for most of the afternoon at the hospital even though I was cleared to leave fairly early this morning. I needed it though. My body ached so badly when I woke up this morning, I'd have rather gone through childbirth again. It's the headache that got me. Like someone taking a screwdriver to my temple and twisting. Slowly.

When I woke from my afternoon sleep it had, thankfully, eased off a bit. It's still there though, pulsating in the back of my brain, even now we're pulling up outside our house. I sit rigidly on the back seat with Mason, one hand holding his, the other clenched in my lap. My eyes are fixed on the front door, but I can feel the tug of Fraser's house in my periphery like a magnet. I fight the urge to look. What if he saw us pull in? What if he's watching from behind his curtains right now?

The thought makes my skin crawl and my head throb. Really, I know it's not just the residual effects of the Rohypnol making me feel this rough. It's the stress. The self-doubt. The gnawing fear that won't leave me alone. It's everything that's been on my mind, building up, over the past few days. If anything, I'm more confused and worried now than I was when I first saw Fraser with that suitcase on my doorbell camera.

Nothing the police have said has put my mind at ease, nor the insistence from Lee that I'm overreacting. But now, even Priya is doubting me, so I have no one to discuss my theories with. They're just stuck swirling around in my brain with nowhere to go. An echo chamber of paranoia and unanswered questions. It feels like I'm going to explode. Being home, which should be a relief, is only increasing that sensation, because now I am, once more, just a few walls away from Fraser.

I shift in my seat, glancing down at Mason's little fingers curled around mine. I chose to be in the back with him, while Priya is in the front with Lee. I wanted to be close to Mason, to be able to hold his hand, but I forgot how loud little boys can be on car journeys. Lee can clearly see my discomfort, as he's quick to scoop Mason up into his arms and away from me as we move towards the door, and thanks Priya for babysitting in a way that tells her she is not to stick around to chat. Part of me feels bad, I know she must be desperate for one of our good old gossip sessions, but the desire to be home and calm is superseding any guilt I feel.

Desperate to distract myself, I insist on doing the bedtime routine with Mason, despite Lee telling me to lie down. It works for a while. He splashes in the bath and asks me to pretend to sip on lattes made of bubbles in miniature plastic cups, and I smush it into my nose so that I have a bubble moustache which makes him cackle with laughter, and we have fluffy towel snuggles on the bathroom floor before I get him dressed in his favourite Spider-Man pyjamas and slippers. It feels normal, for the first time in a very long time, and that helps.

But the moment he's settled and I slip out of his room, the normalcy starts to crack. As I walk down the hallway, I pass the landing window and feel the pull of it. *Don't look.* That's what I tell myself. Looking won't change anything. It'll only feed the panic clawing at my insides. But my feet slow anyway. I hover beside the window, biting the inside of my cheek, fighting the impulse.

I glance. Just a flick of my eyes. Quick. Almost careless. Except it's not. The street is still, shadows stretching long in the lamplight, wildflowers and foxgloves swaying gently in the evening breeze. Fraser's house sits quietly next to ours, curtains drawn tight.

Nothing to see. But my heart is still pounding.

'Did Mason go down okay?' Lee's voice behind me makes me jump.

I spin around, cheeks reddening as if he's caught me watching something inappropriate on TV.

'Yep, out like a light.'

'He hated you not being here,' he says.

'I hated it too.' Hated is an understatement. It felt so wrong not being home with him, knowing he must have been worried sick about his mummy being in hospital. It was probably that knowledge that caused another of my episodes last night.

It was so much worse than it's ever been for the simple fact that Lee wasn't there to talk me down. When I first opened my eyes and realised I couldn't move, I thought I might die. That my heart was beating too fast and too hard and that it would just shut down. I tried to do everything my therapist told me to do. I counted the squares in the suspended hospital ceiling, the signs on the wall, the beds on the ward, but nothing worked. I was just stuck there in literal hell for what felt like hours, drowning in panic. When a nurse did finally come, she had no idea what was wrong with me or how to help. She'd probably never seen it happen before. And while she ran to get someone else, I never wanted to be back with my family, with Lee and with my sweet boy, more than I did in that moment.

'You okay?' Lee says now, snapping me out of the memory. My eyes flick up to his and I know they're watering. I haven't told Lee about last night's episode, and I don't plan to. He worries. He's already carrying too much of my weight. I don't need him worrying more than he already is.

'I just missed you both so much.'

'Anyone would think you were gone for weeks.'

He's making light of it, which is fine. It makes me feel better. Overcome by a sudden surge of gratitude for Lee being Lee, I step forward and wrap my arms around him, holding him close. His returned embrace is strong, safe, and I melt into it.

'I love you,' I whisper, pressing my lips to his. Then, before he can respond, my hands make their way up underneath his shirt. My fingers slide across his warm skin, and he kisses me deeper in response, more urgently.

Just as I'm about to start unbuttoning his shirt, he jolts away from me, holding me at arm's length.

'I don't think we should. You've only just got back from the hospital.'

I look at him longingly. 'I feel better when I'm with you.'

The truth of that statement rocks me. We've been married for five years. We have a five-year-old. I've been in and out of sleep therapy. Our sex life hasn't exactly been thriving recently. Between everyday life and him working longer hours since his promotion, not to mention my, shall we say, paranoia about the neighbours, intimacy has taken a back seat. But right here, right now, all I want is him. I want him to be my sanctuary for a while.

He doesn't need a whole lot of convincing. When he sees how much I want it he's back kissing me, moving those kisses from my mouth to my neck to my chest. We move as one into the bedroom, closing the door quietly so as not to wake Mason, and fall onto the bed. We remove our clothes at record speed and then his mouth is back on me. I arch my neck, allowing my head to fall to one side. My eyes rest upon my bedside table. I frown.

'Have you been in my drawer?' I say.

He doesn't seem to understand my question properly, as he says a muffled 'hmm?' in response while not once stopping what he's doing.

'Lee, why is this out?' I twist on the bed, reaching to the bedside table so that he has no choice but to pause. I point at what caught my attention. My bottom drawer, the one with all my underwear in it, is open, and the one piece of sexy lingerie that I own that I break out on our anniversary is lying on top of my bras and granny knickers.

Lee leans over and peers at the drawer.

'You can put that on if you want,' he says, misunderstanding what I'm trying to say entirely.

'No, I mean, why has it been pulled out of the drawer? What were you doing with it?'

'I didn't get it out of the drawer...'

'Well, I didn't.'

He sits back, all traces of the mood gone.

'You must have done. Why would I go in your underwear drawer?'

'Lee, I'm telling you, I didn't! I haven't been here, have I?'

'You must have opened it before you went out with Priya. Or maybe Mason was messing around in there?'

I blink at the drawer. Could it be that innocent? It doesn't *feel* innocent.

'Mason never comes in our room,' I say quietly.

Lee shakes his head at me, clearly bewildered. 'It's fine. You don't have to put it on.'

The frustration that he's not understanding what I'm trying to say is spilling out of me. I shimmy out from underneath him, body trembling with annoyance and confusion and fear.

'Lee! You're not *listening* to me. If Mason never comes in

here, and I didn't pull it out of the drawer, and you didn't pull it out of the drawer, then who did?'

His gaze flicks between the lacey one-piece and me a few times, as if he's trying to make sense of what I'm saying. A muscle twitches in his jaw. After a few seconds, his eyes grow wide.

'I don't believe this,' he says, standing up and grabbing his trousers. 'After all we've been through that's where your mind has gone?'

'What?' Now it's my turn to be confused. I stand up with him, not bothering to try to re-dress but instead making a grab for my dressing gown.

'You really think I'd do something like that? Even if I did, you think I'd do it while you were in hospital?'

I understand now what he's getting at. He thinks I'm accusing him of having another woman in here, that I've convinced myself she's been wearing my lingerie. The idea is so far from what I had been thinking that I do something completely inappropriate; I start to laugh. He watches me as I chuckle in my dressing gown, still half annoyed, half confused. His expression only makes me laugh harder.

'What's funny?' he says eventually.

'I'm sorry,' I say through fits of giggles. 'It's not funny. It's really not. It's just... that's absolutely what I should be thinking. When I've been away and I come into the bedroom and it's clear that someone has been in our bedroom, my first thought should absolutely have been that you've had another woman in here. But that's not what I thought at all.' At that, I burst into another fit of laughter, and Lee begins to look less annoyed and more scared of me.

'It's not?'

'No.' I wipe tears from my eyes as I continue to laugh.

'What did you think, then?'

The laughter finally starts to subside, and I perch on the

edge of my bed, holding my hand to my forehead. The ache is back, worse than before. Lee comes to sit beside me.

I look at him. He doesn't really need an answer. He already knows that my first thought when I saw that drawer open was that someone has been in our house, uninvited, snooping around. *Much like how I was snooping around in Fraser's house the other day*, I think, though of course, I can't say.

Lee lets out a long, slow sigh. The kind that makes it clear he's exhausted, of this conversation, or perhaps just of me.

'I think you need to go and see your therapist again,' he says after a moment.

I ignore his comment. 'He could have used the spare key.'

'How would he have known where to look?'

'It wouldn't take a genius to find, would it? Besides, Beth told him the day they moved in that everyone keeps a spare hidden. Check on the doorbell app. I bet we'll see him finding it and using it.' I pull out my phone and navigate to the doorbell app. If Fraser broke into our house, it will have been caught on camera. I'll have conclusive proof.

But as I tap into the app a message pops up.

*There is a problem with the connection. Please check your Wi-Fi and try again.*

'Why is this stupid thing not working?' I say, jabbing at the refresh button.

'Miranda, stop.' Lee's hand covers the screen and lowers the phone to my lap. 'I removed the doorbell.'

'You *what*?'

'I don't think it's healthy for you. Even before all of this you were constantly watching the neighbours. You're so paranoid all the time and having a constant video stream of our street is not going to help.'

'Who are you to decide what's healthy for me or not?'

'Hence why I think you need to go back to your therapist!'

I turn away from him, unable to maintain eye contact, and we fall into an uneasy silence. I focus my attention on the clock on our windowsill, watching the second hand tick.

'Do you think I'm crazy?'

'No.' He takes my hand and squeezes. 'I think your mind makes up the worst-case scenario because you're scared.'

'So not crazy, just delusional.'

He doesn't say anything to that. His silence is an answer in and of itself. A tear drops down and splashes onto my thigh.

Lee is wrong. Between the doorbell footage and the bloodstained shirt and the Rohypnol and the thought that someone may have been in our house without our knowledge and the fact that neither he nor my best friend nor even the police will believe a word I say, I'm not scared. I'm bloody terrified. And worst of all, I'm completely alone in it.

'What if it *was* him?' I whisper. The words seem dangerous, as if by saying them out loud I might accidentally make them real. 'What if he's been in our home, Lee?'

'You're talking about Fraser, I assume?'

My stomach clenches as I picture it: him letting himself in here somehow and roaming around our room, looking at our family photos, rummaging through my underwear drawer. Everything around me feels tainted.

'I know you think I'm making a bigger deal of this than it is, but what if I'm not? What if he did kill Anna that night?'

'The police said—'

'The police have barely looked into it!' I don't mean to shout but it bursts out of me, all the frustration that's been building inside of me. I take a breath and bring my voice back to a normal level. 'They think the same as you, that I'm some crazy, paranoid woman and that it's not worth their time.'

'I told you, I don't think you're crazy.'

'What if you're all wrong and I'm right? Just answer me that, Lee.'

He leans back on the bed and lets his head fall back so that he's staring up at the ceiling, as if the correct thing that he should say is written on it.

'I'm going to book you an appointment with the therapist,' he says, and with that he stands up, pulls his shirt on, and leaves the bedroom.

I stare after him and wait for him to come back. He doesn't. I realise with a heavy heart just how well this is all working out for Fraser. It wouldn't surprise me if this is what he had planned all along: to ostracise me, to make it so that I have no support system, so that I feel totally alone. Even before Anna disappeared it started. Sitting there at that dining table being overly friendly with Lee and making me feel like I was an unwelcome third wheel tagging along. If I didn't know better, I'd say they had been best buddies for years.

And then, like poison, a new thought slithers into my head. It's a ridiculous thought, but it's there now, whispering in the back of my mind.

Lee is so quick to dismiss what I'm saying. To make me feel like I'm overreacting, imagining things. To look at me with that mix of pity and concern like I'm not entirely stable. Like maybe I *am* the problem. He also seems desperate for this theory of mine to be squashed as quickly as possible.

So then... what if it's not just concern for my well-being?

What if Lee is helping Fraser to cover up Anna's death?

## TWENTY-TWO

'You sure you don't want me to come with you?' Lee says as he pulls his coat on, ready for work.

'I'm sure. It's not like it's my first time seeing him.'

The real reason I want Lee to go to work and not accompany me to my therapy appointment is because I have no intention of going to see my therapist. And I need privacy in order to do what I want to do. I can't have him hovering over me. Watching. Questioning. Reporting back to Fraser, if that's what he's doing.

I don't want to believe that. I really, really don't. Every time I think about the possibility that my husband knows what Fraser has done, and is helping him to get away with it, my heart feels like it might give out. That's not Lee. He's not the type of person to get involved with things like that, and he wouldn't try to make me think I'm crazy, not after everything we've been through together. But I'd be lying if I said I trusted him anymore. Not fully. Not with this. So I paste on my best 'I'm fine' smile, give him a kiss and a cuddle, and wave him off to the car.

He winds down the driver's window. 'Don't forget!' he calls. 'I might not be back until later tonight.'

'Yep!'

I wave, watching him drive away, and then allow the smile to drop. Forty-five minutes later, I've dropped Mason at school, rushed past Fraser's house, not wanting to spend any longer out on the street than I absolutely have to, and am finally alone in our home. Even in the safety of our four walls, the air feels heavier than it should. I always thought the devil was restricted to being just outside my home, but now there's the possibility that he's living with me too, and that's more than I can bear.

First things first, I locate the doorbell. It's easy to find. Lee didn't make much of an effort to hide it. He's going to be annoyed when he comes home to discover it reinstalled, but I don't care. It's my house too. If he wants to act like I'm losing my grip on reality, that's his problem, not mine. I'll tell him my therapist said there was nothing wrong with having it up there, that it's good for my paranoia, or whatever Lee thinks I have, because it's a way of validating or disproving what I'm imagining. Yes. That sounds like something a therapist would say.

I have to pull a YouTube video up on my phone to figure out how to get the thing working, but before too long I'm greeted by the familiar sight of the street view on my app. A prickle of satisfaction spreads through me. I do have a minor panic when I wonder if having it disconnected like that may have wiped the footage of Fraser putting the suitcase in his car, but to my relief it's still there in the archive. Thank God for the Cloud.

Already feeling better, and pleased with myself for my tiny act of rebellion, I slip on my shoes and head over to Priya's. Ordinarily I'd go to hers straight after the school run, so the delay of putting the doorbell back up probably has her thinking I'm still too weak from my hospital stay to resume our usual routine. On the contrary, I can't wait to talk to her. I figure the incident with the lingerie will probably be enough to rekindle her interest in our theories about Fraser.

As I approach her house, I notice her bay window is wide open, and I can just about see her sitting inside. She's not alone, either. My pace slows until I'm stood close enough to her house and at the right angle to have a clearer view, without her being able to see me. There are two others in there with her. Ellen and Beth.

A stab of jealousy hits me. Beth and Ellen hang out without me all the time. They're like a mirror-image of me and Priya. But I don't remember a time when Beth, Ellen, and Priya hung out without me. Why wasn't I invited?

I press my lips together, annoyed. I don't really want to go in there if Ellen and Beth are visiting too. I get on with them well enough, but they're not the sort of people I want to be discussing my Fraser theories with. Aside from anything, secrets told to Ellen and Beth have a funny way of getting around the entire town in a matter of weeks.

I'm just about to head back to my house when something makes me stop in my tracks. I hear my name. Cocking my head, I take a step closer to the bay window. Beth's voice drifts through the opening.

'Do they have any idea who did it?'

'Not that I know of,' comes Priya's voice. 'Miranda's got some wild theory that it might have been Mr Dreamy across the road.'

'What? Why would she think that?' Ellen says.

'Oh, I don't know. I think she's got a bit of an obsession with him. Literally does not stop talking about him. It's doing my head in.'

A lead weight drops in my stomach.

'I don't blame her,' Beth pipes up. 'I certainly wouldn't mind watching him mowing his grass, if you know what I mean.'

The three of them descend into cackling laughter at that,

the sound of it slicing through me. They think my worries are *funny*. I can't listen any more. I move away from the house quickly and quietly, holding the tears inside until I am well and truly over the threshold of my front door. Once I'm inside I allow them to fall, except they don't. Instead, a shriek escapes from my throat, a guttural scream of frustration.

Trembling, I sweep over to the kitchen table and power up my laptop. My fingers hover over the keyboard, fists clenching and unclenching. Priya wants to joke around and make me out to be some crazy, obsessed stalker? Fine. I can act like one. Once the laptop wakes up, I navigate to Google and type Fraser's name into the search bar. A page of seemingly useless results show up. There's a news report about a teenager with the same name in New Zealand and a few random Facebook profiles that don't look anything like him. I close my eyes and wrack my brains for another detail to include in the search that might narrow down the results.

Anna said something the day we took the welcome basket round. She told us where he worked. Where was it? Orbit-something? Orbit Solutions? No, that's not quite right.

Unable to remember, I take a chance and simply add 'Orbit' to the search query. The top result sparks something in the depths of my memory.

Orbital Solutions Group.

That was it. I'm sure of it.

Sucking in a breath, I tap through to the result. It's a blog post written by the company, not particularly telling, but it mentions Fraser midway through the article as having given a quote about something very techy that I don't understand, and it has a picture of him accompanying the quote. At least that means I'm on the right track.

Hands moving faster than my brain can think, I navigate over to the 'Find Us' tab and squint at the address. It's an office in Birmingham. Miles away. Surely he's not commuting back and forth every day? It would take him hours. Perhaps he works from home a lot. That's common these days, isn't it?

I sit back in my chair and twiddle with a strand of my hair, wondering what to do next. My foot bounces restlessly on the floor. I'm not entirely sure what my plan was in googling him. I wanted to find out more about the man, but all I've managed to learn is the name of the company he works at, and I technically already knew that. The truth is, no amount of googling is going to tell me who Fraser Coles actually *is*. The only people who can tell me that are those who know him. Those who knew him before he moved to this street.

There's a lump forming in my throat that I struggle to swallow down, as an idea formulates. I peer over at the time in the corner of the laptop screen. It's still early. Just coming up to ten. Plenty of time before I need to be worrying about picking Mason up from school, and even more time to spare before Lee comes home from work.

I pull up the Maps app on my phone and type in Orbital Solutions Group. It tells me the drive would take me just over three hours in current traffic conditions. I rock back and forth on my chair as I count back the hours from school-run time to see if I could make it.

It will be tight, I know that. But I also know I've already made up my mind.

## TWENTY-THREE

Orbital Solutions Group is, as it happens, a global tech powerhouse specialising in enterprise AI, cybersecurity, and Cloud infrastructure.

I only know this because I downloaded a bunch of YouTube videos about the company and had the audio playing in the background during the drive down here, thinking it might give me a better idea of the sort of work Fraser does. I'm still not sure I understand the purpose of the company, but it all sounds very important.

The skyscraper office is exactly what you'd expect: glass and steel as high up as the eye can see. It's sleek and intimidating. A giant LED screen flashes promotional messaging on the face of the building and, from the road, I can see the glass-encased lift taking workers up and down the floors. I think if I worked at Orbital Solutions Group, I'd be fired on my first day for throwing up in the lift. Heights, particularly those separated from me by just a pane of glass, are not my favourite thing. Just looking at it makes my head spin.

I park in a Pay and Display, making sure to only put twenty

minutes on the ticket. That means I won't be tempted to stay any longer and risk not making it back in time to pick up Mason. I then make my way over to the main entrance, wishing I had thought to put on some smarter clothes before I left. School-run mum vibes do not match this place in the slightest.

The interior of the building matches the exterior perfectly, and I feel as if I've stepped into the future. Everything is very white. The vast reception area's high ceilings and polished marble floors reflect the glow of LED panels that stream stock prices, news updates, and corporate achievements in a constant, silent loop. Behind the minimalist reception desk, a massive digital art installation shifts and morphs. I'm not sure what it's supposed to be but it's captivating, at least.

The receptionist barely glances up as I approach. She's talking. At first I think she's speaking to me, but when I get closer I realise she's talking into a Bluetooth earpiece. She looks rather fed up. I clock her name badge. Esme.

'I'm going on my lunchbreak in ten minutes. I'll have to do it when I'm back,' she says to her ear, and then, to me, 'Please sign in at the kiosk.' She nods towards a touch screen to my right.

Bold black letters on the screen ask me who I'm here to meet with. I ponder this for a moment, then tap the letter F, hoping it may show me what floor Fraser works on. A whole bunch of names pop up, none of which are Fraser's. Perhaps it's surnames. I try the letter C instead, but still, when the names appear, I can't see Fraser's anywhere. I turn back to Esme, determined to not let this have been a wasted journey, and wait for her to finish her phone conversation.

'Excuse me,' I say once she's done, and Esme looks up, clearly surprised to have been spoken to. She's pretty, with big, doe-like brown eyes. She actually looks a bit like Anna, which is disconcerting to say the least. 'I don't actually have an appointment.'

'Who was it you wanted to speak with?' she asks.

I pause. Who should I even ask for?

'I wanted to speak to someone about Fraser Coles.'

Esme blinks.

'I'm sorry?'

'Um... Fraser Coles? I wanted to chat to someone about him. Is there someone who works with him that I can speak to?'

She's giving me such a strange look you'd have thought I was talking in another language. I shuffle from foot to foot, not sure what to say. In fact, she doesn't just look like she doesn't understand me. Her face has completely drained of colour, as if I've walked in here wielding a machete.

After what seems like an eternity of just staring at me, she returns to tapping away at her computer.

'I'm afraid there's nobody here by that name.'

I blink, taken aback. 'He's the vice president of the company,' I say, with more of a tone of 'you don't know what the hell you're talking about' than I had intended.

'Mr Eric Marston is the vice president of Orbital Solutions Group.'

She says it with such certainty that I wonder if maybe I've come to the wrong building. I pull up the blog post on my phone, cheeks flaming at the thought of coming all this way because of a typo on the map. No. There he is. A quote from Fraser Coles, Vice President, and the logo matches. It's there in black and white. I'm not imagining things.

Fighting the sinking feeling in my gut, I turn the phone to face the receptionist.

'Does the company have more than one headquarters, maybe? Because he's listed here on your website.'

Esme glares at the phone, and then something flashes across her face. Nerves? Anxiety? Fear? It's too quick for me to be sure.

'As I said, there's nobody by that name at this company.'

'But could you—'

'Is there anything else I can help you with today?'

I want to ask her to answer my question about the multiple headquarters. I want to tell her she should advise her HR department to put in some more customer service training for their receptionists. But I say neither of those things. There's something in her face that's telling me not to push the matter any further.

'No, thank you.' I retreat away from the desk and, heart in my mouth, I head back towards the main doors. Something's not right, but I can't put my finger on what. As I approach the doors, I peer back at Esme. She's glugging a glass of water and there's a slight sheen to her forehead that wasn't there before, as if our brief, awkward conversation has made her break out into a sweat. She's rattled. And that rattles me.

I do not drive away from Orbital Solutions Group. Instead, I sit in the driver's seat, hands gripping the steering wheel, and watch the building, eyes focused on the glass doors. I can see the receptionist through them. She said on the phone she was about to go on her lunchbreak, so theoretically she should leave the desk any minute now. I'm just hoping she's going to leave to have lunch at one of the local cafés or coffee shops and not at some private, swanky canteen that only employees can access. To my relief, after a brief wait, Esme stands and heads towards the glass doors. I seize my moment and leave my car, moving swiftly to follow close behind. She takes a left, heading towards the high street, and I speed up my step.

'Excuse me? Esme?' I say once I'm near enough for her to hear me.

She turns. The flash of horror-filled realisation on her face when she recognises me is enough to make me realise how psychotic I must seem to her, so I'm quick to raise my hands in an effort to show her I mean her no harm.

'I'm sorry. I know this isn't appropriate—'

'What the hell do you want?'

She's scared. And not just in a 'this crazy woman has followed me' kind of scared. She's been scared from the moment I mentioned Fraser's name. That was what I saw on her face when I showed her the picture. I recognise it now.

'I just want to talk. You know him, don't you? I can tell from the way you're acting.'

'I don't know what you're talking about. You need to leave me alone, or I'll call the police.'

My body stiffens at the thought of someone else making a report about me. How many times can that happen before I'm locked up in some kind of psychiatric facility? I have a history of mental health issues. Surely it wouldn't take much. One too many calls. One too many accusations...

'I will go. I promise, you'll never see me again after today. But please, I'm begging you. I'm worried about his wife. If you know anything at all about Fraser that I should be concerned about, or that I should be going to the police about, please tell me.'

The panic in Esme's face is lessening slightly. Perhaps she can tell I'm just as freaked out as she is. She brings her thumbnail to her teeth and starts to chew. Then, without a word, she turns and begins to walk off.

'He lives on my street!' I call, desperation seeping into my voice. She stops but doesn't turn back to face me. 'I have a young son. I'm just trying to protect him. Please. If you know anything that can help me, you have to tell me.'

There is a long, excruciating silence. I watch her shoulders rise and fall, her eyes darting around as if she's checking for witnesses. There is a burning, overwhelming desire to shout and scream at her to stop being so selfish, but I know that will just scare her off. Instead, I bite down on the inside of my cheeks, forcing my mouth to remain closed, and wait.

Finally, Esme turns and strides back to me. She comes so close that I can smell her fruity perfume.

'If you know what's good for you and your son,' she says in a low voice, 'you'll stay away from Fraser Coles.'

The words punch through me, cold and sharp, and before I can even think of a suitable response, she runs off and disappears around the corner of the building.

## TWENTY-FOUR

I'm late. I'm so, so late.

If the journey back home had been as smooth as the journey to Birmingham had been, I'd have just made it in time to pick Mason up from school, even with the delay of waiting for the receptionist to go on her lunchbreak. But there have been two car crashes on the motorway causing backed-up traffic for miles that I've had to fight through, and now I'm still eighteen minutes away and should be there picking him up right now. Every red light, every slow-moving car, feels like a personal attack. I'm so stressed at the thought of him standing in the playground with his teacher watching all his friends being picked up and wondering why Mummy isn't there that I can't even think about what the receptionist said to me. All that matters is that I get there. I'll deal with the rest later.

As the estimated time of arrival creeps up on my satnav, the panic inside me rises alongside it. Mason is a sensitive kid, and he jumps to the worst-case scenario just like I do. It's one of those things Lee always reminds me I've passed on to him. I'm never late picking him up, and the fact that I am late means he'll undoubtedly be thinking I'm lying dead on the side of the road or something awful like that. The thought of it brings tears to my eyes.

'Okay, Google,' I say, voice trembling, and my phone responds with a ding. 'Call the school.'

It rings and rings, and after a few moments a mechanical voice tells me I've reached the school's office voicemail and that I should leave a message.

'Hi, it's Mason's mummy. Mason Jennings in Caterpillar class.' I trip over my words and shake my head, trying to collect my thoughts enough to at least leave a coherent message. My nails dig into the steering wheel. 'I am on my way. I got stuck in traffic. But I'll be there soon. Please tell Mason so that he's not worried. Thank you.'

Leaving the message has done nothing to help with my anxiety. Who knows if they'll even receive the message in time? Clearly no one is manning the office right now. I glance at the clock. Another minute lost. I press my foot harder down on the accelerator, breaking the 30mph speed limit.

My tyre clips the pavement as I speed into the car park a whole twenty-two minutes late. I half expect to see Mason standing outside the gates with an angry-looking teacher, but there's no one to be seen. Usually when I do the school run the area surrounding the school is heaving, a swarm of small bodies in blue cardigans and their parents. Pulling up this late is eerie. It feels like a ghost town.

I jam my handbrake on right outside the reception entrance. It's a disabled space but I'm only going to be here for a few seconds and there's no one around. When I burst in through the entrance door, I catch a glimpse of my reflection in the window. I look slightly deranged. Flushed cheeks, wild eyes, hair sticking to my forehead.

There doesn't seem to be anyone manning the desk, so I lean across and call, 'Excuse me?'

After a few seconds the office manager appears. She hasn't

liked me since I forgot to hand in a permission slip for a school trip one time, and I pointed out that it would have been helpful for the school to send an email reminder to parents. She purses her lips at the sight of me.

'Mason Jennings,' I say when she approaches. 'I'm here to collect Mason Jennings. Sorry I'm so late.'

'Is he at an after-school club?'

'No, no. I'm just late picking him up from school.'

'Oh, okay.' She peers behind her, to the little waiting area adorned with kids' drawings and paintings. There's no one there. A single crayon has been abandoned on the table, a red scribble left unfinished on a colouring sheet. 'No one has brought him to the office. Remind me what class he's in? I'll go and see if he's still there.'

'He's in Caterpillar class.'

The office manager disappears down the hallway and I find a chair to slump down into. You'd have thought that they'd have him, bag packed, coat on, ready to go. My fingers tap anxiously against my knee as I glance around the empty reception. My head drops back and I stare at the clock on the wall as I wait. As long as we're back before Lee is home, that's all that matters. Lee cannot know that I was late picking Mason up or he'll want to know why. I'll have to bribe Mason with some sweets on the way home to keep him quiet. A fizzy drink too, maybe.

Except when the office manager returns, Mason isn't with her. Instead, Mason's teacher, Miss Donelly, is walking beside her. Her hands are clasped tightly in front of her.

Something is wrong. I can see it on their faces. Instantly, my mind reels. The first few months of Mason starting school I'd constantly descend into panic attacks, picturing him getting hurt while he was in the care of other people and me not being there to help him. I got used to him being away from me eventually, but now, seeing their expressions, I'm imagining the worst.

Surely, nothing could have happened to him while he was at school? They'd have called me.

'Mrs Jennings, hi.' Her face is creased with concern. 'Are you here for Mason?'

'Yes.' My hands bunch into fists. What a ridiculous question to ask me. Who else would I be here for? I have to fight the urge to shake her.

'It's just... your husband picked him up earlier. At the normal pickup time.'

My mouth drops open. Lee picked him up? No. That's not possible. Lee doesn't get off from work for another hour and a half. Besides, didn't he say something about being home late today?

I shake my head slowly. 'I don't think so.'

'Could you call him and check? Someone definitely collected him. I watched them go.'

At her words my blood runs cold. The walls of the reception area seem to tilt. I pull my phone out of my pocket and tap onto Lee's number. It rings. And rings. And rings.

Then voicemail.

Swearing under my breath, I try again with the same result. Of course he's not picking up. He's still at fucking work.

My breath starts to come to me in sharp, shallow bursts. I step forward and grip the edge of the desk. The wood is smooth, solid. The only thing keeping me upright.

'Are you absolutely sure it was Lee?' My voice comes out a strangled hiss.

'I... I think so.' Miss Donelly takes a step back, her face mirroring my own panic.

'I need you to be *sure*! Are you positive that the man who picked up my son today was my husband and not another man?'

'It looked like him. I'm not...'

My legs weaken beneath me.

'Call the police,' I say through gritted teeth.

The office manager flicks her gaze between Miss Donelly and myself, eyebrows raised. 'Are you sure there was no one else expected to collect him today, Mrs Jennings?'

'Are you *deaf*?' I shout. My voice cracks. 'Somebody has taken my son from the school grounds. He was your responsibility, and you let him be taken by someone that was not me. Now *call the police!*'

Terror flashes through both of their faces as they finally realise the severity of the situation. The colour drains from Miss Donelly's cheeks. She nods and picks up the phone on the desk. Her hands are trembling.

I step back. My fingers twitch, useless by my sides, desperate for action. I need to do something. I need to act. Miss Donelly is already through to the police, but my heart is pounding so fast I can't hear or concentrate on what she's saying through the force of it. The blood rushes in my ears, drowning everything out.

'Mrs Jennings,' the office manager calls as I move to the door. 'You should stay. The police may want to talk to you.'

But I'm already gone. The door slams behind me. My feet hit the pavement outside at a run. I can't just stand and wait for the police to turn up and ask a bunch of questions before finally going to look for him, and probably putting just as much effort into it as they did with Anna.

No. I know who has Mason. It's just a case of figuring out where he's taken him.

## TWENTY-FIVE

The sound of my fist battering Fraser's door splits through the quiet of the afternoon. Each impact sends a dull ache up my arm. The noise is jarring against our sleepy cul-de-sac. If anyone were to look out of their window right now, they'd probably think I'm some kind of madwoman standing here causing such a disturbance, but I'm too high-strung, too desperate to care.

No one comes to answer the door. I'm not surprised. If you're going to kidnap a child, you're not going to bring him back to your house, are you? Not when the mother of the child lives next door. Besides, his car isn't here. But I don't know where else to look. I don't know anything about Fraser. Even the job Anna told me he did seems to hold more secrets than answers. I think about the way the receptionist's face drained of colour when I mentioned his name. What did he do to her to make her so scared? Why is he no longer working at that company, and why is it seemingly so hush-hush?

I don't have time to think about these questions right now. I slam my fist against the door a few more times and, when there's still no answer, I start inspecting his windows. One of them has to be open. I can climb through again, like I did last time, and get in there. Not necessarily to search for Mason – I'm not naive enough to think he'll be in there – but to search for clues. There has to be something. A note. A receipt. A trace of his plans. Some indicator of where he may have taken my son. There just has to be.

I race around the side of the house to the utility room window I climbed through last time. It's closed. I try the other side of the house, the side that the office would be on. Closed. Everything is locked up tight. Tears springing from my eyes, I return to the front of the house and lift the doormat, run my hand along the top of the door, inspect the creepy-looking gnome and other garden decorations, rummage through the bushes. No spare key. He probably knows how dangerous they can be since he used ours to break into our house.

Helplessness washing over me, I turn and slide down the front door until I'm sitting on the ground. Suddenly I'm bawling, tears streaming down my face, snot bubbling at my nostrils. My body shakes with each heaving sob. I cry and I bang my head against the door, and I squeeze my arms around my legs. This cannot be happening. I should have been there. I should have been waiting outside of Mason's classroom to pick him up. It was my duty to make sure that he, of all people, was safe. And now Fraser's taken my little boy, and I can't even bring myself to think about Anna and whatever became of her.

I try phoning Lee one more time. Still no answer. I haven't heard anything from the police yet, either. They're probably still at the school, wasting time asking the clueless staff questions and taking pointless notes. The thought of it causes something to settle over me. A new type of resolve. Something raw and animalistic. The kind of no-inhibitions thinking that only comes from a mother knowing that her child is in danger. Clambering up from my spot on the floor, I round the side of the house until I'm face to face with the gate leading to the back garden. I look it up and down, then without hesitation I pull Fraser's green wheelie bin and push it up against the gate. With a heave I'm up. As I kick off the bin it topples, landing on its side, but I'm already over the fence. No hesitation. No second thoughts.

Their conservatory juts out of the back of the house, connected to the dining room. I saw it when we were round for dinner. It's old. Single-glazed. One that was probably tacked onto the house in the late nineties and really needs knocking down and replacing. It's a weak spot. I don't allow myself to think about what I'm doing, because if I allow my brain to get involved, I'll stop. I'm just operating on pure adrenaline at this point. There's no room for doubt.

I grab one of the garden chairs, metal with a fancy, floral design, and swing. The hard legs impact with the glass of the conservatory door and bounce off it. I swing again. This time there's a cracking sound, but I can't tell if it's the door or the chair.

Again.
*Thwack.*
My arms shake.
Again.
*Crack.*
I grit my teeth.
Again.
*Smash.*

The glass shatters into tiny, blunt fragments, forming a glistening carpet at the foot of the door. Someone will have heard it. Herring Row is so quiet, any kind of disturbance is noticed. I dive inside the conservatory quickly, glass crunching underfoot, and make my way, laser-focused, to the office. There was something in there. Something Fraser did not want me to see. It may not lead me to Mason, but if it's even in the slightest bit incriminating it should be enough for the police to take me seriously, and once they've arrested him, they'll find Mason.

I'm not careful with my search. There's no need to be. He'll see the smashed glass. He'll know someone's been in the house. I pull drawers straight out of his desk and leave them emptied out on the floor. Letters scatter. Pens roll under furniture. I rummage around in the antique cabinet on the far-right side of the room. I search through the files and the paperwork, even his briefcase. There's nothing jumping out at me.

This can't have all been for nothing. There's something here. There just *has* to be. I can't have been imagining the way he was when he caught me looking in here. But then, maybe whatever it was is gone. Maybe he got rid of it the second the police knocked at his door. Maybe I'm too late.

I slump against the desk, not knowing what to do next. A hollow ache swells inside me. There is nothing. I'm out of options. All I can do is return to the school and answer the questions from the police and hope and pray that they're going to take this more seriously than they did Anna's disappearance. I can't fix this. I can't keep my son safe. It feels as if a chunk of me has been carved out and plucked from my chest.

As the thoughts spiral my breathing grows erratic. No. Not here. Not now. I need Lee to talk me down, to stop me freezing, to stop my body shutting down. But Lee will never find me here. Fraser will. He'll find me, lying in a hyperventilating puddle on the floor, weak and helpless, and God knows what he'll do to me. The panic rips its way through my body until it's all I can feel. The worry for Mason is gone. The anger at Fraser is gone. All replaced by just sheer, endless panic.

What would Lee tell me to do? I squeeze my eyes shut and grip onto the edge of the desk as I try to replay his soothing words in my ears.

*Breathe. Focus on your surroundings.*

I squint through half-closed lids at what's around me. Papers. Lots of sheets of paper strewn about the place. And a leather book. No. Not a book. A photo album.

Wait. A photo album.

The curiosity of what's inside it distracts me just enough to take the edge off the panic attack. My breath steadies ever so slightly. I shimmy over to it and start flicking through the glossy pages. Anna must have put this together. It doesn't seem like the sort of thing Fraser would do. But maybe that's a sexist generalisation. The last few days have proved how little I know about him. Maybe he is the photo album kind of man.

The first few photos are just as you'd expect. Him and Anna in various exotic locations. Tropical beaches. Classic touristy shots. A bunch of their wedding day. And then there, after the honeymoon pictures, is the photo that makes me stop dead in my tracks. My breath catches. My fingers grip the edge of the page. I pull the album closer to me, blinking a few times to make sure my eyes aren't deceiving me. They're not.

It's Esme. The woman from the receptionist's desk at Orbital Solutions Group. The one who looked on the verge of passing out at the mention of Fraser's name. In the photo she's standing between Anna and Fraser, their arms wrapped around each other. Friendly. Familiar. They all know each other well.

I flick to the next page and my hands flies up to my mouth. A choked noise escapes me. I nearly drop the album, I'm so taken aback. My stomach twists.

The next set of photos are not smiling holiday photos or snapshots of grinning days out with friends. They're sex photos. Selfies. Point of view shots. Photos that have clearly been taken with the camera propped up so that it can capture the full sordid picture. The glossy pages gleam under the light, the images so sharp they feel like they've been burned onto my retinas.

But it's not the fact that the album is full of sex photos that's shocked me. I've taken a risqué photo or two for Lee in my time. It's the fact that these are not just photos of Fraser and Anna having sex.

They're photos of Fraser, Anna, and Esme having sex.

## TWENTY-SIX

My fingers are slick with sweat. They stick to the plastic photo holders as, unable to stop myself, I flick to the next page.

More of the same. Page after page of it. Every fantasy you could possibly imagine played out in snapshots. Some tame. Some utterly depraved. A few of the pictures are so graphic, I have to look away, yet still I flick through. It's like watching a car crash. I'm horrified, but unable to stop. It's not just what they're doing in these photos that's so shocking to me. It's the fact that they've been captured like this and stored in this album to look back on whenever they please.

I flick to the last page of photos and frown. This is a different woman with Fraser and Anna. It's not Esme. How many women have they managed to convince to be involved with this?

As this thought goes through my mind, my phone starts to ring. The sudden noise makes me jolt. I pull it out of my pocket and let out a strangled cry as I realise it's Lee calling me back, finally. I stab my finger at the answer call button.

'*Lee!*' I sob down the line.

'Miranda? Are you okay? I've just seen all the missed calls.'

'No, I'm not okay. Are you home?' The reality of the last couple of hours settles on me like a ten-tonne truck and I crumple under the weight of it, my body descending into shakes.

'We've just got home. What's the matter? What's happened?'

'It's Mason. I was late getting back and...' My words trail off as something stirs inside me. 'Wait... What do you mean "*we've*" just got back?'

'Me and Mason. I told you this morning I might not be home when you got back from your therapy appointment because I was going to take him to football tryouts, remember?'

My mouth opens and closes like a goldfish. My thoughts feel scrambled. Puzzle pieces that don't fit. I cast my mind back to this morning. He'd been asking if I wanted him to go with me to my therapy appointment. And then, yes, he did say something about not being back until later today, but I'd been so eager to get him off to work so that I could play detective I didn't really clock what he meant. But now I do. Now I remember him mentioning football tryouts to me last week.

The phone drops to my side, tears blurring my vision, and then I'm on my feet, my legs moving of their own accord. I race to Fraser's front door and go to yank it open. My shoulder jolts as the lock fights against me. Swearing under my breath I scramble to unlock it, nearly pinging the chain lock into my eye in my desperation to get it open. The door flings to the side so hard it smashes against the wall.

They're there. Lee and Mason. By our house. Lee still calling my name down the phone while Mason looks up at him inquisitively.

'*Mason!*' My voice cracks. I barely recognise it as my own. I nearly trip over myself as I run to him.

Lee spins on the spot. He clocks me sprinting towards them from Fraser's house, then my face, and his expression twists.

'Miranda? What's happened?'

I ignore him. I can't talk right now. Can't do anything except scoop my boy up into my arms and vow to never let him go again.

'Mummy,' Mason whines under my grip, 'you're squeezing me too hard!'

I release him but only a tiny bit. I need to know this isn't a dream. I need to feel him squirm against me and be sure that he's really here. That he's real. Solid. Safe.

'I made the team,' he says, peering up at me. A laugh bursts from me, and I kiss his forehead, then each of his temples, then his cheeks and then again on his forehead. He giggles and tries to evade my lips.

'Miranda.' Lee's voice is suddenly stern beside me. Still, I keep my focus on Mason. 'Miranda, what's going on? Why were you in the neighbours' house?'

And then it hits me. I'd been so relieved, so full of absolute ecstatic joy to see Mason safe and sound, that my brain had just ignored everything I've done. Everything I'm going to have to try to explain. My head twists back to the direction of Fraser's house. I picture the smashed conservatory. His front door is still wide open from where I rushed out.

'I...'

I'm still crouching on the floor with Mason so I can't see Lee's reaction, but I hear the slow exhale of breath.

'Mase, go inside, will you?'

'Why?'

'Because I said so.'

'But why can't you come in with me?'

'I need to talk to Mummy for a bit, okay? Just go inside and you can have a biscuit and watch TV, okay?'

There are no more arguments from Mason. The promise of a biscuit and TV straight after school, which is usually not allowed, is enough to send him skipping into the house.

Lee's hand slides under my armpit and he hoists me up. My knees feel like they've disappeared from underneath me and it's a struggle to stay standing. Lee grips both of my arms and forces me to face him. His fingers dig in, steady and firm.

'Miranda, look at me.' I do. My bottom lip quivers. 'What did you do?'

'I thought he had Mason,' I whisper, tensing under his hands. The words taste like ash. I'm outside and yet somehow, I feel claustrophobic, as if the clouds themselves are descending upon me, pressing down, smothering me. 'I thought he had Mason and I... I smashed his back door.'

The colour instantly drains from Lee's face. He stares at me, and I feel like I should say something else, elaborate further, but I can't think of anything to say so I just stare back at him. There is a long, long silence.

'Jesus Christ, Miranda.' A vein pulses in his temple. He presses his fingers to his eye sockets and then drags his hand down his face, before grabbing my hand and yanking me towards the front door. 'Inside. Now.'

I stumble slightly as we cross the threshold. My feet barely keep up with my body. Mason doesn't even look round from the TV as we pass the living room. He's lost in the screen, blissfully unaware. We head straight upstairs to our bedroom. Once there, Lee closes the door behind us and pulls the window shut. For a few seconds he stands by the window, head buried in his hands, and I have no choice but to watch him and see what he's going to come out with. Eventually, he spins around.

'Did you go to your therapy appointment today?' he snaps.

I hesitate. My silence is answer enough for him.

'Miranda, I'm begging you. You have to stop acting like this. You have to see what's happening—'

'That's precisely why I've been acting this way: because I seem to be the only person who can see what's really going on!'

'No, not what's *really* going on,' he shouts. 'What you *think* is going on in that deluded head of yours!'

I feel as though I've been slapped. All this time, ever since I started going to therapy for my panic attacks, Lee was the one who made me feel sane. He rationalised everything, telling me it was a perfectly normal response to what we went through, that he'd be concerned if I *didn't* exhibit signs of a stress reaction to it. But now? Now I'm crazy?

He knows how deep his words have cut, because he steps towards me and tries to take my hands. I snatch them away.

'I'm sorry, I didn't mean that,' he says.

'Yes, you did.'

'I didn't. I just... it's not healthy, Miranda. Constantly focusing on this guy, convincing yourself that everything that happens is just him out to get you. I mean, for Christ's sake, you smashed his god-damned window. You broke into his house. Surely you see that...' He pauses, searching for the right words. 'Surely you see that you need help?'

My skin prickles with cold, even in the warm room. I take a small step back.

*Or maybe you need me to get help so I'll stop asking questions. Stop poking around. Stop wondering if you and Fraser have been in this together from the start.*

He looks like the same man I've shared a life with, but now I'm not sure what that means anymore. I'm not sure who exactly I've been sharing it with. I have no words. Nothing to say that won't make things worse. I know what he wants to hear from me, but even if I said it, even if I believed it, he'd never believe that I meant it. So instead, I sink down to sit on the edge of the bed. Deflated. Drained.

Lee makes a move as if he's going to come and sit next to me, but before he can, our doorbell rings. My phone buzzes in my pocket and I pull it out, opening the doorbell app. Lee's gaze flickers between me and the screen, suspicion tightening his features. He raises his eyebrows at the sight of the app. He evidently missed the fact I had reinstalled it while he was out because he was too distracted discovering what a maniac his wife was, but he doesn't say anything about it. The loading wheel spins for a second, and then the picture comes into view.

Fraser is at our door.

## TWENTY-SEVEN

'Oh my God, oh my God...' My pulse is racing too fast, too hard. I'm getting déjà vu from when Fraser caught me climbing into his utility room. 'What do I do?'

I'm more talking to myself than to Lee, but he takes charge nonetheless. He steps in front of me, placing his hand under my chin and tilting my head so that I'm looking straight at him.

'You're not going to do anything. Do you understand me? You're going to stay here and stay silent while I deal with him.'

Ordinarily I'd argue with him, my need to be involved superseding any nerves I have, but right now I can't think of anything I want to do less than go down and talk to Fraser.

'What are you going to say?'

Lee thinks for a moment. The doorbell rings again. The sound makes me flinch.

'Dad!' Mason's voice calls from downstairs. 'There's someone at the door.'

Lee takes my hand and squeezes it. 'You're not home, okay? You haven't been home all day.'

With that, he disappears down the hallway. I listen to the gentle thud of his footsteps going down the stairs. My heart is so conflicted. Part of me is convinced that I can't trust Lee, but the other half of me wants him to protect me, to sort this whole mess out.

I return my attention to the doorbell app. Fraser is still there, hands buried in his pockets, face set like stone. The collar of his jacket is turned up and it makes him look a bit like Dracula. There's a rustling sound as Lee opens the door. I'm quick to turn the volume right down so that Fraser won't hear me watching upstairs.

'Oh, hey.' I hear Lee's voice through the app. I can't see him. I can only see Fraser as he gives Lee a forced smile.

'Hey, sorry to disturb you. Is Miranda home?'

My mouth grows dry.

'No, sorry, mate. She's at some kind of wellness retreat thing. I don't know. She tried to explain it to me and I just nodded, you know what I mean?'

Fraser and Lee both let out a stilted laugh. Lee is surprisingly good at lying. Disconcertingly so, actually. So natural and casual.

'Okay, well, maybe you can help. I've just got home to find my front door ajar. Looks like someone's been in my house. There's stuff everywhere. And my conservatory door at the back has been smashed too.'

'Oh shit. Sorry to hear that. Is there anything I can do? Have you called the police?'

My jaw clenches. What the hell is Lee playing at, suggesting Fraser calls the police? Maybe I should have gone down there. Sitting here, unable to say anything, unable to get involved, is torturous.

'I haven't, no. I wanted to check here and see...' There's a pause, as if Fraser is trying to find the right words.

*Go on, say it,* I think. *You wanted to see if I did it.*

'I wanted to see if you guys had seen or heard anything?'

I hear Lee exhale deeply from behind the camera. I can tell he's choosing his next words carefully.

'Afraid not, mate. Actually, now that I think about it, I did see a group of dodgy-looking kids down this road earlier. Hoods up, smoking, you know the type. I thought it was odd because they had no reason to be down a cul-de-sac. But, sorry, I didn't watch them for long. No idea what they did or where they went.'

'Kids, huh?' Fraser nods slowly, taking in Lee's lie. His expression barely shifts, but something about the way his eyes narrow makes my skin prickle.

I chew on my nail, willing him to believe it and walk away. Each second stretches unbearably. I wonder if Mason can hear any of this conversation from the living room. That would be just my luck: him bounding up to the front door and saying, 'Mummy's not at a wellness retreat, she's upstairs!' But his lack of appearance suggests that he's too engrossed in whatever he's watching on the TV to clock on to the fact that his daddy is telling a bunch of big fat porkies. For once, I silently thank the hypnotic power of children's television.

Finally, after what feels like forever, Fraser speaks again.

'Can I please take a look at your doorbell footage? Maybe if I've got a video of these... kids... it will help them track down the culprit.'

Oh my God. The doorbell.

I gasp so loudly it's a wonder they don't hear me downstairs. Frantically, I slam my hand to my mouth and squeeze, fingers digging into my cheeks, to stop myself from making any more sound. Cold floods my body.

It will have recorded everything. Me swerving into the cul-de-sac after being at the school and thinking Mason had been taken. Me battering my fists against the front door. Me disappearing around the side of the house and then, ten or so minutes later, bursting out to find Lee and Mason in the street. Every desperate, reckless move, caught on film. Lee had disabled it. He'd taken the blasted thing down which meant it would never have captured anything, but I had to go and put it back up. It's the thing that started this whole mess. And now it's going to be the end of me.

My stomach twists and my mouth fills with saliva. I picture myself in prison, with Lee bringing Mason to come and visit me every other weekend. Or maybe he wouldn't let him visit at all. Maybe he'd say it's too much for a little boy to cope with. Maybe Mason would stop asking about me altogether. Kids grow up so quickly. I'll go into prison with my baby boy clutching my knees and I'll come out to a completely different child.

I drop the phone onto the bed, unable to look at Fraser on the screen any longer, and clutch my knees, trying to suck in deep breaths.

'Ah, I'm sorry,' I hear Lee say. 'It won't have recorded anything. It's been broken for a while. I've been meaning to fix it. We just keep it there to scare anyone off breaking in or stealing our Amazon packages, you know?'

He doesn't sound as convincing as he did when he told Fraser I was at a wellness retreat. His voice wobbles, just slightly, but enough to make my stomach drop. I wouldn't believe him. But then, maybe that's because I know he's lying. I peek over my shoulder at the phone. Fraser's expression isn't giving anything away. I can't tell whether he's buying this or not. He blinks slowly, eyes scanning the scene as if he's trying to spot a crack in Lee's story. Maybe they're not working together, after all. Or maybe they are but Lee just wasn't anticipating having to cover up something I had done as well.

There is a long, agonising pause. I simultaneously can't bear to watch and can't bring myself to look away. Just as I'm about to run downstairs and confess everything if only to put an end to this torture, Fraser lets out a slow exhalation.

'Well, if you remember anything else, can you let me know?'

'Sure thing. Sorry I couldn't be of more help. Are you going to call the police?'

I throw my head back in dismay. *Stop mentioning the frigging police, Lee!*

'No,' Fraser says. 'Like you said, it was probably just kids.'

And just like that, to my utter disbelief, he walks away. I nearly collapse back onto the bed. There's the sound of the front door clicking shut and I think I might pass out with relief. But then, just as Fraser reaches the end of our driveway, he turns back to look at our house once more.

No, not our house.

He's looking directly at the camera.

Directly at me.

## TWENTY-EIGHT

My finger is bleeding by the time Lee returns to our bedroom. I've bitten past the nail right down into the skin. I feel like I've aged twenty years in the past two weeks. Lee doesn't appear much better. He closes the bedroom door behind him and slumps against it, looking absolutely exhausted. His shoulders sag and his face is pale and drawn.

'I've called the school,' he says after a while. He's so out of breath as he says it, he sounds like he's just run a marathon. 'Told them Mason is fine and explained that it was just a miscommunication. Fraser's gone. Just stick to the story and it will all blow over.'

I shake my head, astonished that Lee thinks that's that, and now all's well that ends well.

'Don't you think it's odd?' I ask.

A pained look flashes across his face. 'What?'

'That he's not going to the police?'

'Do you *want* him to go to the police?'

'No, of course not.' I roll my eyes. 'But surely, it's what he should do? You would, if you came home to find your conservatory door smashed.'

Lee shrugs and moves from the door to the bed. He throws himself down on it, still fully clothed, and puts his head on the pillow, staring up at the ceiling.

'How should I know, Miranda? The guy's loaded, isn't he? Maybe it's less of a hassle to just replace the door.'

'Lee, you're not seeing the big picture...'

I can see the life being sucked out of him the more I push, but I can't help it. I'm not Lee. I can't just stick my head in the sand and pretend I haven't noticed things.

'If he's got nothing to hide, he would have called the police. He would have done that first, before even thinking about coming round here. That means he doesn't want the police sniffing around. Why?'

'Stop. Please. I'm begging you.'

I stiffen, my mouth twitching. I don't want to say what I'm thinking but the words are piling up on top of each other, spilling out of my mouth.

'Lee, I have to ask you something, and I need you to tell me the truth.'

He looks at me, one eyebrow raised expectantly. I take a deep breath.

'Are you helping Fraser?'

He flinches, a look of confusion flashing over his face.

'What?'

'Do you know something? Are you trying to help cover something up?'

There's a long, long pause. I can see the vein in his temple pulsating. For a moment, it looks as if he might hit me. I feel myself shrink a little even though I know he would never do that.

'You think I'm buddied up with a guy I barely know and I'm helping him to cover up his wife's murder?'

As the words leave his mouth, I hear the stupidity in them.

'It's just... every time I try to talk to you about it you shut me down.'

'For God's sake, Miranda!' He sits up very suddenly then, and I flinch. I don't think he's ever shouted at me like that. He's got angry, sure. We've argued plenty of times over our years of marriage. But he's always been the cool-headed one. If anyone is the type to shout like that, it's me.

He realises it too, because he buries his head into his hands. 'I'm sorry. I just... You've got to stop. We can't keep on living like this, with your obsession or whatever it is taking over everything you do. It's not good for you. It's not good for me. And it's not good for Mason.'

My eyes gloss as I think about the little boy downstairs watching TV, completely oblivious. 'I'm doing this for him. If it was just me to think about, I wouldn't be so scared.'

I look at my phone, my grip tightening on its edges. The desire to pull up the footage of Fraser again is strong, but I'm not sure it will help matters. Lee has already seen it and didn't seem to think anything of it. Nor did the police.

'There's an album in their house,' I say after a moment, realising with a jolt that I have a new piece of information to share with him. 'It's messed up. They've got all these pornographic images of them and—'

'You went through their photo albums?' Lee's voice rises, growing more urgent, more horrified.

'Yes, but...'

'So, in your panic thinking that Fraser had Mason, you somehow found the time to go looking through their stuff?'

'Lee, listen to me—' I rake my fingers through my hair, gripping hard. He's totally missing the point.

'No, I'm done listening to this, Miranda.'

'See? That's what I mean. You won't even let me talk! There were other women in these photos. Two other women. They've got some kind of bizarre open marriage.'

'I don't care what they do in the privacy of their own home!' His hands slam down on the bed and his shout echoes around the room.

There's a creak at the bottom of the stairs. 'Mummy? Daddy? Why are you arguing?'

Lee shoots me a glare. We hadn't even noticed the TV going onto mute.

He breathes deeply. 'We're not arguing, bud. Go back to watching TV. We'll be down in a second.'

The room falls silent as we wait for the sound of the TV. When we do, I wipe my face with my sleeve. Lee looks deep in thought for a few minutes. The vein in his temple pulses, something that only ever happens when he's trying to decide between two equally awful options. I try to guess what he's attempting to decide between, but I can't. It's like I've lost touch with the man I've always known so well. I can't read him like I used to, and he can't read me.

'I'm going to take Mason to see my mum for a few days,' he says eventually, quieter this time, so as not to alarm Mason again.

I frown. 'Again? You've only just been to see her.'

'You need to see your therapist. And until you're willing to accept the fact you need help, I don't want him around you. Not while you're like this. I'll drop him there and come home so that I can be with you. He'll only miss a couple of days of school and then it's the summer holidays anyway.'

A dull heaviness settles into my core. It drags through me like wet cement. Lee's words circle my brain. *I don't want him around you.* They stab me and slice at my skin, taking little chunks out of me each time I replay the sentence.

'You can't.' My voice is hollow, strained. 'You can't take him away from me.'

'I'm not taking him away from you. But I know you, Miranda. You won't get the help you need unless you're faced with an ultimatum. This is it. Go see your therapist, sort yourself out, and I'll bring him home. That's the deal.'

The tears are welling up again, threatening to burst free. My throat burns with the effort of holding them back. 'Please,' I beg. 'Don't do this. I'm sorry I accused you, okay? This is all just getting too much for me.'

My head throbs. Now, talking to him, my gut is telling me that he isn't involved in this after all, which means I've just made things unbearably worse for myself.

Lee shakes his head, the lines in his face deepening. 'I know. That's why I have to do it. I'm sorry.'

He hauls himself off the bed and moves into the en suite, where he splashes his face with water. I watch his reflection in the mirror. The water drips from his chin, soaking into his shirt, but he doesn't seem to care.

Maybe he's right. I've spent so long convincing myself that Fraser is evil, that Anna is lying rotting in a freshly dug grave somewhere, maybe I'm looking for things that aren't there. After all, I thought he'd collected Mason from school when he hadn't, and look how that's turned out. I even started to convince myself that Lee himself was in on it. How many more theories will I come up with?

Maybe it is all in my head.

## TWENTY-NINE

Mason has been gone for two weeks, but it feels more like two years.

I don't know why this has affected me so much. Whenever Lee has taken him to see his mother and I've stayed home before, it's been a welcome break. I'd be catching up with Priya, having wine and popcorn nights, and going out shopping without having to worry about watching the clock or cries of 'Mummy, I'm bored!' A small, selfish part of me had always relished the quiet, the space to just be by myself again.

But this time, it feels different. Two weeks is much longer than I've ever been away from him, but more to the point, this time he's been taken from me against my will. I've had no idea when to expect to see him again. We've FaceTimed every single evening, of course, but it's not the same.

Thankfully, he has no idea what's going on. When he found out he was going to visit Grandma again so soon after the last trip and that he'd even get to miss the last couple of days of school before the holidays, he was so excited I barely got a cuddle goodbye. I did from Lee, though. He held me and stroked my back and whispered well-rehearsed reassurances into my ear.

'It's all going to be okay, Miranda. We're going to get through this.'

I nodded into his chest. Let him take my son. Played my part.

Since that day, I've been good. I've done everything Lee wanted me to do. The day after he dropped Mason off, we went to see my therapist together. I was the remorseful wife, the anxious mother, the woman finally seeing sense. It was disturbingly easy to slip back into it. Like no time had passed. Like I had never even gotten better, and I was still in the throes of PTSD from the break-in. My therapist agreed with Lee that my conviction that Fraser is a cold-hearted killer is likely a symptom of my lingering anxiety.

'Ever since the break-in you've been so afraid of the world,' my therapist had said, 'you look for things and people who could be a threat, even if they're not.'

I sat and I nodded, and we went to get my prescription for anti-anxiety pills, the same ones I've been taking since the break-in time but stronger. I had initially considered slipping them under my tongue and holding them there until I could get to a toilet to spit them into, but I decided against it in the early days, just in case Lee caught me. He's been watching me like a hawk these past two weeks. I needed to be a good little patient. He needed to believe that I've started to accept that I've fabricated my suspicions of Fraser and that any 'evidence' I have on him is circumstantial. It's not been easy. Every time dark thoughts inch into the corners of my mind or I feel that creeping temptation to check the doorbell app, I've been doing something to distract myself. Reading a book. Cleaning. Clipping my toenails. Anything. The desire subsides eventually. Most of the time. I even managed to stop myself from spying when he got workmen in to fix his conservatory.

Although it's been tough, it's worked. When we went to see my therapist again yesterday, he said there had been a marked improvement already. Lee was so pleased with me he rang his mum as soon as we got home and said he was going to come and collect Mason today. And that's what he's doing. Driving down to his mother's house to bring our son home. He only left ten minutes ago, which means I have a few hours until Mason will be back with me where he belongs, but at least I know he's coming back. I have an actual time to look forward to. A sense of certainty.

The sense of relief from Lee leaving the house is immense, not just because my plan to make out like all is back to normal has worked. It's a relief to not have to pretend for a little bit. I sit at the kitchen table, the pill packet in my hands, foil crinkling under my fingertips. I pop one out. It skitters along the table like it's trying to escape. I pinch it between my thumb and forefinger and stare at it.

It's tiny. Insultingly so. Just a dot of chalky white with a scored line down the middle. You wouldn't think something so small could numb you the way it does, would you? Could make you feel so sluggish and drowsy and so not yourself.

My phone flashes up with a message from Priya. I peer at it out of the corner of my eye. I can only see the first line of it.

*Hey, how are things going? Want to pop round for...*

I return my attention to the pill. I haven't spoken to Priya since I heard her and the others laughing about me. I can't forgive her. Not yet. Eventually I probably will. Once I've proven to her and everyone else that I'm right. Once they've acknowledged that they should have listened to me.

I imagine Lee tapping his fingers on the steering wheel, humming along to Led Zeppelin, congratulating himself on how well everything is going. On how obedient I've become. I move to the sink and run the tap. Cold water rushes out. The pill tumbles from my fingers, sticks briefly to the stainless steel of the sink, then slides down the drain with a flick of my finger.

*Gone.*

I slide the pill packet back into the box and place it on the top of the fridge where it always sits, out of reach of little hands. I don't need them. I am not crazy. And I have a plan. Next week, once things have calmed down and Lee has relaxed, I'm going to find Anna's body. It's the only way to make everyone believe me. She has to be close enough to drive to and from in ten minutes, because that's how long Fraser was gone that night. That only leaves so many potential burial spots.

But that's next week. Now? Mason is coming home. That's all that matters.

I'm going to do something nice for him. A welcome home party. That would make his day as he steps through the door. I'll get some balloons and some of his favourite snacks. Nothing fancy, but just enough to show him how much I missed him and make him realise that, despite what he thinks, I'm way cooler than Grandma.

The thought of it makes me even more excited for his homecoming, if that was even possible. Picturing his little face as he feasts his eyes on Party Rings and cocktail sausages and macaroons. He'll shriek with joy, throw his arms around my waist, tell me I'm the best. I can't wait.

I slip my jacket on and step outside, heading purposefully towards the end of Herring Row, briefly glancing at Fraser's house as I pass it. It doesn't look like there's anyone home, but I get a horrid prickling sensation at the back of my neck nevertheless. I ignore the sensation, instead focusing on what I want to do. No point getting distracted now. This is the first time during the two-week period that I've left the house without Lee. A small victory, but a victory all the same. Wandering to the shops on my own feels somewhat alien.

Tesco is bustling. Everywhere I look there are parents trying to wrangle their kids. It's the end of the second week of the school holidays, when parents have already done the days out and spent a king's ransom on keeping the little ones entertained, and are starting to run out of ideas and money. My heart aches with longing, but I tell myself that it's okay. Mason is coming home. He's coming home.

I initially grab a basket and start dropping things into it, but quickly realise that I need a small trolley instead. I pick up a two-litre bottle of Dr Pepper, something that we'd never ordinarily have in the house but that I know Grandma gives Mason at her place, and wedge it in beside the crisps and the sweets. I have far too much for one welcome home party for three, but I don't care. We'll live on sugary leftovers for the rest of the week. Mason will never want to leave again.

Once I can't fit any more snacks into the trolley, I hop on the travelator to head upstairs to the homeware section. Balloons will be up there. Mason will be so excited. He adores playing keepy-uppy with Lee. This is good. This is where I need to be putting my energy this morning. Normality. I can deal with the rest another time. Today, I won't even think about uttering the name...

*Fraser.*

He's here. In the homeware section. I stop as if I've walked slap bang into a brick wall and start backing out of the aisle, pulling my trolley with me. I round the corner backwards and slump, relieved that he didn't spot me over the handlebar. It's then that I notice an elderly lady opposite is staring at me. Clearly, I look like a maniac. I give her a small smile and she's quick to avert her gaze, disappearing down the bedding aisle.

Chewing on my bottom lip, I lean forwards and peek around the corner. He's still there, perusing the tools hanging up on the pinboard shelf. I squint at his shopping basket.

There's no sign of food in there. Rather, it looks like a DIY fever dream. Tape, a plastic sheet, and is that... rope?

A familiar chill slinks down my spine. I shake my head. Don't do this. Not today. At least let Mason get home before I go off the deep end again. There could be a completely reasonable explanation. Just because the contents of his basket look like the sort of thing you'd see on a serial killer's shopping list doesn't necessarily mean anything. Clearly, I've seen too many horror movies. Perhaps he's sorting out his conservatory. That feels like a faint possibility.

'Excuse me.' I nearly jump out of my skin at the sound of a woman's voice behind me. I step to one side, allowing her to pass. When I look at Fraser, he's staring right back at me.

Millions of tiny ants creep along my skin. I duck my head low and push my trolley sharply around the corner. Sod the balloons. The snacks will be enough to make Mason's homecoming special. I just need to get out of this shop. The aisles are suddenly feeling too busy, too narrow, too claustrophobic.

I'm just about to get to the travelator when Fraser appears in front of me. He's headed me off. How? Why? I jolt backwards, arms flying up defensively. My eyes dart around. Thankfully the shop is packed. If he does so much as take a step closer to me, I'll scream so loud the entire customer-base of Tesco will be able to stop him.

'What are you doing?' Fraser says.

'Erm... shopping.' I gesture dumbly at the contents of my trolley. Fraser looks down at it, one eyebrow raising.

'I mean why are you spying on me?'

Oh. He saw me.

'What are *you* doing?' I say, deciding that turning the questioning around on him is the safest play.

'Shopping.'

Touché.

The two of us watch each other for a moment, waiting for

the other to speak. His eyes are narrowed, as if he's trying to read my thoughts. Frantically, I try to think about anything other than smashing through his conservatory door, just in case, on the extremely slim off-chance, he is indeed psychic.

Finally, unable to bear the silence any longer, I say, 'How's Anna?'

My pulse skips but I keep my face neutral. That was ballsy. But I've said it now. No taking it back.

He smirks at me. 'She's fine.'

'Still visiting relatives?'

'Yep.'

'Huh.' I nod, absorbing the information, as if I was expecting any other answer. 'Is she going to be coming home any time soon?'

He tilts his head to the side at that, surveying me. It's unnerving, but I hold my position. I don't want to risk upsetting Lee and making him change his mind about bringing Mason home, but I can at least make Fraser squirm.

After a long pause, he takes a step towards me. I flinch, unsure what he's doing or whether or not I should be afraid, but my plan to scream loudly to attract the attention of the other shoppers fails when he grabs the top of my arm. The sudden movement snatches the breath from me and when I open my mouth, no sound comes out. He leans in close to me and speaks low and quiet, right up against my ear, so that his breath tickles my cheek.

'You need to stop getting involved in our business. Trust me. I don't want anyone else getting hurt.'

# THIRTY

I push Fraser off me with such force we both stumble back. My heart is pounding so hard I can hear it in my ears, drowning out the hum of the supermarket around us.

'Get off me!' I shout, finally finding my voice. A few people glance our way, their faces a mixture of confusion and mild concern. But no one intervenes.

Fraser looks shocked, taken aback, almost as if he wasn't expecting this kind of reaction from grabbing me and threatening me. As if I'd just accept it. As if I owed him that.

'I mean it. Stay the hell away from me!'

'Are you alright there, miss?' A man in a navy coat approaches us, his eyes flicking between the two of us, assessing the situation. It's the momentary distraction I need. Without thinking, I seize the handle of my trolley and shove it towards Fraser as hard as I can. The wheels shriek across the linoleum. It impacts hard with his abdomen, and he lets out an almighty grunt as he crumples, hunching over the edge of the trolley, gripping the frame for support.

Shock ripples through the bystanders, but I don't wait to see what happens next. Before anyone can say or do anything I turn and bolt, weaving past a few bewildered shoppers. The fluorescent lights blur above my head. I catch glimpses of faces, all wide-eyed, all watching. I sprint down the travelator, nearly knocking over a pensioner with a basket of groceries. She mutters something sharp, but I barely register it. The automatic doors glide open just in time for me to barrel through them.

'Hey! *Stop!*' The security guard is shouting after me. He must think I'm shoplifting, but I don't care. I don't stop. I can't. Not with Fraser so close. Not with my body still trembling from the feel of his breath against my skin, my arm still aching from where he grabbed me. I keep on going. Cold air slaps my face, and I suck in gulps of it as I push my legs harder. My lungs burn. My muscles scream. Just a little bit further. I just need to get home and then I can lock myself in and call Lee.

By the time I reach the house, my limbs feel like lead, but adrenaline keeps me moving. My fingers fumble with the lock, trembling so much I drop the chain twice before finally securing it. I spin, chest heaving, and rush to check the windows, yanking at the latches to make sure they're locked. The back door. The kitchen window. Every possible way in. Only when I'm certain that nothing short of brute force will get through do I press my hand against the front window, my breath fogging up the pane. No sign of him. Satisfied that I, at least for now, am safe, I move to the kitchen and collapse into the chair at the table. Lee has to take me seriously now. Even if he is somehow entangled in all of this, surely, *surely* he won't take kindly to his wife being threatened. If he doesn't take my side now, I've just about sealed my fate as Fraser's next victim.

My phone is slick with sweat as I pull it out of my pocket, leaving damp fingerprints on the screen as I tap through to my contacts. My vision is still shaky, my breath unsteady. I press Lee's name. I haven't even got the energy to hold it up to my ear, so instead I turn on the loudspeaker. The ringing circles the kitchen.

'Hi, this is Lee—' comes his voice.

'Lee! Thank God. You need to—'

'I can't come to the phone right now, but please leave a message and I'll get back to you as soon as possible.'

A growl escapes my throat. I wait for the beep, tapping my foot. When it comes, I just tell him to ring me straight back, before jabbing at the end call button. I press my hand to my forehead. Should I call the police? The thought flickers through my mind, then vanishes just as quickly. It's certainly what I'd tell anyone else to do in this situation, but I'm not anyone else. I'm the crazy lady who seems to have some kind of grudge against her next-door neighbour. I'm the one who was literally told by a police officer to stay away from Fraser. Would they even care if I told them he had threatened me at the shop? Would they even believe me?

Frustrated with them and myself, I stand and begin to pace the kitchen. I need something to distract myself. To calm me down enough to think properly. The washing. That's a good, mindless task. I put it on before I went out, so it will be finished by now and ready to put in the tumble dryer. Plus, getting it out of the way now means I can focus fully on Mason when he gets home. I grab the wet clothes out of the washing machine and transfer them over. It's funny; ordinarily I hate washing our clothes. It's one of those tasks that just grinds me down, probably because it's so never-ending. But here, now, going through the motions, it's calming in a way I never thought it would be.

I'm just about to empty the lint tray when my phone starts to ring. I spin around. Lee's face is dancing around on my phone screen. A rush of relief and dread hits me at the same time. I snatch the phone up and slide to answer. It's clear he's not yet on the road with Mason. I can hear his mother laughing and Mason squealing in the background. She must be tickling him. The joyful sound feels foreign. Out of place.

'Hey, sorry I missed your call. We're going to be leaving in about an hour. Mason just wanted some lunch before we left.'

'Lee...' My voice cracks and I have to clear my throat. 'Lee,' I try again. 'Please come home now.'

'What was that? Hang on. Mase! Keep it down, will you?' There's rustling on the other end of the line, the sound of him moving to a quieter spot. My fingers twitch at my side while I wait. I jab at the start button on the tumble dryer and it spins to life, just as Lee comes back to the phone. 'Sorry, Miranda. What did you say?'

'Please can you come home now.'

'Now? Why?'

'Because...' I falter, the emotions of the day finally crashing over me. 'Because I need you.'

There's a pause, and when Lee speaks his tone has shifted, his voice suddenly low and serious. 'Miranda, what's happened?'

'Fraser... he...'

My explanation is snatched away by the doorbell ringing. The sharp sound cuts through the air, jolting me like a slap. My stomach twists. Slowly, I turn my head to look at the front door. Ours isn't like some of the neighbours'. It doesn't have glass in it, so it's impossible to see from here who is on the other side. That's partly why we got the video doorbell. The front door has never seemed so ominous, so terrifying to me. Even when we first moved in and I would flinch at every knock, convinced it was someone coming to rob us, I don't think I ever felt fear like this.

Another ring of the doorbell sounds. It vibrates through my bones.

'Miranda?' Lee's voice calls through the phone. 'Are you still there?'

Eyes still locked on the front door, I grab the phone and switch off the speaker. 'Just come home. Now.' I hang up and swap over to the doorbell app. The buffering wheel circles, agonisingly slow. I will it to load faster. It might not be Fraser. It could be the postman for all I know, or maybe Priya. Actually, the smart thing to do would have probably been to go to her place instead of mine. At least then I wouldn't have been alone. But it's too late now.

The feed flickers to life. My eyebrows draw together as I squint at the shadowy figure standing on the doorstep. I place my finger and thumb on the screen and zoom in. My heart stops. My body goes ice cold.

A single breathless word escapes my lips.

'*Anna.*'

## THIRTY-ONE

Anna.

She's alive. And standing on my doorstep, staring at my doorbell camera.

I blink a few times, thinking I must be imagining things. This can't be real. This must be a bizarre trick of my mind. I can't believe what I'm seeing. But I am seeing it.

As my eyes open again, she's still there. Her hand raises and she presses the doorbell a third time. It chimes through the house. She then moves her knuckle to the door and starts knocking, hard and frantic. She looks around, checking the street behind her.

I snap into action. I race to the front door and go to yank it open. My shoulder jolts as the locks fight against me. Swearing under my breath, I scramble to unlock it, nearly pinging the chain lock into my eye in my desperation to get it open. The door flings to the side so hard it smashes against the console table and the lamp wobbles.

I'm half expecting her to be gone when I open the door, for the hallucination or ghost or whatever it was I was seeing to have dissipated, but no. As soon as the door opens, she rushes inside. I slam the door closed once more behind her and redo all the locks.

We stare at each other. My mouth hangs open and tears gather in my eyes.

'Hi,' she whispers.

And then the dam breaks. The tears spill down my cheeks and I hunch over, gasping for breath in between sobs. I didn't even know the woman that well. But I can't stop crying. Relief, fear, confusion –

they all crash into me at once.

Anna places her hand on my back and rubs it in slow circles. It's strangely soothing.

'Let's get a cup of tea,' she suggests.

We move into the kitchen, her hand still on my back. I feebly reach for a couple of cups while she grabs the kettle and fills it up. As she does so, I can't help but watch her. My eyes are glued to her face, to her plump-with-life face. The rise and fall of her chest. The flush of her cheeks. Every time I've thought of Anna lately it's been of her in a ditch, skin growing hollow and grey, sinking into her. I was so sure that when she eventually was found she'd be half-decomposed, and yet here she is, making us a cup of tea in my kitchen.

'I thought you were dead.' The words fall out of me with no preamble. I'm not sure how you lead up to announcing something like that, but there's nothing else I can think to say. She flinches at my words, hand hovering above one of the cups with a teabag. Her expression is tight, strained, as if she expected this but still wasn't ready.

'I would have been if I'd stayed.' She drops the teabag into the cup and does the same with the second, before pouring the boiling water over them and heading for the fridge.

'Were you with relatives?'

'No.'

'Where have you been then?'

She hands me my cup of tea, which, I realise, she made entirely by herself while I just stood and watched. I continue to look at her, waiting for an answer to my question. She clutches her own cup. Her knuckles are white against the handle.

'I ran away. I've been... in hiding.'

My mind reels.

'Why?'

'Because I was scared. I had to get away, or I would have been killed. Fraser, he's...'

At that moment, the doorbell rings again. I jump so wildly my tea spills over the edge of my cup and scalds my skin. I hiss through my teeth as I slam it down on the counter and snatch up my phone, still open on the doorbell app from where Anna had appeared on the doorstep.

'Oh God.'

I turn the phone to Anna. Her face pales when she sees the camera.

*Fraser.*

'Pretend we're not here,' she whispers.

There's a scuffling sound at the door, and for a moment I think Fraser is trying to get in. He's disappeared from the view of the camera.

'Miranda?' His voice echoes through the house and I realise he's calling through the letterbox. I gesture at Anna to stand back so that neither of us are in view. 'Miranda, if you're in there, I just wanted to say sorry for freaking you out earlier. I shouldn't have grabbed your arm like that. I get why you reacted the way you did. But I really do think we should talk. There's a lot going on that you don't know about.'

I think this may be the most he's ever spoken to me. His voice seems different, too. Less full of hatred, more tinged with concern. He's a master manipulator. Every word feels like bait to trap me.

'Miranda, I know you're there. I can see your reflection in the fridge door.'

My hands bunch into fists. Stupid stainless-steel fridge.

'You need to leave!' I shout, peeking around the corner so that my eyes meet his through the letterbox. 'Right now. I'm with Anna—'

Anna shakes her head wildly at the mention of her name, but it's too late.

'I know what you tried to do to her,' I continue. 'We're calling the police!'

'Wait. Anna's with you?' His eyes grow wide, and he makes a feeble grab at the locked door handle. 'Miranda, open this door now. You don't know what you're doing.'

'I'm going to call the police if you don't get away from my house this instant!'

'Do it. Call the police! But you have to let me in. You're in danger. You've locked yourself in there with a murderer!'

His words reach me at the exact same time as the sharp pinching sensation in my neck, like a wasp's sting. I turn, coming face to face with Anna. She grips the tops of my arms, holding me steady.

'*Shhh.*' She strokes my hair as my legs disappear from underneath me, an unnatural weight dragging me down, and she lowers me to the floor. 'It's okay.'

The world around me swims and blurs, reality slipping through my fingers. My thoughts turn to thick mud.

The last things I see before I close my eyes are Anna's face, and the needle she's clutching in her hand.

PART TWO

# THIRTY-TWO

## ANNA

Two Years Ago

I'm sitting across the table from Fraser and Esme, the receptionist at Orbital Solutions Group, and have never been more confused.

I thought Fraser and I were going to eat at the Ivy as a date. It's not like we have many of them anymore. Our marriage is stale, lacking excitement, and we've had one or two conversations about needing to *do* something. We need to re-learn how to enjoy our time together. Not just live in an endless cycle of going to our respective jobs, working ludicrous hours, and ignoring each other on our phones for the evening until bedtime.

We used to love each other hard. There was a time we couldn't get enough of each other. Now, we've reached the point where when Fraser mentioned going to dinner, I actually got excited, that is, until his receptionist walked in. Once she joined us, I wasn't quite sure what to make of this evening, and I'm still not.

She's nice, though. Far more personable than some of the

more senior members of staff I've met from Fraser's work. Pretty, too. She also seems just as confused as to why she's here as I am. I wonder if she can afford this place on her receptionist's salary, and decide that Fraser has probably offered to pay.

Every time he speaks to her, I squint, trying to decide whether or not he's flirting with her. She looks a little bit like me, but younger, which is cause for concern in itself. Also, he insisted that instead of calling him Mr Coles, as all junior members of staff are expected to call the vice president, that while she's here she can call him Fraser. Also suspicious. I can't help but wonder what kind of conversations they have when I'm not around. Are they light-hearted, flirty chats by the coffee machine or late-night texts that linger too long on his mind? I've never been one to check his phone. Maybe I should start.

But what I can't for the life of me figure out is, if he is indeed screwing his receptionist – and I wouldn't put such a cliché past him – why am I here too? Is this some bizarre attempt to make me jealous? Make me up my game for fear of losing him to a younger model? If that's his plan, he's going to be sorely disappointed. I can't be manipulated like that.

After a couple of hours of, admittedly good, flowing conversation, Esme excuses herself to go to the bathroom. Fraser and I both watch her go. Her hips swing side to side when she walks. I always thought it looked ridiculous when people walked like that, as if they were trying to imitate a model on a runway, but on her it looks natural. I wonder if Fraser has noticed it too, if his eyes follow her the way mine do now.

Once she's gone, Fraser turns to me and grins.

'What do you think?'

I raise an eyebrow at him. 'What do I think about what?'

His shoulders droop, and his cheeks go a little bit red as he realises he's going to have to elaborate. He leans forward, resting his elbows on the table.

'Remember what we discussed the other week?'

I shrug, still not sure what he's getting at, and his blush deepens. I don't think I've ever seen him blush before. Maybe once when we first started dating.

'We, um... well, you...' He averts his gaze so that it's fixed on the tablecloth. 'You suggested adding a bit of... *fun*... to our marriage.'

I blink, suddenly understanding what he's getting at. We had a conversation about what's happened to us, about where our sex life has disappeared to, and I suggested we try livening things up a bit. I had listed a few options: introducing toys, trying out some light bondage, filming or photographing ourselves, and...

My eyes widen.

'You want to have a *threesome* with her?'

Fraser looks at me in shock, and for a moment I think I may have got this wrong, but when he shushes me I realise that he just doesn't want anyone overhearing.

'I heard her on the phone with her friend,' he whispers. 'She's into that kind of thing.'

My head spins. When I had suggested a threesome, it was one of those things that you say but never actually do. I mean, who actually has an open marriage? Surely, it's just the same as cheating? The idea of it had been a flippant suggestion, a passing thought born from desperation to reconnect. I had never in a million years expected him to go ahead and *source* someone for the deed. Let alone someone he works with and sees every day. Clearly his ears perked up when I mentioned it far more than I had realised.

Seeing my expression, he shakes his head. 'Don't worry if you don't fancy it. It was just an idea. We can do something else...'

Before I can respond, Esme comes back from the ladies and Fraser sits back in his chair, looking, quite frankly, mortified, even though Esme has absolutely no idea what we've just been discussing.

Although, does she have no idea? Maybe she knows *exactly* why she's here. Maybe her trip to the ladies, leaving Fraser and I alone to discuss, was part of their master plan that they've concocted to win me over. She's a good actress, if that's the case. Although, looking at her now, I'd say she's about as clueless as I was five minutes ago.

I tilt my head, allowing my eyes to roam over her as she peruses the dessert menu. I try to picture her in our bedroom. How would it work? Would we take it in turns? Both please Fraser at the same time – her kissing him and me down below, and vice versa? I bet he'd love that.

I consider the alternative. Why should Fraser get everything? I've never been with a woman, but looking at Esme now, it's not a terrible idea. In fact, picturing us together, with Fraser watching, is making me rather hot under the collar. It's a feeling I haven't had in some time. Very rarely do I get an aching desire to make my way to the bedroom.

Maybe that's saying something...

Maybe, just maybe, this could work.

## THIRTY-THREE

Six Months Ago

Esme, Fraser and I have been in an open marriage now for eighteen months. Eighteen *glorious* months.

I wasn't there when he pitched the idea to Esme. Fraser knew her better, and it seemed like it would be less intimidating for him to suggest the idea quietly over coffee rather than have the two of us corner her. I wish I'd been a fly on the wall, though. How do you even approach the subject? Whatever he said, it worked, because that evening she came round, and it was the start of something beautiful.

Fraser and I have never been happier. Who would have thought that inserting another woman into our marriage would help it so much? I'm not sure what it is. Maybe the added layer of excitement, that sense that we're doing something that we really shouldn't be, or perhaps it's simply the fact that we both get to experience another person's body that's not each other's. There's a delicious thrill to it.

I'll give Fraser credit, too. He's asked me if I'd like to find a man to experiment with. He's said he won't be jealous, that I've been so amazing at welcoming Esme into our lives that the least he can do is return the favour. What he doesn't realise, though, is I have no need or desire for another man. I'm quite happy with Esme and Fraser. More than happy.

She's coming round tonight, and I can't wait. Perhaps I should head to town in my lunchbreak and purchase a new set of lingerie for the occasion. Esme always looks so good. As soon as I make the decision, I'm counting down the hours. I finish up my paperwork at record speed and as soon as one o'clock hits, I hop in the car and drive to the shopping plaza.

Orbital Solutions Group is right near here. I could pop in, see if Esme is around to join me for lunch. I've just about figured out her shift pattern now, having watched her through the glass doors plenty of times. She should be there.

No, don't get distracted. I'll be seeing her later, anyway. Besides, that's not part of the agreement. We spend time together, not in couples. If I were to have lunch with Esme without Fraser, it's crossing a line, tiptoeing into affair territory. The only way this arrangement works is if we all trust each other.

I make my way to the Ann Summers shop and select a piece that cinches in at the waist and will give me all the right curves in all the right places. It's silky smooth to touch, and I imagine both Fraser and Esme's fingers running over the silky fabric. My skin tingles with excitement. I can already envision their faces when they see me in it, the hunger in their eyes, the way their hands always seem to find me at the same time.

It's as I'm heading back to the car that I see them. I spot Esme first. She's sitting at a table in Costa, sipping on a large cup of what looks like a cappuccino. My eyes are inadvertently drawn to her lips and my mouth waters. But then my gaze pans across to the person she's sitting opposite.

It's Fraser.

They're having coffee together. Not just having coffee

together. To anyone who doesn't know the circumstances of their relationship, they'd probably think they were on a date. They're leaning in towards each other with an air of familiarity. Esme's foot is playing with Fraser's under the table.

Sucking deep breaths through my nose and out through my mouth, I try to be rational. They're work colleagues. That's all this is. Two colleagues getting coffee together. Except, they're not just work colleagues. I've seen them together in the bedroom, naked bodies grinding against each other. It didn't bother me then because I was a part of it. It was my sordid secret, too. But now?

Then, as Fraser cracks what I assume is an incredibly funny joke, Esme throws her head back with laughter and lowers her hand to his. Her fingers stroke along his knuckles. The touch is light, casual, yet unmistakably intimate. A gesture of tenderness. Something that should belong to us, not just to them.

This is not just coffee. This is a date. It's a date without me.

How often does this happen? How often does Fraser see Esme outside of our evenings together? I grip the handle of my Ann Summers bag so tightly it leaves indents in my skin. The thought that they might have their own secret world, their own private moments, makes a sickly taste creep up my throat.

He's wearing the blue shirt I got him for his birthday, the one I always ask him to wear because it shows off his arms so well. Is he wearing it for her?

On autopilot, my hand drops to my handbag and fishes out my phone. I tap Fraser's name and press the phone to my ear. His own phone flashes on the table in front of him. I think, initially, that he might let it go to voicemail, but after a moment he picks it up.

'Hey, what's up?' So light. So carefree.

'Not much. Just wanted to chat. I'm bored at work. What are you up to?'

'I'm just at lunch. Thought I'd grab a Costa.'

Not a lie. But not the whole truth.

'Sounds nice. Is Esme still coming over tonight, do you know?'

'I believe so.'

That was his chance, right there, to tell me he was with her now.

'Okay, well, I guess I'll see you at home?'

'Yep, see you later.'

'I love you.'

'You too.'

He hangs up first. My hand hangs by my side.

This is not acceptable. I had been restrained. I had wanted to invite Esme to lunch but I stopped myself out of respect for Fraser and our marriage. Esme is not Fraser's plaything. She's not his opportunity to cheat on his wife without repercussions. We had an arrangement. An understanding. Boundaries that we all agreed to. Boundaries that now feel blurred and compromised.

This is a betrayal from both of them.

I managed to get through the rest of my workday without breaking down entirely, and now I'm home, waiting. I've been sitting on our bed for forty-five minutes, staring at the clock on the wall, watching the seconds tick by.

Fraser and Esme should be arriving any second now. He always gives her a lift when we're supposed to be seeing each other in the evening. Sometimes they're late, as they are today, and it's never occurred to me before now why that might be. I've always just assumed it's because they've got caught up at work, finishing up a last-minute pile of paperwork or taking a phone call too late in the day. I've always pictured Esme sitting in the staff room, waiting for Fraser, bundled up in her coat and bag by her ankles. Now I'm picturing all sorts of different scenarios.

I swallow the thoughts down and pick up the album from my bedside table. I have to distract myself. Perhaps it's not as bad as I think. Perhaps it was just coffee, and the familiarity I saw was just that which came from our evenings. They have slept together, after all. Of course they're familiar with each other. Who is to say that, just because they had coffee without me, they're doing anything else without me? And *technically* he didn't lie to me when I asked him where he was. Still, the doubt lingers. Jealousy gnaws at my gut as I start to flick through the pages of the photo album.

We started photographing ourselves a few months into our arrangement. It added yet another layer of excitement, and it meant I had something to look back on when I felt like it. Normally, my focus would be on myself when looking at these pictures. How it looks having two sets of hands on my skin. But this time I'm focusing on Esme and Fraser, and the way they're looking at each other.

I lift a shaky hand and place it on one of the photos, so that I am completely covered. My breath snatches in my throat. Without me in the picture, they look exactly the same. Just as happy. Just as besotted. I try to convince myself that it's just a trick of perspective, but the weight of what I saw earlier presses heavy on my chest.

I recognise the sound of Fraser's Range Rover pulling up on our drive. They're home. I don't move. Instead, I stay sitting on the bed, waiting for them to come upstairs.

'Anna?' Fraser's voice calls as he comes through the front door.

'Upstairs.'

There's the rummaging of coats and shoes being removed, then some inaudible chatter, laughter, then footsteps on the stairs. My body tenses.

When they come through the bedroom door, they can tell instantly that something's wrong. Concern flashes across both of their faces. Their worry should reassure me, but instead, it feels like a performance.

'Is everything okay?' Fraser says.

'Did you have a nice coffee date today?' No mincing my words. I don't have the patience for that.

Fraser looks confused for a moment, brow furrowed as he searches for understanding, and then realisation hits him, and he glances at Esme.

'You saw us?' he says.

'I saw you.'

'Why didn't you tell us you were in town?' Esme says, her sweet voice like sickly honey. It drips with false innocence. 'You could have joined us.'

Oh, that's very clever.

I lean back on my hands and tilt my head. 'Would you have wanted that?'

'Of course.'

I don't indulge that with a reply. The room falls into an awkward silence, and Fraser and Esme exchange a glance.

'Maybe you should go home,' Fraser says to her after a moment.

'No, don't let me spoil *your* evening.' I stand up, the anger I've felt since the moment I spotted them in the coffee shop bubbling up inside me, spilling out of my mouth. 'Here, would you like me to sit in the corner and film you both? Or would you prefer I went downstairs and just left you to it?'

Esme grimaces, and it feels like a gut punch. 'I don't know what your problem is, Anna, but I can't be bothered with this.'

She turns and heads to the bedroom door.

'Where are you going?' I call after her.

'Home. Life is too short, it was fun while it lasted.'

'Don't you *dare* leave this house!' The words come out

louder than I mean for them to, more a screech than anything, the rawness of it hanging in the air. It makes Esme stop in her tracks. Even Fraser looks shocked.

Esme turns slowly on her heel. 'Excuse me?'

'You don't get to just walk away from this. From us.'

'And why exactly is that?'

Something flips inside me at that, a switch that I didn't know existed until now.

'If you leave, I'll share all of these photos' – I pick up the album and allow it to fall open in my hands, the photographic proof of our sordid fantasy laid bare – 'with all of your friends and family.'

## THIRTY-FOUR

One Month Ago

I'd forgotten what it felt like. The butterflies. The excitement of meeting someone new. It's a heady rush, one I haven't experienced in too long.

I have to say, when we arrived at Number Seven Herring Row, lugging boxes through the narrow hallway and pretending to be excited about shelf space and wall colours, I wasn't filled with the usual thrill of a fresh start. I didn't feel the hopeful flutter that used to come with every new postcode. There was no escape this time. No sense of reinvention. Just quiet shame, wrapped in a pretty bow.

We didn't move because we wanted to. We moved because we had to. Because I pushed things too far.

It's a pretty village. Quaint. Picturesque, even. The sort of place my mother would have killed to live in. She used to dream of living in a village like this, with its flower baskets hanging from lamp posts and cobbled streets and the old church spire poking into the sky beyond the wildflower meadow. If she were alive, she would have spent every waking moment nagging me to invite her for tea.

We always live in beautiful places. It's the one thing I can't fault Fraser for. His eye for locations is impeccable. Every house we've ever lived in has been just the sort of thing I'm looking for, and he's always furnished them wonderfully, sourcing decorations from antique markets and obscure little shops tucked away in back alleys, finding pieces that give our home a unique character. I've grown so used to his flair for interiors that I've grown numb to it. It's expected. Predictable.

But meeting someone *new*. Now that is exciting.

I haven't met anyone new in a couple of months. I thought I might never feel it again. After the fiasco with Esme, I wasn't sure we'd ever find anyone else to slot into our marriage. Esme called my bluff. Left the house and never came back, despite my assurances that I would destroy her if she did. I wonder, sometimes, if she ever felt even the slightest flicker of fear. If she truly believed I wouldn't follow through on my promise. Maybe she thought Fraser would stop me. Maybe Fraser thought he would, too.

Of course, it backfired somewhat. I should have thought things through more. When I leaked the photos, I wanted to humiliate her. I wanted to punish her. I didn't expect it to cost Fraser his job. The whispers spread fast through Orbital Solutions Group, moving like wildfire from one department to the next. The vice president caught in an ongoing affair with the receptionist? Worse, an affair his wife was part of? It was the kind of scandal the company couldn't afford to have associated with its name. He was marched into a joint HR and PR meeting so quickly his head spun. He was to leave the company quietly and he would receive a large severance pay to soften the blow. Esme was allowed to keep her job upon signing an NDA. I haven't seen her since. Sometimes I think about her. Less so, since we met Julia.

We met Julia in Greece. After Fraser lost his job, it was obvious he blamed me. He never said as much, but I could tell. It clung to the air between us, thick with resentment. So we decided we'd make the most of his unexpected additional annual leave and take a holiday. A sun-drenched last-ditch attempt to save our marriage. A week in a boutique hotel with too many cocktails, forced laughter, and long, tense silences broken by the occasional spark of something that almost felt like us. Julia ended up in our bed one night after a few too many cocktails in the hotel bar and a flirtation that escalated far quicker than any of us anticipated.

I was hooked again. That rush, the electric thrill of the forbidden, the feeling of something new. I craved it. Julia filled that void. The best bit was, because we were on holiday, I could keep an eye on the both of them. Fraser was never out of my sight. When we returned home, she became our next secret indulgence, my reason to smile in the middle of a dull workday. The only downside is she lives too far away. Forty-five minutes is inconvenient. We can't have the same effortless, easy nights we had with Esme.

Although, perhaps it is a blessing in disguise. Fraser can't just take Julia to lunch in the middle of the day. He can't see her without driving a good distance, or arranging for her to come here. It's trickier to have our evenings, but it's easier for me to keep tabs on them. It's a more contained situation.

I'm very aware that I sound like a crazy, scorned wife, but I can't help it. I watch Fraser when he talks to her. The way his eyes light up. The easy charm in his voice. The same lilt he used with Esme before everything fell apart. I try to tell myself it's nothing. That he wouldn't cross that line again, not after what it cost him.

But I don't trust him. Not anymore. And certainly not with Julia. It was supposed to be something that brought us closer, but lately, I feel like I've invited a stranger into our bed and handed her the keys.

And then came Miranda.

Miranda was a surprise. A thrilling, fabulous, wonderful surprise. She was a breath of fresh air when she turned up at our door, welcome basket laden with goodies balanced on her forearms, and I almost laughed at the quaintness of it. How thoughtful that was. A rarity in today's culture. She matches the village perfectly. She's sweet, warm, unguarded, and beautiful, though she doesn't seem to realise it.

The best bit of all is she doesn't work. She said something about doing hair for that Ellen woman, but it was clear it's more of a casual arrangement than an actual job. That suits me perfectly. It means she'll have plenty of time. Time for long, lazy afternoons at the spa, for yoga classes and lakeside cocktails, for whatever else I can dream up. More importantly, it gives me a reason to call her. I'll ask her to do my hair. If ever you want an opportunity to chat to someone, it's getting a haircut. It's the perfect excuse to sit down with her, to talk, to learn everything there is to know about her. Ordinarily, I can't stand the inane chatter that comes with getting my hair done, but for Miranda, I'll make an exception.

She's coming round to dinner tomorrow night and I can barely contain my excitement. Fraser, on the other hand, is livid. I know that just from the silent treatment he's given me since I extended the invitation, from the way he's been moving around the house, his jaw set in a tight line. Why do men do that? Why can't they just come out and say what's bothering them instead of making it clear we've done something wrong but not elaborating. I'm not entirely sure why he's so annoyed. It's not like she'd discover anything I don't want her to just by coming round to dinner. All that will come in good time. Besides, she's bringing her husband and son with her. What exactly does Fraser think I'm going to do? Pounce on her over the dining table? Steal her away before dessert?

Maybe he can sense it. My excitement. Maybe he saw the way my eyes lit up when I first saw her, the way my body hummed with anticipation. He can tell how much I'd love to bring Miranda into our marriage. But so what? There are no rules to say we can only have one addition to our bed. Julia is incredible, but she's not here enough. Maybe once a month, if we're lucky. Miranda could fill the space she leaves behind. Maybe eventually – my heart begins to pound just thinking about it – we could have them both. Miranda and Julia here together, at the same time.

Fraser can sulk all he wants. I'm the kind of wife any man would kill for. Not only am I happy to bring another woman into our marriage bed, I'm willing to accept more than one. Not just willing, I'm actively *sourcing* potential takers. How could he not be over the moon about this? I wonder if he ever stops to appreciate the effort it takes on my part.

He can go and do one. I'm bringing Miranda into this marriage, and there's absolutely nothing he can do about it.

## THIRTY-FIVE

After Miranda and the other women leave, I spend the rest of the morning getting the house ready for her to come round for dinner tomorrow. I wish Fraser would stop sulking around the house. He's dampening my excitement.

At lunch, he has a face like he's swallowed a wasp. His fork scrapes against his plate as he finishes off his bacon, the sound like nails on glass.

'I've got to go out after lunch,' he murmurs, more to his empty plate than to me.

'Now? We've only just moved in.'

'I've got a job interview. I nearly forgot about it with everything going on. It was arranged before we had a move-in date.'

'Oh? Where is the interview?'

'A company just outside of town.'

I nod, my mind twitching. *A company just outside of town.* Ambiguous. Nondescript. Is this just him being moody, or is he purposefully being vague?

I smile back, pushing my tuna salad around my plate. 'What role is it?'

He shrugs. 'Similar to what I was doing before. Senior consultant-type thing.'

'Okay. Well, good luck.'

He grunts some kind of thank you, and then stands to dump his plate and cutlery in the dishwasher. My eyes follow him as he moves around the kitchen.

'I'm going to have a shower,' he says, disappearing into the hallway. His footsteps are heavy on the stairs.

I roll my eyes, annoyed. Whatever's going on with Fraser, he's treating me like a bit of dirt on the bottom of his shoe, and that is not okay. He doesn't get to treat me like this. I have a PhD. I work myself to the ground in the gym every week to keep my body the way it was when we first met. I'm the sort of woman who always has eyes on me. Fraser should consider himself lucky to be with me.

And yet, he's drifting from me. He drifted with Esme. And now I feel like ever since we met Julia, it's got even worse.

It's with this thought in my mind that I creep upstairs and into the bedroom. My ears prick up as I enter, making sure that I can still hear him in the shower. His phone is on charge on the bedside table, as usual. He never takes it into the bathroom with him when he showers. I sweep past the en suite and pick it up. For a moment, I think he may have changed his passcode, but on the second attempt his phone unlocks.

First, I check his messages for any sign of communication with Julia. I never used to have to do this. This is what he's done to me – him and Esme. They've turned me into one of those wives. There's nothing on his phone apart from the texts we've sent together to organise our evenings together. I check his calls and Facebook Messenger too, but nothing jumps out at me.

The shower stops.

*Crap.*

My fingers fly over the screen faster, tapping into his emails and scrolling through to find some mention of a job interview.

There. The fourth email down. I open up the email, eyes quickly scanning the details. All looks as he said. An interview for a consultant job about half an hour from here. He was telling the truth.

I let out a half laugh, realising how stupid I'm being. He's not doing anything he shouldn't be doing. I'm letting what happened with Esme taint what we've got with Julia, what we could potentially have with Miranda. I come out of his emails and lock his phone, ensuring to place it back in exactly the same place on his bedside table so that he doesn't realise I've had it. I scamper from the bedroom just in time to avoid him coming out of the en suite and seeing me.

As I'm tiptoeing down the stairs, however, something stirs within me. A gnawing realisation. I frown, trying to lock onto it. My eyes widen. It's the address of the company. That's what's bothering me. Something heavy drops into the pit of my stomach.

His job interview today is just ten minutes from Julia's house.

I wait exactly forty-five seconds after he leaves.

Long enough for him to pull out of the drive and make it to the end of Herring Row. Long enough to not be obvious. I don't even bother brushing my hair, just pull on shoes, grab my keys, and slide into my Range Rover.

I see his car up ahead as I turn into the high street. My foot eases off the accelerator, letting a delivery van slide between us like camouflage. My heart thuds against my ribs as I follow him through the next roundabout, then another.

Ten minutes from Julia's house? It's too neat. Too convenient. As I drive, I think about how he described this job interview. All so generic. He's always been good at plausible vagueness. The way he keeps things just on the edge of believability. Just enough truth to coat the lies.

I kept telling myself I'm being ridiculous. Paranoid. But still, I need to know.

As we get closer to where the interview is supposed to be, I stay a little further back, two cars now between us. He pulls into the company car park and I coast past, pretending to check my mirror, pretending not to be the kind of woman who follows her husband.

But I am now. I am that woman. And I hate myself for it.

I drive across the street from the car park, pull up on a double yellow line, and sit there, engine humming under me. Waiting. He goes into the building and is gone for what feels like hours. All okay so far. As long as he comes out after his interview and goes straight home, it'll all be fine.

Eventually he appears again at the door and strides back to his car. He sits in the driver's seat for a few moments, then turns on the engine and starts to drive. He leaves the car park.

And then he turns right. The right turn you'd take if you were going to Julia's house.

I feel the blood leave my fingers. I drive in the direction he went, clutching the wheel so tightly my knuckles hurt. My car swings out onto the main road, and I scan the sea of cars.

I can't see him.

He's gone.

The question is, where?

## THIRTY-SIX

I never found him. I drove all the way to Julia's house, expecting to see his car parked up outside, but it wasn't there.

I had no choice but to come home and finish unpacking and getting the house ready for tomorrow's dinner. Wherever he went today after his interview, I will not allow it to ruin our evening with Miranda. But now he's come home and the tension still hasn't eased up.

Even as he slips into bed beside me, Fraser doesn't even say goodnight. What is his problem?

'Goodnight, then,' I say, not willing to stand for it a moment longer. I am his wife. He can't treat me this way. The least he can do is explain to me what I've done that's so wrong.

'Night.'

A one-word answer. Not good enough.

He leans over and switches off the bedside lamp, but I immediately turn it back on. He squints up at me.

'What are you doing?'

'Are we not going to talk about why you've been so off with me all day?'

He sucks in a deep breath through his nose and lets it out slowly through his mouth. 'I'm fine. Let's just go to sleep.'

'Fraser, you're *not* fine. You've been sulking like a child all day, ever since Miranda came over.'

He stares at me at that, incredulous, then sits up. I've got his attention.

'Why do you think that might be, Anna? Have a wild guess as to why I might not be thrilled at the prospect of you getting friendly with another woman.'

So I was right. He could tell there was an instant attraction there. But I still don't understand.

'It's just dinner,' I say.

'But it's not *just* dinner, is it? Any more than it was *just* cocktails with Julia.'

He swings his legs out of bed and leans forward, his elbows on his knees. From this angle I can see his fingers raking through his hair. That was one of the first things that attracted me to him. His hair. It's thick and dark and floppy. Even when he's old he won't lose it. I can tell. He'll be a silver fox. When we first met, I couldn't resist running my hands through it. I'm not sure when that stopped.

I place a hand on his bare back, and he flinches under my touch. That stings.

'I don't understand. You're the one who suggested we have an open marriage in the first place. You're the one who found—'

'Esme?' Fraser finishes my sentence for me. 'Yeah, I did. And look how that turned out. I still haven't found another job.'

'Well, now that we're here you can get serious about the job hunt. There's bound to be jobs around here for someone like you.'

He shakes his head. 'That's not the point.'

I wait for him to elaborate, to tell me what the point of all this is, but he just continues to sit on the edge of the bed, head hung.

'Please talk to me,' I say after a moment. My voice sounds small, hesitant. Qualities I've never associated with myself before now.

He looks at me then, and his eyes are different. Sad and exhausted.

'I don't think we should have ever had an open marriage.' He sighs. 'And we certainly shouldn't again after... not after what happened with Esme.'

My hand drops from his back. 'But that's never going to happen again.'

'Really?' He raises one eyebrow. 'Because you've been spying on me.'

'What?'

'You're not as subtle as you think you are. I caught you in the rear-view mirror. I know you were following me today.'

My face pales. I thought I had been so careful. Clearly, I wasn't careful enough.

'I wasn't with her, you know,' he continues before I can reply. 'I know you think I was, but I did genuinely have a job interview.'

Yeah... and I invited Miranda to dinner out of the kindness of my heart, I think.

I purse my lips, wondering whether or not to attempt lying about following him. I could claim he's being paranoid, that it wasn't me he saw. But he'll know in his gut that he's right and all that will do is make him trust me less.

I opt for the mature route instead. 'I'm sorry.'

His face softens and he takes both of my hands in his. 'Let's just stop. We don't need anyone else. It can be just you and me again.'

Just me and Fraser. I think back to how it was when it was just me and Fraser. Stale. Boring. Every time we had sex it was out of obligation, moving through the motions but lacking any real passion. The idea of going back to that, of returning to a life where our bodies touched out of habit, not desire, feels like being buried alive. I stand up and begin pacing the room.

'I don't want to stop,' I say.

'Why not?' He stands too and blocks my way. 'Why can't you just have a normal marriage? What is wrong with you?'

'What's wrong with *me*?' My hands move on their own accord, no thought process going into the movement at all. I place both palms on his chest and shove him. Hard. 'What's wrong with *you*?'

I'm not strong enough to have made him stumble back far, but my Pilates has obviously paid off enough that I can take him by surprise if I need to. He takes a few steps back to steady himself, then looks at me, shocked.

'Any other man would give anything for this arrangement. For a wife like me.'

'But I just want you. Don't you see that? I don't care about being with other women.'

'Well, I don't just want you!' I fly at him then, arms flailing. My hands smack against his arms, his shoulders, his head. I don't know what's come over me. I'm overcome with a desperation for him to shut up, for him to pipe down and just do as he's told.

'Stop!' Fraser calls from underneath my slaps. He raises his forearm to act as a shield, so I go under it, punching him in the stomach. He lets out a grunt. When he straightens up again, it's like he's had an injection of adrenaline. He grabs me by the tops of my arms with a newfound strength.

'I said stop!'

He pushes me back and I crash against the wall. My head impacts with the framed photo of us on our wedding day. I hear the glass crack. For a second, a sharp, cold silence hangs between us, like we're both realising what we've just done.

'Anna... Oh God, are you okay? I didn't mean to push you back that hard.'

He reaches a hand out to me but I snatch mine away. 'Don't touch me.'

Regret pulls on his features, and I almost feel sorry for him. He slumps back down on the edge of the bed, head in his hands. I make a move to leave the bedroom, leave him to feel sorry for himself as always, but as I do, something pulls my attention to the window. I look up, narrow my eyes.

Our window is open, and the window across the street, the one that would be Miranda's bedroom if the layout of their house matches ours, is open too. I can just about see a faint blue glow coming from the room. Almost like one from a phone screen.

Someone in that house is awake.

How much did they see?

## THIRTY-SEVEN

I can't concentrate at work.

I actually love my job. Sleep disorders is a fascinating business. It's not something I ever thought I'd get into. I had originally planned to be a paediatric surgeon, but I read an article at university about a man who had been diagnosed with 'sexsomnia', which, despite the name sounding rather comical, is a genuine infliction that causes people to act out their sexual dreams while they're still asleep. From that moment, I was sold on this particular branch of medicine. The complexity of the mind's vulnerability during sleep, how the body can betray itself without conscious thought, has always captivated me.

But I'm due to see my second patient of the morning in an hour's time and I'm just not with it. My brain feels foggy from everything that's happened over the past few days, which isn't ideal when I'm supposed to come across as a highly qualified professional. Patients expect clarity and confidence. They need to trust that I can help them. Today, though, I feel like a fraud.

First, there was the nightmare of a dinner on Saturday. Fraser couldn't have been more off with Miranda if he'd tried. I've never been so humiliated in my life. I wanted to launch across the table and jab his chopsticks into his eyes. Even after she, Lee, and Mason had gone, the tension between us didn't ease up.

Then there was my failed attempt at wooing her over a haircut on Monday. I hadn't even thought about the fact she'd want to take my cardigan off to put the hairdressing gown on, and I'm convinced she saw the bruises. Just great. Of course, she doesn't know the origin of the bruises. She doesn't understand that I only got them because Fraser had been holding me back, trying to stop me from attacking him. I think she might think he's one of those awful, controlling, abusive husbands. Not ideal. She's never going to want to join us if she thinks that of him. I need to figure out a way to reassure her. To make her realise that he's not that type of guy at all. He'd never lay a hand on me. Damage control is needed.

'Megan?' I poke my head out to the reception. Megan shoots her head up from the computer eagerly. She's still pretty new here, just out of college, I think, and she worships the ground I walk on.

'Yes, Doctor Coles?'

'I'm not feeling great. Could you please rearrange the rest of my consultations for today?'

'Of course. Are you going to go home? Do you think you'll be in tomorrow?'

I can already see the panic surging through her at the thought of having to inform patients that their appointment has been moved at the last minute. I don't blame her. It was always the worst part of the job when I first started out.

'Yes, I'm sure I'll be fine tomorrow. Thank you.'

Relief washes over her and I retreat back to my office, wondering if I should actually go home or not. I'm not sure I want to. Fraser will be there. Fraser is always there now that he doesn't have a job. Our home feels smaller with him in it all day, as if his unemployment has inflated his presence. He went out yesterday for another job interview, this time a good hour away from Julia's house, and it was glorious. I took full advantage of his absence and invited Miranda to the club for a spa day, making sure to cover the bruises with makeup, just on the off chance she hadn't seen them. It was the perfect opportunity to figure her out. She's happy in her marriage, but I wouldn't say blissfully so. Certainly not so much that she would never even consider joining our little situation. And she's easily led. I got her into that plunge pool easily, even though she really didn't want to do it to begin with. That means I can persuade her.

The only slight glitch of the day was when Fraser called. She's started to feel a little uneasy around him, I think. She seemed quite happy with my excuse, something silly about Fraser not wanting me to spend money on the membership. While that's probably true – now that Fraser doesn't have a job we're living on just my wage which, while high, is not really enough to sustain the lifestyle we've become accustomed to – that's not the reason I didn't want him knowing what I was up to. I didn't want him realising I was out with *Miranda*. Just like I have to convince her to join us, I have to convince him that it's a good idea to have her join us. Bringing someone new into our world requires delicate precision. One misstep, and the entire balance could shatter. I wonder if I'll have to convince Julia, too?

But I can't figure out a plan for that right now, not while my head is as fuzzy as it is. I need to go home, have a nap, shake off whatever this is, and then maybe I can call Miranda this evening. Julia is supposed to be coming over tomorrow, so perhaps having them meet would be a good first step to introduce Miranda into our world without being too explicit about it and scaring her off.

I'm pleased with this idea and already feel a little bit better by the time I pull into Herring Row. My eye drifts, as it always does these days, to Miranda's bedroom window, just on the off chance she may have left her curtains open. She has, but I can't see her inside. It's a small disappointment, a missed chance to catch a glimpse of her private world.

I'm so busy looking at Miranda's house that the black Mini parked up on the side practically jumps out of nowhere. I slam my foot down on my brake and the car stops with a jolt. Luckily I wasn't going fast down our cul-de-sac, but it's sent my heart thrumming in my chest all the same. There are hardly ever cars parked up on the pavements down this road. Everyone has their own driveway. It's only when there's guests that you'll see this, hence why I hadn't been expecting a car to be in my way.

The penny drops.

That Mini is parked outside our house. It's our guest. And though it's usually only ever parked outside where we live in the evenings, when it's too dark to properly see, I recognise it. It's *Julia's* Mini. Julia is here. At our house.

I pull up behind the car and take a moment. There could be many reasons why Julia could have come over while I was supposed to be at work. Perhaps she's had to move our evening to tonight and so she thought she'd get here early to surprise me? Maybe she wanted time to have a look round the new house? It's a whole four hours before I'm due home, but it's a possibility. A slim one.

Regardless, it'll do me no good to rush in there all guns blazing. If there really is nothing going on and I do that then not only will it be the end for us and Julia, Fraser will never in a million years consider adding Miranda into the equation. I can't afford for suspicion to unravel everything.

I climb out of the car and close the door as quietly as I can. Before I put my key in the front door, I press my ear up to it and listen. I don't know if you can ever actually hear anything through a front door, but I certainly can't right now. The key slides in slowly, silently, and there's a soft click as I turn it.

As I step over the threshold I listen some more. Still silence.

In fact, if I didn't know any better, I'd say there was no one here at all. Maybe Fraser and Julia have gone out. My stomach churns as I remember seeing him with Esme in Costa. The way they played footsie under the table like a young couple in love. Sickening. No, that's not what's happening here. Fraser wouldn't do it to me again.

*'Once a cheat, always a cheat.'* My mother's words reverberate around my head. That was what she told me when me and Fraser first got together. There I was practically glowing about the fact that he had left his wife for me, and she had to go and put a damper on things. I had ignored her warning for years, and even when we started our open marriage, I didn't think it was something I needed to worry about. Now, the certainty I feel is waning.

I force myself to breathe slowly, steadying the anxiety that threatens to crawl up my throat. Esme could have been a one-off. Correction – she *was* a one-off. I have to believe that. Anything else is unthinkable.

I tiptoe up the stairs, concentrating on avoiding any creaky spots. I'm about a third of the way up when I can hear it. Heavy breathing. I turn my head in the direction of it. It's coming from our bedroom. I follow the sound, my heart pounding. When I reach the top of the stairs I stand for a moment outside our door. It would be so easy to turn back. To pretend I hadn't heard anything. To go back to work and see my patients and not have to deal with this. But if I do that then I'll never know, and I think that might drive me insane. My gaze drops down to the handle.

Maybe it's not what I think. Maybe Fraser is in there on his own. It wouldn't be the first time I walked in on him giving himself a little extra relief.

But Julia's car is parked outside.

I reach out and rest my fingertips on the door handle. It takes me a good few seconds to work up the courage to open the door. I imagine a thousand different scenarios, some ludicrous, some painfully plausible, each one twisting the knife a little deeper.

And when the door swings open, I know it's the beginning of the end.

## THIRTY-EIGHT

They're so into it they still don't hear me to begin with.

It's only when Julia drops her head to one side and her eyes flicker open that she spots me. She gives Fraser a shove to get him off her and disappears, legs and arms scrambling madly, under the duvet. Fraser, meanwhile, totally confused as to why he's been interrupted, spins around.

I think I actually see his heart stop for a moment. I think mine does too. Our eyes meet and my breath is surprisingly steady. I'm not sure what I'm feeling. Shell-shocked? Angry? Sad? Probably a concoction of all the above. The room feels unnaturally still, a vacuum where sound should be. Even my own heartbeat seems muted, as though my body can't decide whether to fight or flee. My fingers grip the hem of my jacket.

Fraser is the one to finally break the silence.

'Anna,' he says, pulling himself up off the bed and hurrying to cover his rapidly fading hard-on with his boxers. I wait for the next part of the sentence. *Anna, I'm so sorry. Anna, it's not what it looks like.* But nothing comes. He doesn't say anything because there's nothing to say. He can't talk his way out of it like he did with Esme. He can't make out like it's all in my head. This is undeniable, tangible betrayal. No room for misinterpretation.

I watch him in disgust as he gets dressed. He pulls his shirt on but leaves the buttons undone. Julia gets dressed too, pulling her bra and thong on and slipping her silky dress over the top. I step out into the hallway, not to give them privacy, but because I can't bear to look at their half-naked bodies. Once Fraser is fully dressed, he comes to join me in the hall so that we're face to face.

'I told you we should have stopped this. We should never have brought someone else into our marriage,' he says.

I tilt my head, surveying him for a moment, wondering if I've heard that correctly. The audacity is staggering, almost laughable.

'Are you actually trying to blame *me* for this?'

'No. That's not what I mean. It's just... of course it was going to end like this. I've... I've grown to care for you both.'

My right eye twitches. I glance over at Julia, who is huddled in the corner of our bedroom, avoiding eye contact at all costs. She almost looks a little afraid. It's crazy. Any other time I'd have been delighted to have seen her in my bedroom. Fraser is wrong. We could have made this work. All he had to do was stick to the rules. It was either him and me or the three of us, but never him and her. That is the difference between our arrangement and flat-out cheating. It was only ever okay if I was involved and consenting, too.

I don't even quite realise I've grabbed him until I hear the rip of his shirt. I want to shake him, I want to hurt him, I want to flay him alive with my nails. My love for him has been snuffed out in the heat of my jealousy. It's a primal, uncontrolled fury.

'Anna, what the fuck are you doing?' He pushes against me, but my rage is too far gone. I hit and scratch and kick. Anything to make him understand just a tiny bit of how he's made me feel. I want him to feel the raw pain.

'*Stop it!*' Julia's voice is high pitched, frantic. She runs at us and tries to grab my wrists, getting in between me and Fraser. Getting in the way.

'Get off me!' I shriek, yanking my wrists away from her.

It all happens too fast.

She stumbles forwards, knocked off balance by my sudden movement. There is a fleeting second where I catch the look on her face, her mouth widening in shock, an audible gasp escaping her lips, before she tumbles, crashing down the stairs, bouncing off the walls as she descends. There is a sickening thud as she reaches the bottom. Then silence.

Time seems to collapse in on itself. There's a moment where neither me nor Fraser move. We just stare down the stairs in a frozen state of utter shock. It's only when she moves and groans that we jolt into action. We barrel down the stairs after her. Fraser crouches down and lifts her head.

'It's going to be okay. We're going to get you help. Anna, call an ambulance.'

He strokes her hair and his fingers turn red. There's blood seeping out of what looks like a crack in her skull. It must be fairly bad, because her eyes are rolling back in her head, and she seems to be shifting in and out of consciousness. My stomach knots painfully. I can't tell if it's guilt, fear, or the residual sense of betrayal still festering inside me.

Fraser looks at me, eyes ablaze. 'Anna! Call an ambulance! *Now!*' I've never heard panic like that in his voice.

I'm not sure why I'm not panicking. I should be panicking, shouldn't I? There is a severely injured woman at the bottom of our stairs. She could be dying, for all we know. But for whatever reason, it's not hit me yet. I'm hoping it's the shock. I'm hoping it will all rush to me later and I'll descend into a mess. If not, I don't know what that says about me.

Seeing I'm not about to call anyone, Fraser lowers Julia's head to the floor and starts rummaging through his pockets.

'What are you doing?' I ask.

'Looking for my phone!'

'It's upstairs. You had it on the side table while you were shagging her.'

He stops, stares at me. 'We have to call for help.' Each word is punctuated, spaced out, as if he's talking to someone who doesn't speak English.

When I still don't move, he scrambles up onto his feet and shoves past me, bounding back up the stairs. I cock my head and look at Julia, still twitching, still clinging to life on our floor. If Fraser calls an ambulance now, they could well get here on time. She's probably got some kind of bleed on the brain, but they might be able to save her.

But there's something churning in my gut.

I don't want her to be saved.

It's not just the fact she slept with Fraser and broke our agreement. It's not just the betrayal. It's the way Fraser was stroking her hair. Something about it tells me they weren't just shagging. There were feelings there. Feelings that don't involve me. They've crossed a line I can't come back from.

The decision is made before I even realise it. I stride over to the console table that houses our key bowl, the photo of me on my graduation day, and the bust ornament that Fraser picked up from an antique store a couple of years back. It's expensively heavy. Sharp edges.

I return to Julia just as Fraser bursts out of the bedroom onto the hallway.

'I can't find my phone!' he cries, panicked.

That's good. Better that the call hasn't been made.

'Anna... Anna, what are you doing?'

I fall onto my knees beside Julia's head. She's barely conscious at this point. She won't feel a thing.

'Anna, stop!'

But I barely hear him over the sound of Julia's skull crushing under the weight of the bust.

## THIRTY-NINE

Hands grab my shoulders and shake me. I blink three times. Try to focus on what's in front of me. Fraser is in my face. He shakes me so much my head snaps back and forth. He's saying something. Shouting. But his words are far off. His eyes are wild, uncomprehending, like he doesn't know who I am anymore. Maybe I don't either.

Then he slaps me.

The sting momentarily stuns me. I blink. 'Huh?'

'What have you done?'

I look down and that's it. That's when it hits me. That's the moment where I realise what I did. I killed Julia. Cold-blooded, purposefully killed her. At least when she went down the stairs, I could have argued that it was an accident, even if it wasn't really. It would always have niggled at the back of my mind, whether or not it really was unintentional, but it would be the official story. Eventually, if I told myself enough, I probably could have convinced myself that I never meant for her to fall down those stairs.

But there's no arguing this. I went and got that bust. I

brought it crashing down onto her head. There is no accident here.

I scramble back, pushing myself up against the wall, desperate to create some distance between me and Julia's body. It echoes through my bones: the sound it made, that momentary resistance before her skull caved in.

'Oh God,' Fraser says. He looks around him, shaking his head, pulling his hair. There's blood everywhere. On the bust. My trousers. The carpet. Fraser's white shirt. 'This isn't happening. This isn't happening...'

'W-wh-what should we do?' My words come out stuttering, shaking. My teeth clank together as I tremble.

'I don't know.'

'Please, Fraser. I'm sorry.'

'You're *sorry*?' He shouts so loudly I cower back, arms covering my face as if I'm terrified he's going to attack me. Maybe I am. I don't know what to think anymore. I don't know what to do. The look he's giving me is pure hatred.

I reach out a hand and grab his arm, pulling him closer to me. 'You have to help me. This is your fault.'

'What?' Fraser yanks himself away, disgusted. '*My* fault?'

'You did this to me. I would never... I'd never have hurt...' I can't bring myself to finish my sentence. My breathing is growing frantic, panicked. I can't go to prison for murder. People like me don't do well in cells. Just thinking about it causes me to let out a howl.

For a moment, Fraser just stares at me. I can't read his expression. Somewhere between repulsion and shock, I think. My breath grows more ragged, and I clutch my chest.

'Please... help... me...' I rasp. I launch myself forward on all fours, clawing at his legs, desperate for him to come to me, to hold me, to help me.

His face softens a touch.

'Right, calm down. Come here.' He pulls me to him, and I

cling to him like a life jacket. I feel so small in his arms. Desperate for a rescue I don't deserve.

'I don't want to go to prison,' I sob, burying my face into his shoulder. I'm sure I feel a slight recoil from him, but it only makes me hold onto him tighter. Whatever I've done, we are in this together. We've both been living this lifestyle. We've both done things we shouldn't have. He has to stick by me. For better or for worse, wasn't it?

I think he can tell I'm not going to calm down without some kind of reassurance, because he wraps his arms around me.

'You're not going to. We're going to deal with this. No one knows she was even here except for us.'

'Really?' I look up at him, wiping my face with my sleeve.

He peers down at me. His face doesn't look as certain as his words. In fact, I've never seen him look so afraid, but he nods all the same. 'You're right. This is my fault, too. But you have to do exactly as I say from now on, do you understand?'

Ten minutes later, we are armed with the necessary tools.

Bin bags to cover her body and stop the blood from getting anywhere else. Carpet cleaner to address the spots of blood on the stairs, and bleach to deal with the puddle on the wooden floor where Julia lies. New clothes for Fraser and me. Rubber gloves to avoid fingerprints. And our large suitcase, the one we bought for our honeymoon, to serve as Julia's final resting place. The irony is bitter. This suitcase meant for adventures is now trapping a life that I've taken.

'Okay,' Fraser says, looking down at her. He looks about ten years older than he did this morning. His face is practically grey. 'Let's get her wrapped up in the bin bags.'

I do as I'm told. It's awkward. Bin bags are not designed to house a human body. As I pull one up over her leg it tears, and I swear under my breath.

'Go and get some packing tape,' I say. He does. Luckily, we have lots. The perk of having just moved house. I wonder if there's a world record for the shortest time living in a house before a crime is committed. If there is, we've surely won it.

The packing tape makes it easier. I wrap the bags around her like black, shiny bandages instead of trying to fit her into them. My stomach turns as Fraser does her face. I'm not sure why. She's already dead, it's not like the plastic over her airways is going to suffocate her, but the thought of having a bin bag over my nose and mouth makes me feel nauseous. By the time we're done, she looks more like one of those Halloween decorations and less like an actual, real human. Which is good. It makes it more manageable. It's easier to see her as a problem to solve, not a person I killed.

Fraser stands. 'I'm going to line the boot of the car with some bags too. Just in case.'

'Don't leave me.' I grab his sleeve and look up at him, pleading. I don't want to be here on my own with Julia.

'I'll be right back.'

He goes, and I huddle my knees to my chest. I have visions of Julia sitting up still wrapped in the bin bags, horror-movie style. I'm going to be so messed up after this I'm going to need to become my own patient at the sleep clinic.

When Fraser returns, he sees me curled up in the shadows and crouches beside me.

'Are you okay?'

I shake my head. 'What's going to happen to us?' I whisper, still staring at Julia's plastic-clad body.

'What do you mean?'

'I mean, are we going to be okay? Us? Our marriage?'

Fraser lets out a long, slow sigh. 'I don't know. I can't really think about that right now.' Tears prick my eyes at his words. 'But I do want to help you. I saw the signs. I knew this was all too much for you. I knew you weren't coping with it and I went along with it anyway. If I had done my job as your husband this wouldn't have happened. So, let's just get through tonight, let's get you some help, and let's see where we are after that, yes?'

I nod, but the movement is so small it's almost imperceptible. Still, Fraser takes my silence as an agreement. He unzips the suitcase and flops the lid down onto the floor. I peer down into its belly.

'Is she going to fit?' I say.

'We're going to have to make her fit.'

It's a struggle. I have to remove all thought about this being a person as we squeeze her in, bending and shoving and twisting areas to manage it. I tell myself she doesn't feel it, that it doesn't matter, but my stomach still turns at the way her limbs give way so easily. The only thing that keeps me going is the thought of the alternative. I'm not about to start chopping her up into little pieces to get her in there. I'm not that deranged.

Once she's in and we've zipped up the suitcase, I'm instantly overcome with a wash of relief. Even though she's still here, even though it's not over yet, just having her body hidden away and out of sight makes me feel a little better. Like this day might actually end after all. I get to work cleaning the floors and the little bit of blood splatter that landed on the walls as she went down the stairs. The scent of the bleach fills my lungs and stings my throat. There's no room for the bust in the suitcase, so I have to clean that too. I don't put it back on the console table though. I never want to see it again. Instead, I go up to our bedroom and find a bag of items we'd decided to take to the charity shop when we were unpacking the house. Old clothes, unwanted trinkets, forgotten pieces of our old life. The bust can go with those items and find a new home somewhere, somewhere where it likely won't be used as a murder weapon.

When I return to the bottom of the stairs, Fraser has moved the suitcase closer to the front door.

'I'm going to wait until it's dark,' he says. 'Better to do it in the middle of the night when there's no chance of being spotted getting rid of the suitcase.'

'Where are you going to take it?'

'There's a river not too far from here. I go past it sometimes when I go for a walk. There's a massive fly-tipping area, a pile of things people have dumped, mattresses and old furniture and such. It never gets cleared and it stinks like nothing else. I'll put it there. Bury it under some other stuff.'

I nod. It doesn't sound like the best plan. What if someone does decide to clear it? What if a dog smells her rotting body, or a nosy kid stumbles across it and decides to go through the rubbish there, seeing what they can find? I had expected Fraser to bury the suitcase underground somewhere. But then, I suppose, there's more risk of being caught, and more risk that someone would spot a freshly dug grave.

'And we're going to have to do something about Julia's car,' Fraser says. 'It's still parked up outside. I was thinking of dumping it as well as the suitcase, but I think an abandoned car will raise too much suspicion. I'll drive it a few miles away tomorrow and leave it as far from the suitcase as possible. There are no cameras on the country lanes so it should be fairly safe.'

All I can do is nod again. It feels as though we're planning something entirely normal – a trip, perhaps. It doesn't feel like we're figuring out the best way to not get caught for murder. Maybe that's the most terrifying part: how easy it is to go along with all of this.

The rest of the afternoon and evening is spent mostly in silence. We try to turn the TV on to distract us, but it's no good. We're both just staring at meaningless flashing images, not at all aware of storyline or dialogue or even what show we're watching. My thoughts pulse in time with the flickering screen, looping the same words over and over: *Julia. Dead. Julia. Murder.* All either of us can think about is the woman in the suitcase in our hall.

Fraser waits until nearly 3 a.m. before he finally gets up and lugs it outside. I don't watch him do it. I stay where I am on the sofa, even once I've heard the car drive off down the street, pretending it's not happening. Even if this plan works, I'm not sure how to move on from this and stop the memory of it from sending me insane.

To be honest, I'm not entirely sure whether or not I'm already insane. Maybe I crossed that line hours ago, when I brought the bust down onto Julia's skull, or perhaps when I helped Fraser bend and twist her body to fit inside the suitcase.

This thought is interrupted by a loud ringing, harsh and sudden in the early morning quietness. It shatters the stillness like a gunshot. My whole body jolts. For a split second I think it's an alarm. The police coming to haul me away. Maybe they caught Fraser in the middle of dumping the suitcase and he's confessed everything to them. I realise quickly that it's only my phone ringing.

Why is my phone ringing at 3 a.m.?

I lean forward and peer at the screen. A sharp, involuntary shiver works its way from my toes all the way up to my scalp, leaving a trail of ice in its wake and causing the hairs on the back of my neck to stand to attention.

It's Miranda.

# FORTY

Fraser isn't gone for long. Ten minutes maybe. Not enough time to drive far. Not nearly enough distance between us and what we've done. I'm concerned that he's dumped her body far too close to home, that he should have driven further afield just in case someone finds her remains, but I don't say that. He's on my side, for now. I need to keep it that way.

'You okay?' he says once he's safely through the front door. He doesn't mean that really. What he means is, am I about to have some kind of breakdown?

'Fine,' I say. 'You?'

'All taken care of.' He comes to join me on the sofa, collapsing into it and lifting his legs up onto the coffee table. Ordinarily I'd scold him for not taking his shoes off, but things like that seem a bit silly now.

'Miranda called,' I say after a moment. My voice sounds mechanical. Detached. Is this how it starts? The unravelling? 'Twice, actually.'

His feet drop to the floor with a thud. He stares at me, aghast. I had been in two minds as to whether to tell him or not. I don't want to freak him out unnecessarily. But I can't not. It's too much of a coincidence that she would call right at the moment he left the house with a dead body in our boot.

'Jesus Christ.' He leans forward, running his hands through his hair. 'Do you think she saw me?'

'Maybe. But... I don't think it's anything to worry about necessarily. If she did, all she would have seen is you with a suitcase.'

Fraser is quiet for a moment. He stares straight ahead, eyes locked on my phone, thinking.

'Okay, here's what we're going to do. You're going to go away for a few weeks. Get a nice hotel room, or something.'

'What? I don't want to leave—'

'Anna, listen to me.' He turns to me, takes my hands in his. 'You need to get away from all of this for a bit. From this house, from Miranda—'

'From *you?*' I finish his sentence for him.

His eyes meet mine. He looks as if he's about to cry. 'We need some space. After everything that's happened, it will be good for us. Then you can come back in a few weeks once we've had a chance to process everything and you've cleared your head. Just lie low for a bit and when you return, we can try to fix us.'

My bottom lip quivers. 'What about Miranda?'

'Like you said, all she would have seen is me with a suitcase, if she saw anything at all.' He shrugs, trying to look nonplussed, but I know him. I can tell from his posture he's stressed. 'I'll just tell her that you've gone to visit relatives.' He gives my hands a small squeeze. 'It'll be fine, Anna. We will be fine.'

I desperately want to believe him.


I did what Fraser said. Phoned in sick to work. Packed a bag. Disappeared.

Miranda was definitely suspicious, though, of what I'm not

entirely sure. She turned up at the crack of dawn at our house, and I had to hide upstairs while Fraser got rid of her. I've been staying at this hotel for a few days now, and I've been very good. No phone, as per his instructions. No contact with the outside world.

I know why he told me to shut myself off like this. He's worried that Miranda is going to try calling me again and I won't have the willpower to stay away. He's probably right, to be fair. The first day that I was here, I woke up thinking it was all some kind of terrible dream. It didn't feel real – not finding Fraser and Julia in bed together, not watching her tumble down the stairs, none of it. But then once I realised where I was, that I wasn't in my own bed but two hours away hiding out in a hotel, I knew it was real.

I am a *murderer*.

I spent the entire first day locked away, jumping any time footsteps sounded in the hall. Even when I ordered room service and knew someone would need to knock at the door in order to deliver the food, I was convinced it was the police coming for me. The second day, I filled my hours by watching the news on the television in the room dressed in the hotel's plush white dressing gown, just in case a report about a body being found in a suitcase in the Cotswolds popped up. It never did. But now it's the third day, and I've started to grow restless. Antsy.

The worst part of all of this, the bit that is really concerning me, is I don't even feel that bad for what I did. Panic, yes. Every couple of hours I'm hit by a wave of fear and nausea, that churning in my stomach that tells me all is not well. But it's not because of guilt over what I did to Julia. It's because I'm scared I'll get caught. It's self-preservation. And the fact that the concern for myself is stronger than the regret of what I did? That terrifies me. There's something deeply wrong with me, and I'm not sure what to do about it.

I decide to go down to the buffet this morning, instead of ordering room service. Even though I've opted for a beautiful room with a garden view and queen-sized bed, I'm starting to get cabin fever only ever seeing the same four walls. Even just seeing the staff helps. Fraser's logic of having me go into hiding for a bit is sound, but the trouble with this plan is I'm on my own. That's dangerous. It gives me time to think about everything. To replay it all in my head, over and over, like some kind of sick highlight reel. I glance around at the other guests, mostly couples laughing and chatting away with each other, and wonder how long Fraser expects me to stay away. He just told me to lie low for a while. How long is a while?

After stuffing my face with sausages, bacon, scrambled eggs – all the food I'd ordinarily avoid – I decide to take a dip in the pool and indulge in a sauna to take my mind off everything. Perhaps I could even get a massage, really work those worries out of my shoulders? But it's a mistake. As soon as I step foot into the hotel spa I'm thinking about Miranda, about our spa day that we had together at the club. It feels simultaneously like it was years ago and only yesterday. The memory causes a sense of longing to tug at my insides.

Abandoning the spa idea, I go back to my room and rummage around in the rucksack I brought with me, pulling out my switched-off phone and laying it on the bed. My fingers tap on the unresponsive screen. It feels wrong, unnatural in this day and age to not fill quiet hours with mindless scrolling. I had thought maybe this would be a nice break from technology. People do it, don't they? Switch off from the world. A digital detox. A retreat. But that's for people looking to find peace, not people trying to outrun their own actions. I'm not finding it restful. The desperation to check to see if Miranda has tried calling me again is too much to bear.

It wouldn't hurt, would it? I could just switch it on for one minute. Long enough to quickly glance through any notifications and then I can turn it straight back off again. Just a second. That's all. It doesn't take long for me to convince myself. Before I know it, I'm holding down the power button and watching the Samsung loading screen flicker to life.

I chew on my lip as I wait to see if anything will pop up. A couple of meaningless notifications do. A missed alarm. A calendar reminder to send an old friend from school a birthday card. And then...

My breath catches in my throat.

*Miranda. 6 missed calls.*

## FORTY-ONE

'Mrs Coles? There are a couple of police officers in reception. They'd like to talk to you.'

I nearly drop the phone. The police are here. *Oh God.* This is it. I'm going to prison. This is the end of my life as I know it.

The concierge coughs on the other end of the line. 'Mrs Coles?'

'Yes, sorry. I heard you. I'll be right there. I just need to get dressed.'

I place the phone down on the receiver a little too hard. I don't know what to do.

My first instinct is to try to make a run for it. This hotel is massive. I could easily dash out of one of the back entrances unseen, run across the golf courses to the car park, and just hope to God that there aren't more officers waiting to catch me trying to get away. But that would only make things worse, wouldn't it? Running is as good as confessing. And then what? They chase me down, drag me away in handcuffs?

I have no choice. My legs are like jelly as I shimmy out of my dressing gown and pull on proper clothes, and they continue to feel like they're unable to hold me up as I walk towards the hotel reception. I tell myself not to look so guilty, to carry myself like I have nothing to hide, but my body doesn't seem to want to do as it's told.

The two officers at the door smile at me as I approach them.

'Morning, Mrs Coles. Sorry to disturb you. I'm Sergeant Hargreaves and this is PC Danvers. The concierge has very kindly given us this room to chat in. Is that okay with you?'

They gesture at one of the meeting rooms and I peer in. No additional officers. No guns. Not even a set of handcuffs waiting for me. From the way they greeted me, it doesn't sound like they're coming to arrest me. But then, if that's not the case, why on earth are they here?

'Sure,' I say. 'Is everything okay?'

'Nothing to worry about. We're just doing a welfare check.'

*Welfare check?*

'Okay...'

We move as a group into the living room. I'm praying they can't hear how fast my heart is beating. It's like a drum in my chest, each beat louder than the last. I sit on one side of the meeting table while the officers sit on the other.

'We've had a report from a concerned neighbour,' Sergeant Hargreaves says. 'They were worried about you and asked us to check in. Your husband informed us that you're staying here whilst visiting relatives, is that correct?'

My palms begin to sweat. *Miranda.*

'Oh, really? That's odd. Yes. I often take little getaways, to recharge the batteries, you know, and to visit some elderly relatives who live nearby. We've just moved house, so I needed a break. And I'm fine, as you can see.'

'And you're safe and well here? No one is pressuring you to stay or stopping you from leaving?'

Only my husband, who wants me as far away from Miranda as possible.

'No, no. I just needed some space. But I'll be heading home in a few days.'

Sergeant Hargreaves nods, seemingly satisfied, and PC Danvers taps something into his tablet. The faint clacking of his fingers on the screen sends a shiver down my spine.

'Would you be comfortable giving us a phone number where we can reach you directly?' he says. 'Just in case we need to follow up?'

'Sure.' I reel off my number and PC Danvers logs it. I suppose I'd better keep my phone on from now on, just in case they try to ring me.

'Just to confirm,' Sergeant Hargreaves says, clasping his hands together, 'nobody has harmed you or made you feel unsafe at any point?'

'No. Unless you count the trainee chef's cooking. Nobody's safe eating that.' I laugh, but when I realise I'm the only one laughing I chew down on my lip. The air in the room tightens.

'Your neighbour expressed concerns specifically about your husband. She said you'd been arguing a lot. That there were bruises on your arms that looked like fingerprints...'

Oh God. Is that what Miranda thinks? That I'm out here because Fraser has been beating me around?

'No. Nothing like that. We had an argument a couple of nights ago, but it was nothing to be concerned about. Probably just our neighbours being nosy. You know how it is.' I force a light chuckle, but it comes out wrong, stilted. I feel my cheeks redden. I'm hoping I haven't just got Miranda in trouble for wasting police time, but the more I can convince them that there's absolutely no reason to be sniffing around, the better. 'Sorry you got dragged over here for nothing.'

Sergeant Hargreaves nods. 'That tallies with what your husband told us.'

'Oh?' My ears prick up. 'What did he tell you?'

'He explained that he didn't want to tell your neighbour

where you were staying. That she has become a bit obsessed with you lately, never leaving you alone, inserting herself into your business. Would you say that's accurate?'

My entire body tenses. What? Why would Fraser say that? My blood is rushing hot and fast in my ears. This was not the plan. The last thing I want to be doing is incriminating Miranda. I want to pull her closer to us not push her further away. The only reasoning I can think of is that he told Miranda I was visiting relatives, like he said he would, and when the police started poking their noses in, he needed an excuse for why he lied to Miranda. But surely there could have been another way. He could have told her I'd changed my plans or... anything other than this.

'Mrs Coles?' Sergeant Hargreaves prompts, snapping my attention back to him. 'Is your neighbour causing you issues?'

I desperately want to deny it, but I can't. Doing so will only prompt more questions about why Fraser said something that isn't true.

'A little. She showed up at the last spa day I tried to take. I just thought it was easier to not let her know I was attempting another, in case she wanted to come to this one too.'

More tapping into the tablet. Oh God, what have I just done?

'Sorry to have disturbed your break,' Sergeant Hargreaves says. 'We'll give her a verbal warning, tell her to keep her distance from you and your husband. If she continues after that you can call us and quote this number, and we'll escalate things. Does that sound okay?' He writes a number on a card and slides it across the table from me. I take it, swallowing hard.

*Does* that sound okay? Miranda being told to stay away from me? No. That doesn't sound okay at all. It sounds absolutely awful. But I have no choice but to feign gratitude.

'Thank you,' I croak.

The two officers stand, straightening their jackets as they do so. 'Not at all,' Sergeant Hargreaves says. 'If anything changes or if you ever feel unsafe, please don't hesitate to call us, okay?'

'I will. Thank you for checking in.' I shake both of their hands, concentrating on keeping my grip firm and steady.

I maintain my composure until they're out of the hotel, then half-run to my room. I burst through the door and throw myself on the bed, grabbing a pillow and burying my face into it. My fingers grip the edges of the fabric as I scream.

This is all so messed up. I came here because I trusted Fraser to deal with this situation, but all he's doing is making things worse. He's taking matters into his own hands and making stupid, rash decisions.

Well, if he can't be trusted to sort this out on his own, I'm going to have to return to Herring Row.

# FORTY-TWO

Monday morning, I wake before the sun has even risen in the sky. It takes me just three hours to pack up my bags, check out of the hotel, drive back to the Cotswolds, and locate Miranda.

She looks even better than I remember. She probably thinks she looks rough. Her hair is thrown up haphazardly in a bun, and her clothing choice would suggest she just grabbed the nearest joggers and top she could find. But to me, her beauty shines through. She'd turn heads in a strappy black dress.

She's clearly running late. Her jaw is tight, her movements clipped. She's dragging her poor child along the pavement so fast his arm looks about ready to pop out of its socket. I won't try to talk to her now, not while she's so flustered. I'll wait until she's dropped him at school. She'll be calmer then. Easier to talk to.

I spent the entire drive over here planning what I'm going to say to her. Every word, every pause, every gentle smile, scripted and rehearsed in my mind to perfection. It's a delicate balance. I have to reassure her enough that she's going to drop this suspicion of Fraser. I can't have her involving the police anymore, even though she seems to have got entirely the wrong end of the stick.

Clearly, Miranda didn't call the police because she knows about Julia. If she had, that would have been an entirely different conversation with Sergeant Hargreaves yesterday. But she knows something is up. She thinks she's protecting me, that's the irony of it. I think Sergeant Hargreaves seemed satisfied when he left. He shouldn't bother us anymore. But I'd still rather not risk it, especially not with Fraser clearly getting himself in such a tizz about all this. If she stops poking her nose in, then he'll stop saying she's some kind of crazy stalker. Flattering as the idea may be, it's not a helpful complication.

Besides, if Miranda doesn't stop thinking Fraser is some kind of monstrous wife beater, she'll never want to join us.

She's stopped walking. Something has distracted her inside the coffee shop. Or someone. I keep my pace steady, matching the natural rhythm of the street. I move in unison with the other people strolling along the street so as not to draw attention to myself, pulling my sun hat further down over my face just in case she looks over. My eyes narrow as she goes into the coffee shop, squinting to see through the window. What is she doing? I thought she was in a rush to get to school?

And then I realise. A slow, creeping dread curls around my ribs. She's talking to Sergeant Hargreaves.

I dive into the park that's across from the coffee shop and sit myself on a bench, forcing my breathing to stay even, my posture relaxed. I try to look as nonchalant as possible by pressing my phone to my ear and pretending to have a conversation. I wish I could hear what's being said in that coffee shop. But there's no way I could get in there without one or both of them noticing me.

My head turns ever so slightly and I peek sideways, past the rim of my sun hat. A subtle movement. I can't see that well, certainly not well enough to attempt reading their lips, but he seems to be growing a little impatient with her. His arms fold, then unfold. His fingers tap against the table. Good. That means he thinks she's making a mountain out of a molehill. That means he believed me yesterday. Relief trickles through me, but I don't fully let it settle. Not yet. I return to my fake phone call, wishing I'd had a chance to speak to her before she spotted him.

When she leaves the coffee shop she crosses the road, coming to stand right outside the park. She's dangerously close. All she'd have to do is look to her left and she'd see me sitting here. I tilt my head so that the sun hat covers more of my face, feigning distraction, pretending to focus on my imaginary caller.

She's talking on the phone. I can just make out the brightness in her voice. Something about going to a cocktail bar tonight. My ears prick up at that. *Interesting.* Maybe that would be a better time to talk to her than right now. In fact, it would be perfect. I could explain why I've been away and apologise for making her worry, and then we could spend the rest of the evening together at the bar. Alcohol would smooth things over, lower her guard. She'd certainly be more open to the idea of joining our marriage with a few drinks inside of her. At that thought, another idea stirs inside me, and a flutter of dangerous excitement journeys through me, making the hairs on the back of my neck stand on end.

I pull my phone away from my ear and pull up Google Maps, searching for local cocktail bars and hoping there's not too many to choose from. There are only two that I can see, and one of them has only just opened. I assume that's the one she's talking about going to, probably with Priya. Even if it's not, if I turn up and she's not there I can just check the other one. One way or another, I'll find her.

I'm just deciding that this is how I'm going to be spending

my evening when a car horn blares. I flinch, looking up. There's a commotion by the school. Looks like Miranda just nearly got hit by that Range Rover. Jesus. She needs to be more careful. Thankfully, she's fine. She's back on the pavement, hugging her son and having a good old cry. The way her shoulders shake, the way she clings to him... she's breaking. I can see it. Cracking under the pressure. She's clearly got a lot on her mind, bless her. She needs me. More than ever. If anyone knows how to have a bit of fun and loosen up, it's me.

Already feeling excited about the evening ahead, I tap over from the map to the news page I've got pinned in my favourites. A habit. Just in case. I've been refreshing it every few hours since the police visited me at the hotel. I scroll through mindlessly for a few moments, my brain elsewhere, focused on how this evening might play out. The music, the atmosphere, the way she'll look at me when she finally realises she's meant to be with us.

I'm shocked into consciousness by a news headline buried right near the bottom of the page. Only a small block with just a few lines. Clearly not a big breaking news story. Not sensational enough to be on the main page. Insignificant to most. But not to me. It's there: three tiny lines of text accompanying an image of Julia, smiling broadly at whoever is behind the camera.

> *Twenty-seven-year-old Julia Porter has been reported missing by her family after she failed to return home after a night out. The police are searching for her and have encouraged anyone who knows anything about her movements on 16 July to come forward. At present, no persons of interest have been identified in her disappearance.*

My lip twitches. It's okay. We knew this would happen eventually. Her family were sure to notice she was gone at some point. The important thing is there is nothing tying her to us. I just need to focus on getting Miranda on side and this will all be over, like waking up from a particularly bad dream.

And just like that, I'm excited again for this evening.

## FORTY-THREE

The cocktail bar is perfect. Just the sort of environment you want for a conversation like this. Dim lighting, music loud enough to blur words, bodies moving in a steady rhythm. A place where decisions are made impulsively, where inhibitions slip away.

I find myself a booth right in the corner, where I won't be seen until I'm ready. Timing is everything. I force myself not to think about the news report. There's no point in getting all worked up about it. All that matters right now is seeing Miranda.

It's not long before she and Priya enter. Miranda snatches my breath away. She's not wearing anything crazy. Just a pair of skinny jeans and a flowing, strappy top and heels, but I've never seen her dressed up for a night out. She should do it more often. She will, once things are how they're meant to be.

I keep on worrying what Fraser will say when I tell him Miranda's agreed to join us. He's going to freak out initially, I know that much. He'll say it's too soon after Julia, that we're being reckless. But he worries too much. If he saw her tonight, looking the way she does, I'm sure his hesitance would dwindle. He wouldn't be able to resist the idea. No one could.

From my booth, I watch as Priya orders their drinks. Miranda is distracted, her eyes darting, checking her phone, not fully here. She opts for a gin and tonic. A shame. G&Ts are more a slow sipping drink. Cocktails are much more likely to get her loosened up faster. It would've made it easier. But that's what contingencies are for.

My fingers brush over my backup plan in my pocket. I brought it with me as a little insurance just in case she's not quite as loose as I need her to be. And that is a definite concern. Even here, amongst the music and the crowd, with Priya excitedly bouncing around beside her, she's still on edge. I can tell from the way she's sitting on the bar stool with her shoulders hunched, her body language closed off, guarded. She needs a good massage. Next time I take her to the club I'll treat her to the full-body experience.

By the time Priya has drunk three G&Ts and begun drunkenly flirting with the barman, Miranda is still finishing up her first. This is so frustrating. She's holding back, too busy checking her phone to get properly into the swing of things. After a moment, she stands and moves towards the front of the cocktail bar, pressing her phone to her ear. She's probably checking in on Mason. I glance back at the bar. Priya has ordered two large cocktails – good girl. She's also not paying the blindest bit of attention. Her back is turned to Miranda's drink while she leans across the bar, ensuring the guy behind it has a good view of her cleavage. Perfect. A willing distraction. She's done her part beautifully. This is my chance.

I glide over to the bar. Not too fast. Not too slow. Nothing that will attract attention. Priya may be well and truly captivated by the barman, but I don't want anyone else clocking what I'm doing. Once at the bar, I take a second to check my surroundings. One stray glance, one flicker of curiosity, that's all it takes to ruin everything. But no one is paying the slightest bit of attention to me. Everyone is too busy with their own drunken conversations to watch me.

That's the beauty of places like this. People get wrapped up in their own worlds. Their own little dramas. I check the CCTV cameras. They're angled at the middle of the bar and the main space with all the tables, not the end that I'm standing at. I'm in a blind spot. I lean against the bar, pretending to peruse the selection of bottles in the fridge, and pull the little plastic baggie from my sleeve. A practised movement. Quick. Effortless. The seal pops open. The powder that I prepared earlier slides, tips out of the bag, lands in Miranda's drink. I give it a quick stir with the straw. The Rohypnol disappears instantly.

I realise it's somewhat morally ambiguous. I'm a doctor, after all. Snatching a couple of pills from the pharmacy at the sleep clinic and crushing them into a powder for use as a roofie is frowned upon at best. But morality is flexible, isn't it? Besides, who better than a doctor to know exactly how much is just enough? I only needed a little bit. It's a powerful drug. The amount I have is just enough for her to become loose enough to be open to the idea of joining our marriage. Right now, she's about as tight as a clamp. As soon as the drugs have started to take effect, I'll pull her away from Priya, give her some made-up excuse for why I've been away, and then I'm just going to do it. I'm going to kiss her. Once we've crossed that barrier it'll be easy to convince her to join us. But there's no way she would even consider a kiss while she's all wound up. That's why I needed my backup plan.

'Hey.' A man appears beside me, his face lopsided in the way that often happens when someone has taken drugs. Pupils blown wide. Alert and sluggish at the same time. My stomach constricts. Did he see what I did? Is he about to alert the staff?

'Can I buy you a drink?' he says.

I exhale, relief washing through me. Just an idiot. A nuisance, nothing more. 'No, thank you.'

I move to head back to my booth, but he steps to one side, blocking me.

'Come on. A pretty little thing like you shouldn't be drinking alone.'

A pretty little thing like me? How pathetic.

'I'm not alone,' I'm quick to say, hoping that might be enough to realise he's wasting his time.

He doesn't move. He's too close now. Too eager. From here I can smell the stench of his breath. Beer mixed with weed. Cheap aftershave trying and failing to mask the sweat beneath it.

'You sure look like you're alone.'

Oh shit. This is all I need. A confrontation that's sure to cause a scene and attract the attention of everyone around me. I glance quickly back at the front door, peering through the glass. Miranda is still outside with the phone pressed to her ear, but I can't imagine she'll be out there for much longer. She cannot see me. Not yet. Not until the Rohypnol has kicked in a bit.

'My husband is in the bathroom,' I say, flashing my wedding ring in his face.

Before he can say anything else, I shove past him and make a beeline for the booth again. I slide in and duck my head low, praying that he won't follow me over here. After a minute or so I risk a glance in his direction. He seems to have given up, and is now focusing his efforts on a blonde girl who, from this angle, looks as if she may not be wearing any underwear.

But someone else has caught my attention now. Miranda is back. She sweeps over to the bar, still looking tense and on edge, and appears to chastise Priya for ordering cocktails. I watch. And wait.

Rohypnol doesn't take long to kick in. It's really a small amount, barely enough to matter, but it should start to smooth her sharp edges within a matter of minutes. That's all I want. Then I can swoop in, show her I'm fine, pull her away from Priya, who – let's face it – seems to be far more concerned with the barman than with Miranda, and start what is going to be something amazing.

They go to sit at one of the high tables, where Miranda drinks the entire cocktail, much faster than she did with the G&T. I track every movement, every shift in her expression. I start to worry that perhaps I didn't put enough in, that she's not going to feel the effects at all and I'm going to have to try to talk to her when she's all high-strung. But as she finishes the last sip, she sets her glass down and licks her lips, her gaze trailing lazily around the room. Yes, there it is. That's the beginning. I wait for that flicker of ease, that moment her shoulders might relax, that hint of warmth in her expression.

But something else happens instead.

Miranda's hand goes back to her drink, gripping it like an anchor. Her other hand jerks toward her chest as if trying to dig something out from behind her ribs. Something is wrong. She stands, grips the table. Her face is changing. Eyes wide. Lips slightly parted, like she can't quite pull in a full breath. Priya asks if she's okay but she doesn't respond. She just sways again, blinking rapidly.

'*No,*' I whisper.

And then she's on the floor. I'm on my feet before I realise I've moved. People are turning now, murmuring, a couple stepping forward to help.

'Call an ambulance!' Priya shouts.

I freeze, stomach folding in on itself. My fingers still tingle from where I held the packet. The stupid, crinkling plastic that had seemed harmless when I pulled it out of the dispensary. Just something to help her relax. That was all it was. I've given much higher doses to patients before and they've been absolutely fine. It's a one in a million chance that she would have a reaction like this.

She's barely conscious, staring with wide eyes at one of the men in the crowd. I wonder if she knows him. With the way she's looking at him, I'd say she was terrified of him. But before I can think any more about it her body convulses once, and then she goes terrifyingly still.

The barman is kneeling beside her now, checking her pulse. Someone else is on the phone to 999. The room is too loud. Deafening. The scrape of chairs, the shuffle of feet, the shrill sound of Priya sobbing. I can't hear my own thoughts over the roar of it all.

No, no, no. This wasn't how it was supposed to go.

There's a group of people leaving, clearly not concerned enough for Miranda's welfare to interrupt their night out. I take one more look at her lying on the floor, and move to tail the group that's leaving.

I follow them straight out the door and don't look back.

## FORTY-FOUR

I watched to make sure she got loaded into the ambulance and taken to the hospital. I needed to know she was still breathing, that I hadn't actually killed her. I'm not a complete monster. I care about her, after all.

But then I was stuck. I couldn't go home. If I did, Fraser would have figured out that it was me, that I'm the reason Miranda ended up in hospital last night. But I also couldn't go back to the hotel. If I left and she took a turn for the worse while I was two hours away, I'd never forgive myself. So, with nowhere else to go, I slept in my car a couple of streets down from the hospital. Tried to sleep, at least. I think I only got a few broken hours. I've a crick in my neck and my spine feels like it needs to go in a stretching machine.

Amongst the sleeplessness, I've been checking her social media every hour or so, waiting to see if there would be some kind of update. She's not got her accounts locked down like I have. She's careless. When I go to her Instagram I see a flood of smiling photos of her, Lee, and Mason. She really should adjust her privacy settings. You never know who is looking at your personal pictures.

The more I check to see if she's posted, the more of a rabbit hole I descend into. I scroll back for a little bit and there's a few shots of her on the beach, her curves on show in a white bikini. A little bit more, and there's a photo of her sipping lattes in a park in London, where, I remember, she told me she used to live. I can't quite picture her there.

The more I scroll, the more I seem to know her. The more I can't stop thinking about her even when I'm not looking at the phone. It's like she's seeped into me. Like she's taken up permanent residence in my mind. And the more the guilt gnaws at my stomach. A relentless, churning sickness. I can't believe I'm the reason she's ended up in hospital. My amazing, brilliant plan has gone so terribly wrong it's almost laughable. Is she awake yet? She's going to be so utterly terrified. As far as she's probably concerned someone was trying to hurt her, perhaps even date rape her. She won't know what my true intention was. She doesn't know that I would never, ever hurt her, that all I wanted was for her to loosen up enough to have a bit of fun. If she did, she'd understand.

I'm starting up the car engine before I even realise what I'm doing. I have to check on Miranda, to make sure she's okay. It wouldn't be weird, would it? Me visiting at the hospital. After all, we're friends. She would do the same for me, I'm sure of it. I drive pretty much on autopilot, rounding the few corners between me and Miranda. My car creeps towards the car park, then slows to a stop.

There are police cars outside.

My stomach drops. No, it's fine. I don't need to be concerned. That's quite normal, isn't it? Police parked up at hospitals? You always see them when you go to A&E.

But the stark reality settles on me as my foot remains pressed on the brake. They probably are here for Miranda. Of course they are. They'll want to talk to her. They'll want to find out what happened, if she saw anything, if she can remember anything at all about last night. I swallow hard, knock my car into reverse, and leave the hospital car park.

I drive around for a little bit, not really sure where to go. It seems so pointless to have come all the way here just to turn around and go straight back. Like I've wasted an entire day and a half just to scare myself to death and almost kill Miranda. Really, I need to be figuring out what my next move is going to be, but my mind is white noise.

I end up pulling into Herring Row, thinking maybe I can see Fraser and convince him to let me come home. But as I pull up outside our house, I can tell straight away that he's not home. The windows are all shut. He's perpetually too hot and will have every window in the house wide open at all times of the year, even in the dead of winter. Julia's Mini is gone too. Fraser must have dumped it.

I slump against the steering wheel, hands clammy. I'm contemplating what to do next when a movement catches my eye. I peer over at Miranda's house. Lee is at the front door. What is he doing? My eyes narrow as I lean to one side, trying to get a better view. When he takes a step to the side, I realise what he's got in his hand. The doorbell.

Their video doorbell.

Ice floods through my veins. Oh. My. God. They've got a video doorbell. Does that mean it was caught on camera that night when Fraser drove off with Julia's body in the suitcase? Did it record the whole thing? My heart hammers against my chest and my top suddenly feels too tight.

No, I need to calm down. Think logically. Don't spiral. This is not as big a deal as I might think. If they had seen anything, if they suspected anything at all, then surely, *surely* they would have gone to the police. And Sergeant Hargreaves didn't say a word to me about the suitcase when he came to see me. Only that Miranda had expressed concerns for my welfare. This is all fine. They probably never even checked the movement notifications. They must get loads of them, surely. The postman. People leaving for work. Birds. You're not going to sit there and watch every clip, are you? They'll have piled up, ignored. Too many to sift through. And besides, from the looks of things, he's just taken it down. It's probably not even working right.

By the time Lee straps Mason into his car seat, gets in his car, and drives off, I've convinced myself that I'm right, that there is nothing to be concerned about. I sit and I think. Think about Miranda. And Fraser. And what my next step might be. She's clearly looking for me. There must be a certain level of concern for my well-being there or she wouldn't have gone to the police. That, in itself, brings me a small sense of satisfaction.

I pick up my phone and start scrolling through her Instagram again, taking in every little morsel of her personality. I'm not sure how long I sit here. After a while my eyes drift back to their house and up to the top window. The master bedroom window. Miranda's bedroom. God, I wish I could go up there. There's a desire deep in my gut to lie on her bed, to breathe in her pillow, to stare up at the ceiling that she stares up at every night. What does she think about when she lies there? Does she dream about me? Probably not. Not yet.

My feet move of their own accord. I step slowly, cautiously towards the house, glancing around me as I do so to make sure there's no one about. It's just gone nine thirty. Most people will be at work. All is quiet. All is still.

When I reach her front door, I run my fingers over where the doorbell used to be. Its empty plastic holder remains. How funny to think that Miranda has been worrying about my whereabouts, and the day I come back to Herring Row her husband decides to take down the video doorbell. One of life's little ironies. Not unlike hoping I could loosen her up a tad and ending up causing her to fall unconscious.

I slide my fingers along the top of the door, feeling across the top ridge, but all I find is dust. I do the same with the outside light, with the same result. Perhaps they don't have a spare key. I'm not sure it's the norm anymore these days. Everyone's so bloody terrified they're going to get burgled. I bend down and try lifting a few of the rocks, deciding that if I can't find anything amongst these, I will take it as a sign and return to my car. Maybe I will go to the hospital after all, and brave the police. They probably wouldn't want to speak to me anyway. After all, I wasn't even at the cocktail bar last night.

Just as I'm about to give up, I see it. The glint of metal as I lift one of the rocks. They do have a spare key, after all. I pick it up and twist it around my fingers. Am I really going to do this? Though, in all honesty, I've done a lot worse lately. Murder. Lying to the police. Stealing drugs. Spiking someone's drink. What's a little added trespassing?

I move quickly, sliding the key into the door and hurrying inside so that there's no danger of being spotted. The house is dark. I look around, taking it all in. It feels bizarre to me that I've never been here. I feel like I know Miranda so well, and yet I've never stepped foot inside her home, even though it's a stone's throw from mine. She hadn't wanted me to come inside when I picked her up to take her to the spa at the club. I imagine she was worried I'd judge her for it being slightly messy in here. But I don't. It all adds to her charm. She's haphazard, a little scatterbrained. A perfect contrast to me. They say opposites attract.

I'm still standing in the hall after a couple of minutes, and have to shake myself. No point in just lingering here. There's no telling how long Lee is going to be gone for. I move over to the stairs and peer up. They look identical to my own. I have to blink away the image of Julia crashing down them, her head splitting open against the edges, her limbs twisting and breaking.

Not wanting to think about it anymore, I start to ascend the stairs, allowing my hand to slide up the banister as I move. Something is churning in my stomach. At first, I think it's nerves, nerves that I might get caught, or perhaps that I'm going to regret doing this. But as I reach the top of the stairs and push open the door to Miranda's bedroom, I realise it's not nerves at all.

It's excitement.

Her room is just the way I expected it to be. The bed is roughly made. Just a duvet and pillows. No throw cushions or runner at the foot of it. My hand brushes over the fabric as I move around to what is clearly her side, based on the selection of items on the bedside table. A steamy cowboy romance book. A candle. A half-empty glass of water. The smart watch that she owns but mostly seems to forget to wear.

I'm about to sit on her duvet when my eye drops to the drawer in the bedside table. It's ever so slightly open and there's the end of a bra strap hanging out of it. I pull it fully open and peer down into its depths. Her underwear selection will definitely need to be re-examined when she joins us. Perhaps that could be a nice day out for us. We can go underwear shopping together. I pick up a few items and toss them to one side. All designed for comfort, rather than aesthetic.

I stop, my fingers brushing over something rough at the very bottom of the drawer. I pinch it and pull it up so that it's on top of the rest. It's a piece of black lacy lingerie. The bodice has deep red boning running down it, to where it meets with suspender straps. My breath catches. This is more like it. An unexpected side to her, tucked away like a secret. I can just picture her in it. Soft skin against delicate lace. Her fingers trailing over the same fabric I'm holding now. I wonder if she's worn it recently. Probably not, since it was buried at the bottom of the drawer. Maybe not even since she had her son. There is so much she has to rediscover about herself.

Giving in to my fantasies, I lie back on the bed, my head on her pillow, holding the lingerie to my chest, stroking the fabric. I shut my eyes for a few moments as I think about Miranda and what the future holds for us.

A sound outside wakes me, makes me drop the lingerie. The front door. Lee is home. I rush to the bedroom door and peek around the edge. He's there, at the bottom of the stairs, and he's not alone. Miranda and Mason are with him.

I look at my watch. How could I have slept for so many hours?

'I'm going to sort Mase his bath,' Miranda is saying.

'You don't have to do that,' Lee replies. 'You sit down. I can do it.'

'I want to, Lee. It's fine, really. I'm not going to break.'

They take a step towards the stairs, and I duck back into the bedroom. My eyes scan the room wildly. There's no way I'm getting out of here without them seeing me, not until they've put Mason to bed and gone to chill out downstairs. Even then I'm not sure how I'm going to manage slipping past without catching their attention.

There's only one place I can go that doesn't involve leaving the bedroom and stepping into full view. The en suite. I make a beeline for it. There's no time to shut the door because Lee comes into the bedroom, so I have no choice but to hide behind it, burying myself in the towels hanging on the back of it. The scent of fabric softener tickles my nose. I pinch it at the bridge, willing myself not to sneeze. Screwing my face up, I hold my breath and force myself to remain deadly still. Thankfully, he's not in the bedroom for long, but even when he leaves, I don't move. They're still upstairs. I can hear them in the bathroom, then in Mason's bedroom, then in the hallway. I stay behind the door, praying that once they've put Mason to bed they'll go downstairs, and I can figure out how to get out of here.

But they don't go downstairs. There's a rustling sound, and then they're both in the bedroom. It only takes me a couple of seconds to realise what's happening. I can hear it in the soft murmur of their voices, the intimacy of it. My eyes widen. They're going to have sex. They're going to do it with me stuck in here. Heat crawls up my neck. This is not good. What do all men do after sex? Go to the bathroom. Or, more likely, the en suite. Right where I am.

The bed creaks as they fall onto it. I don't know what to do, but there's not really anything I can do. I can't leave. I'm just going to have to wait here and hope that they fall asleep straight afterwards. I squeeze my eyes shut, as if that will somehow make me invisible, focusing on not making a sound.

Miranda's breathing grows heavy. The sound makes all sorts of images flash into my mind. I chew on my lip, telling myself not to, that it's beyond stupid. But the curiosity is more than I can bear. I tilt my head and peek around the edge of the en-suite door, taking in the sight of her body.

But I don't get to enjoy it for long. She sits up suddenly.

'Have you been in my drawer?' she says.

*Dammit.* I dropped the lingerie when they came home and forgot to put it back in my panic. I move back into the towels so that I'm once again fully hidden, and listen. And the more I listen, the more revealing their conversation becomes. I press a hand to my mouth, muffling my breathing as I take it all in. As I stand here and absorb what's been going on while I've been away, how Miranda has got totally the wrong end of the stick and thinks Fraser is behind all of this, a proper plan finally starts to piece itself together in my head.

And this time, my plan does not involve Miranda joining our open marriage. It never ends well when we do that, anyway.

With this plan, I get her all to myself.

# PART THREE

# FORTY-FIVE
## MIRANDA

I've gone back in time. I must have done.

It's exactly the same as waking up in hospital after I got roofied. That drilling in my skull. That urge to keel over and be sick but too little energy to actually do it. Except... it's not the hospital. There's no antiseptic smell. The air feels familiar, yet off.

I try to open my eyes. My eyelids feel like magnets, forcing themselves back together. It takes every ounce of effort to pry them apart, and when I do, the room comes to me in a swirling mess. A white ceiling spinning about my head.

It's too much.

I squeeze them shut again and press my fingers and thumb into my eye sockets, hard enough to make stars dance in my vision. Anything to stop the spinning. After a moment I give opening my eyes another shot. This time, the world is a little steadier. I blink. Then blink again.

I'm in my bedroom. Tucked up under my duvet.

The realisation does nothing to calm me. A deep, unsettling dread sits in my stomach. What happened? Did Lee put me here? Where is he?

I tilt my head to the side. My vision swims, trying to adjust. There's a glass of water on the side table, condensation trailing down its surface. A piece of paper is propped up against it, a single word scrawled on it in delicate letters.

*Drink.*

A chill runs down my spine. That's not Lee's handwriting. I know that for sure.

My throat is raw, aching. My thirst overpowers my desire to figure out what the hell is going on, and I snatch up the glass, gulping down huge mouthfuls of water. It's cold, almost painful as it slides down my throat, but I don't care. I drink until the glass is empty, my breath ragged. Another wave of wooziness hits me, fog creeping over my mind, and then...

A flash of memory. A jolt of electricity through my veins.

*Anna.*

Anna is alive.

The thought crashes over me, knocking the breath from my lungs. She's alive. She came to my door. I saw her on the video doorbell, let her in, warned Fraser to stay away from her, but he had said something that didn't make sense. My hand tightens on the empty glass.

He had said she was a murderer.

I sit up too fast. The motion sends pain exploding behind my eyes, a sharp, blinding stab that nearly knocks me back down. I remember it all now. Every horrifying second. How the last thing I saw was her face as she injected me with something. Drugs? Rohypnol? Is she the one who roofied me in the club? She's a sleep doctor. She probably has access to that kind of thing.

My stomach lurches and before I know it, I'm clasping my hand around my mouth. Acid burns in my throat. I clamber out of bed, forgetting that my limbs are barely working. My legs give way the second they hit the floor. I collapse, my hands slamming against the wall, my stomach clenching in violent protest. I half stumble, half drag myself to the en suite, barely making it in time. My knees hit the tiled floor as I lean my head over the toilet bowl and retch. Tears sting my eyes. I clutch the sides of the toilet, my body wracked with shudders, the sickness coming in relentless waves.

When I've got nothing left to expel from my body I collapse to one side, eyes closed, my entire being feeling utterly wrecked. I lean my head back against the porcelain. Its coolness is soothing against my pounding head. I take a few deep, slow breaths, counting each inhalation and exhalation, waiting for the sickness to pass.

It eases slightly after a few seconds. My pulse slows. The dizziness recedes just enough for me to think.

I open my eyes again.

And then I scream.

## FORTY-SIX

It's Fraser.

He's lying in the bath, his head propped up against the wall, face tilted towards me. His arm closest to me rests on the side of the tub. And there is so much blood.

There's more blood than I've ever seen in my life. It's coated his wrist and his hand. It's gushed down the side of the bath and formed a deep puddle on the floor. It's smeared across the wall and over his face and his arms. The smell of it clogs my throat. It's everywhere.

I scramble back, my back smashing against the radiator. I don't know what to do. Every instinct is telling me to run, get as far away from this room and that bath as I possibly can, but my limbs are still sluggish, still wrecked from the drugs. I crawl on my hands and knees, dragging myself towards the door to the bedroom.

Legs appear in front of me, blocking my route. Bare feet. Toes curled slightly against the bathroom floor. I arch my neck, squinting up. The ceiling lights are too bright, plunging the person standing in my way into a silhouette.

'It's okay, Miranda.'

Anna. That's Anna's voice. I fall backwards, retreating into the en suite. She steps towards me, coming out of the harsh light so that I can see her face properly.

She's smiling.

'It's okay,' she says again, then crouches down in front of me. I try to increase the distance between us, pressing myself against the cupboard under the sink, but there's nowhere to go. This is a small room. I'm trapped.

Her hand reaches out and lands on my knee. I push away more, the sharp edges of the cabinet digging into my spine. Her thumb strokes my skin. It's then that I realise I'm in my pyjamas, the silky shirt and shorts set that Lee got me for my birthday. Every hair on my arms and legs stands on end. Who got me changed while I was unconscious? Anna?

'W-what's going on?' The mere act of speaking causes tears to burst from my eyes.

'I know this is probably a huge shock,' she says, not taking her hand off me. 'But you don't need to worry. He can't hurt you now.'

My eyes flick to Fraser. It's almost like he's staring straight at me. If it wasn't for all the blood I'd expect him to blink at any second.

'What do you mean?' I gasp.

'He was going to kill you, Miranda.' My gaze returns to Anna. Her face is sincere, eyebrows pulled up in concern. 'You knew too much. He killed our friend Julia. That's what you saw that night. He was getting rid of her body in that suitcase.'

My head spins. I think back to the doorbell footage. I had been so sure it was Anna in that suitcase, and everyone made me think I was crazy. But I was at least partly right. It may not have been Anna but there was a body in there. I wasn't just paranoid.

'Oh darling.' She comes to sit next to me and wraps her arm around my shoulders. I shrink under the weight of it. 'If I'd known you were so close to figuring it all out, I'd have come back much sooner.'

The fabric of her blouse is cool against my clammy skin, and her perfume curls in the air between us, syrupy and overpowering. I gag, my stomach twisting with such force I instinctively clutch my middle. I'm sure I'm about to be sick again.

'I had no idea you were in so much danger,' Anna continues. 'But it's okay. I've fixed everything. I'm here now. I got him before he got to you. You're safe now.'

*Safe*.

The word echoes strangely, warping in my head like sound underwater.

'You killed him,' I say, stating the obvious, though my voice is barely there. It cracks under the strain of everything I'm holding in.

She doesn't even blink. She doesn't seem to realise that she's done a bad thing. That's what's really scary. The calm. And she hasn't just killed him. It wasn't an act of passion or self-defence. That's when you stab someone in the middle of an argument or hit them too hard with something. A quick, thoughtless second. An act that you don't even realise you've done until it's already too late. That's not what happened here. She somehow got her own husband in the bath and slit his wrists. That would have taken time. It was calculated. Slow. At this thought, my body goes rigid, breath catching like a hiccup in my throat. How did she even manage to overpower him? Fraser was strong. Taller than her. She must have drugged him too.

'I made sure the syringe has his fingerprints on it, not mine,' she says, as if reading my mind. Her hand gently pats mine where it's trembling in my lap. I can't pull away. 'And the syringe is in the bath with him. The police will think he used it on himself before slitting his wrists to dull the pain. I told you, Miranda. It's okay. They'll never know it was us.'

My breath stutters. *Us?* What do I have to do with any of

this? Her tone is so calm, almost reassuring. It's like she's not at all concerned about any of this. Like the fact she killed her husband means absolutely nothing to her. Worst of all, it seems premeditated. Listening to her now, I'm struggling to believe that any of this was a crime of passion in a last-minute attempt to save me. It all sounds too methodical. Too well thought out.

'I made it look like a suicide,' she continues, 'caused by grief over what he did to Julia. We're free. We can finally be together.'

Something twists inside me at that. A deep, icy dread settles in my gut, heavier than before. Be together? What the hell is that supposed to mean? A shudder works its way through my entire body. I think back to mine and Anna's relationship since she came to Herring Row. Going to dinner, doing her hair, visiting the club. The way she would smile at me. The lingering looks. I never questioned it at the time. Assumed she was just overly friendly and had taken to me more than any of the other women on Herring Row.

Then everything I thought Fraser had done over the past few days. That sense of being watched outside the school. Being roofied at the cocktail bar. And what about Esme? She was involved in some kind of weird threesome with Anna and Fraser. I saw the photographic proof in that album. The pictures flash through my mind, lurid and undeniable. Was Julia the other woman in the photos?

Esme had looked terrified when I mentioned Fraser's name. She warned me to stay away if I knew what was good for me. But perhaps it wasn't because she was scared of Fraser. Maybe she was scared of Anna.

Was all of this down to Anna all along? Did I really get Fraser that wrong?

I try to steady my breathing, but my chest is tight, my ribs aching with each inhale. I tense my body and attempt to slide out from under Anna's arm. She jolts, stares at me, eyes wild.

'What are you doing?' she says.

'I... I...' My tongue feels thick, useless. My throat is closing up, making it difficult to speak, difficult to breathe.

'I've done this for us. You get that, right?'

'I don't...'

My brain isn't working. Nothing is working. My vision tunnels, black creeping in at the edges. It's like the walls around me are closing in, locking me into a tight, claustrophobic box. I let out a small whimper.

Anna's expression turns grave, and she lets out a heavy sigh. 'Oh,' she says. 'I see.'

She removes her arm from my shoulders, giving me a tiny moment of relief from the pressure, and hauls herself up from the floor. She takes a few steps towards the door and for a moment I think she's going to leave, but she stops in the doorway, one hand on each side. Her shoulders rise and fall. She stays like that for a few seconds. When she turns her head to face me, there are tears lacing her eyes.

'You have to decide to be with me.' Her voice is trembling, cracking, like she's about to break down. 'If you don't, all of this was for nothing.'

My head shakes of its own accord, moving side to side slowly.

Something shifts in Anna, something cold and final settling into her features. Her eyes darken. 'Well then, in that case, you'll have to die too.'

## FORTY-SEVEN

The change in Anna is sudden. She lurches forward, making a swipe at Fraser's body. There's a splash. A flash of silver catches the light.

She's got the knife.

She points it at me, her whole body vibrating, her breath ragged. She shakes the knife wildly as she shouts. 'You're an ungrateful bitch! I did all of this for you! How can you not see that? How can you turn me away after everything I've done for you?'

A scream gathers in my throat, but it catches, refusing to escape my mouth. My body locks, muscles tightening, limbs rigid. My stomach turns to cement.

*No. Not now...*

'Are you not even going to say anything?' Anna cries, tears pouring down her face. 'Do I not even deserve an explanation?'

I clench my jaw, trying with all my might to move it, to speak. What Anna doesn't understand is that I'm not refusing to say anything on purpose. I physically can't. Suddenly I'm right there again. Listening to a slow creak of a door. Footsteps. Someone breaking into our flat while I'm stuck. Frozen. Unable to help or do anything or even wake Lee up to alert him. Unable to protect Mason. Trapped in my own body while fear roots me in place.

Except I'm not listening to a burglar. I'm trapped by Anna. Mason isn't here. He's safe with his dad. But they're on their way home. Or, at least, they should be. I asked Lee to hurry.

'Say something,' Anna says, her voice lower now. Coaxing. 'Tell me you understand. Tell me you're sorry.'

My lips part but no sound comes out. I can't even think properly past the dull roar in my ears. Anna's jaw tightens.

'Don't ignore me,' she says.

Nothing.

Her grip on the knife shifts. The blade glints as her knuckles flex. She exhales, taking a step closer. I want to squeeze my eyes shut, to block out the view, to prepare myself for the inevitable pain of the knife slicing through my skin. But I can't even do that. All I can do is stare at her.

She leans forward so that her nose is nearly touching mine. A knowing smile tugs at her lips.

'Oh,' she breathes, almost amused. 'You can't.'

I realise with a sinking dread that she knows exactly what's wrong with me. I told her. During our spa day. I basically revealed to her my biggest weakness. She reaches out, the tip of the blade tracing lightly over my forearm. Not pressing. Just enough to make my skin prickle. Anyone else would jerk away, but me? I can't even flinch.

'I've seen this at the clinic before. I could do anything to you right now, couldn't I?' She watches me, studying me, her free hand brushing over my shoulder. 'And you'd just... let me.'

My mind screams at me to move, to push past her, to fight, but my body doesn't listen. Anna's hand slides down to meet mine. *Think, Miranda, think. What would Lee say to you right now?* He'd tell me it's not real, that my body freezing is in my mind. And if it's in my mind that means I can control it.

'That's good to know.' Her fingers lace with mine. 'That's very good to know.'

My eye twitches. A tiny, almost imperceptible movement. *Focus on your surroundings. Latch onto reality. On something beyond her and this moment.*

Four drops of blood dripping from Fraser's wrist.

Three smears of red on the tiles.

Two cold dead eyes watching me from the bath.

One knife.

'Stop.' It's just a single word. But it comes from my mouth. It's more than I've ever been able to do on my own without someone with me to coax me out of it. It's enough to tell me I can break myself out of this.

Suddenly, a piercing alarm rips through the house. For a moment I think it's in my head, another trick of my panicked mind, but Anna jumps and swerves, twisting around to look in the direction the sound is coming from.

It's the fire alarm.

Anna gives me one last look before disappearing out of the bedroom, taking the knife with her. The world snaps into focus. How? How could there possibly be a fire when we're up here? But I only have to think about it for a few seconds before the realisation hits. The lint tray in the tumble dryer. I was about to empty it but got distracted. I've had a go at Lee so many times for not emptying it, ranting at him about how not doing so is the leading cause of house fires.

I have to make myself move.

My fingers twitch. Then my toes. A slow, stuttering return. Lee and Mason will be home soon. If there really is a fire, they can't come into this. Not to mention if they walk through that door there's no telling what Anna will do. I cannot, will not, allow them to be hurt. I gasp, my nerves flooding back to me all at once. I throw myself forward, landing on all fours and heaving deep, frantic breaths, just as Anna returns.

'Something's caught fire down...' Her words trail off when she sees me. Realisation flashes across Anna's face. I can move and she knows it. My eye drops to her hand, which twitches by her side. She's no longer holding the knife. She must have left it downstairs.

My body moves before my mind can catch up. I take my chance and lunge forward, all muscle, all instinct, smashing Anna into the doorframe with every ounce of strength I have. She crumples. I scramble onto my feet and go to make a run for it. Anna's hand curls around my ankle, vice-like, and I'm flying, hurtling down to the bedroom floor. The impact rattles through me, knocking the breath from my lungs.

I look back at Anna. She's clawing at my leg, her nails digging in, her grip relentless. I try to wriggle free from her grasp, but my limbs are still weak, whether it be from the drugs or the way my body shut down, I'm not sure. I just know I have to do something.

'What are you doing? There's a fire!' I shout. 'We've got to get out of here!'

'No!' Anna shakes her head wildly. Tears spray to the side, landing on the carpet. 'If I let you go, you'll go to the police.'

'I won't. I promise.' I wrack my brains for what I can say to her to make her let go of me, but how do you know what to say to someone who has fully lost her grip like this? I picture Lee and Mason coming home to the house burned to a crisp, the firemen pulling out my cremated, unrecognisable body from the rubble. This can't be how I die.

'Anna, I'm sorry,' I say, reaching a hand back to her. 'You're right. I didn't appreciate what you did for me. But I do now. We could be together. If you just give me time to come to terms with everything we could...'

'Shut up. Shut up! *Shut up!*' The sound that comes from her is half a scream, half a growl. My attempt to pacify her isn't going to work. My eyes travel up to the top of my bedroom door.

Smoke is flooding in through the crack. This is bad. We're running out of time.

I glance back at Anna one more time, muster every ounce of strength I have, and kick. My foot impacts with her face and her head snaps back. She lets out a cry, simultaneously letting go of my leg. I scramble up, unsteady, but she follows me and goes wild. My stomach caves under her fist. My scalp burns as she wrenches my hair and scratches my face. It's like she's suddenly grown five extra hands. I don't know where to protect first. Instead, I just push her as hard as I can. I just need to get her away from me. She stumbles back. There's a crash as she falls into the dresser, then a sickening crack as her head catches the edge of it. Her legs buckle and she collapses.

Her body goes limp. Her eyes close.

She's still.

## FORTY-EIGHT

The room suddenly seems bizarrely calm. Even though the smoke still rolls into the room, growing every second, the lack of Anna's screams makes my ears ring. I hesitate for only a second. I sweep to the bedroom door and tap the doorknob with the back of my hand. It's cool to the touch. No fire on the other side.

Sucking in a deep breath, I pull the door open. Thick smoke billows into the room. It clings to the ceiling, blackening everything it touches. I duck down, shielding my eyes and mouth with my arms. There's definitely no fire on the other side of the door, but downstairs is another story. I take a few tentative steps down the stairs, just enough so that I can peek around the bottom of the stairwell and see how bad it is. My heart jackhammers against my ribs.

The entire kitchen is ablaze. Flames creep over the cabinets, the table, the chairs, even the ceiling. The heat from the flames is too hot to bear. I squint, back away slightly, watching as it licks its way across the top of the door and into the hallway. The wallpaper that Lee and I chose so carefully when we first moved into this house peels and chars. The smoke catches in my throat. I cough and splutter, eyeing up my escape route. But something is stopping me from running to the door. Something is tugging at me, pulling me back.

I twist on the bottom stair and look up to the hall. My bedroom door is still wide open.

Is Anna still breathing?

Do I care?

I should. I should care.

But I don't.

Or do I?

My body sways forward, then back. Trapped between instinct and hesitation. No, I do care. Inside that room is a woman. A live woman, knocked out and unconscious. Helpless. Whatever she's done, however disturbed she is, can I really leave her up there to burn to death?

I've never felt so torn in my life, but I don't have time to stand around deciding. Crouching low and covering my airways with my pyjama sleeve, I scramble back up the stairs. I think I must be insane as I return to the bedroom, but I've done it now. No turning back. Anna is still lying exactly where I left her. I collapse to my knees beside her.

'Anna! Wake up!' I take hold of her shoulders and shake her, praying that she'll come to. I don't think I'll be able to carry her. She's not exactly heavy but I have the upper body strength of cooked spaghetti. The heat is creeping up the stairs. Smoke curls around me. The fire must be catching, spreading. My throat burns, desperate for oxygen. Gritting my teeth, I run to the en suite. With the fire I had totally forgotten about Fraser, so seeing his bloody body once more makes me recoil. I gag, turning my head away from him. I can't look at him right now. I need to keep going.

I move to the sink, cupping my hands and collecting as much water as they can carry. It drips through the cracks in my fingers as I make my way back to Anna, but there's enough that when I flick my fingers at her several large droplets splash down onto her face. She flinches.

'Anna, can you hear me?'

Her face scrunches up and her hand moves to her head. When she pulls it back, there's blood on her fingertips. 'What's going on?'

'We have to move. Now. Can you get up?'

I slide my hand under her upper body and heave with all my might. Even with her lucid, it's an effort to pull her up to a sit, let alone stand. My lungs feel like they're lined with razor blades.

'Anna, I need you to try to put weight on your legs. Can you do that for me?'

She groans as we haul ourselves up. We stagger in sync, moving as one disjointed unit, her with her arm thrown over my shoulders, me trying desperately not to buckle under her weight.

In the time it took me to get Anna, everything has gotten terrifyingly worse. The smoke is thicker, the heat as we descend the stairs is stronger, and when we reach the bottom, I realise the fire has spread through into the hallway, creating a tunnel of flames for us to walk through, and has started to creep into the living room.

I squeeze my eyes shut, refusing to allow myself to think about Mason's drawings from school that I've hung up proudly on the wall, or his bunny on the sofa that he needs in order to go to sleep at night, or the box of keepsakes I have tucked away in the bookcase with cards Lee and I have written to each other over the years and mementos of our memories together. None of that will matter if I'm dead.

A crack splits the air. A groan from above. Something shifts in the ceiling, and I know what it means. The house is losing its fight. I narrow my eyes, setting my sights on the front door directly ahead, at the end of the tunnel of flames.

But then a burning pain like nothing I've ever felt before shoots through my chest plate. At first, I think I've caught fire. I let go of Anna and fall back, landing awkwardly on the bottom stairs. A howl escapes me.

My eyes flick to Anna; my hand reaches out to her. She'll help me. She'll help me just like I helped her. But she's not moving to rush to my side. She's standing, looking down at me, expression blank. I follow her gaze.

And that's when I see the knife sticking out of my chest.

Oh God... she's stabbed me with the knife.

I knew she'd left it down here, but I didn't know where. But she knew.

I'm in disbelief, though I'm not sure why. Just ten minutes ago Anna had been threatening me with it. But I had tried to help her. I had wanted to help her.

'Anna,' I gasp, a fresh wave of agony hitting me as I try to talk. 'The fire...'

But there's no talking her down now. She takes a run at me, hand outstretched for the knife. I throw myself to one side, just barely avoiding her. The force of the movement sends a shockwave radiating through my torso. I look down, terrified that I've made things worse by moving. The knife hasn't hit anything important, I don't think. It's too far to the left. More my shoulder than my chest. My hand grips around the knife handle and I pull. A raw, guttural scream escapes me. I've never known anything like it. The sheer intensity of the pain mixed with the unrelenting heat of the flames makes my vision blur and my head spin.

Blood soaks my top. I shouldn't have removed it. Too late now. I clamber to my feet, turning just in time to see Anna fly at me again. My arm shoots up instinctively, blocking her from grabbing the knife. She claws at my arm and it's all I can do to try to force her back. My breath rasps in my throat. The world slows around me. I look between Anna and the fire, between the fire and Anna. Both hell-bent on killing me.

Sirens sound. Far off. In the distance. Barely audible over the roar of the fire. Perhaps it's only in my head, a yearning for someone to come and save me. But it's enough to give me the one thing I need.

Hope.

Grimacing, I push and kick back against Anna's attack. Her eyes widen and her balance wavers, arms pinwheeling, desperate to catch herself. She stumbles back. Her feet seem to move in slow motion as she tumbles. Another step, and another, and another, until she's smashing into the blazing cabinet behind her. A shriek rips from her throat. There's the sound of wood splintering, already weakened from the fire. The top of the cabinet is glowing orange from the heat. It shifts, tilts.

Anna's eyes meet mine for only a second before the burning wood comes crashing down on top of her.

## FORTY-NINE

'Miss? Is there anyone still inside?'

When I don't respond to the fireman he gives up, moving instead to direct his crew. They rush about, pulling equipment from the fire engine, hurrying to the house.

'Okay, Pete, we'll need some medical attention over there,' he says, gesturing at me and my bloodied shoulder. 'Dan, Oscar, go with Alex. No confirmation on whether there's anyone else inside. Check. But be quick about it.'

The three of them nod and go to enter the building. One of them is young. Not long out of school, by the looks of it. Risking his life. I think about his poor mother. How terrified she must be every time he goes to work.

'There's a woman!' I shout. They spin to face me. 'In the hallway. A cabinet fell on her.'

There's a murmur around me, and I realise I'm surrounded by the other residents of Herring Row, probably now all trying to work out who is missing, and who could be the woman trapped in the burning building. I can't focus on them right now though.

The fireman at the front motions at the others to stay close and they disappear into the smoke and the flames, followed closely by two men with hoses, who try to clear the way for them as much as possible. Another crew attack the house with a giant stream of water. The difference it makes is minimal. The fire is relentless, devouring everything in its path.

A kind-faced paramedic appears in front of me, blocking my view of the house.

'Ma'am, can you come and sit over here so that I can take a look at your shoulder?' She leads me over to an ambulance, its back doors wide open. I hadn't even noticed it arrive. She sits me on the edge and places a mask over my mouth. I breathe deeply, my lungs still craving oxygen. My ribs ache with the effort. The paramedic gently pulls the fabric away from my wound and I hiss through my teeth. When the air hits the raw flesh, I have to fight the urge to jerk away.

'How did you get this wound?' the paramedic asks.

I consider lying. Saying that I fell in the commotion on a piece of broken mirror or something. I'm not sure why. Tripping and injuring myself just seems like something I'll be asked to relive less. If I tell them what really happened there will be a whole investigation, police interviews, statements. What good will it do now? Fraser is dead. Anna is probably dead.

God. Fraser. Yet again, the chaos had caused me to forget about him, and the sudden memory of his bloodied body is a jolt to the system. They're going to find him, for sure, and when they do, there will be an investigation regardless. I can't stop it. I can only brace myself for what comes next.

I turn to the paramedic.

'My neighbour Anna Coles killed her husband, Fraser, and tried to kill me. His body is upstairs in my en-suite bathroom. This is a stab wound from one of my kitchen knives. You'll probably also find Rohypnol or a similar drug in my bloodstream.'

Of course, there are more details. I'll have to tell everyone about Julia's body, hidden away in that suitcase that Fraser dumped. I'll have to explain how Anna had wanted me to join their weird open marriage and that she killed Fraser because he was going to tell me what a psycho she was. I'll have to detail what happened in that en suite and downstairs in the hallway, every terrifying, nightmarish second. But for now, the paramedic knows what she needs to know. I wasn't exactly right about what was going on in our street, but I was close enough. There was someone dangerous living here. There was something I needed to protect my family from.

My attention is pulled away from thinking about what happened inside that house by a shout from the commanding officer still standing out on the street, by the fire engine.

'The roof is unstable. You need to get out now,' he says into his radio, his voice laced with urgency. The crackle of static follows, then a muffled response I can't quite make out.

I stare at the house, at our family home, picturing the roof coming crashing down, just as the cabinet did. Folding in on itself like a house of cards.

'I need a status update, people!' the commanding officer shouts. 'Could she have moved? Have you checked every room?'

My breath lodges in my throat. They can't find Anna.

I strain my ears, desperately trying to listen to the other side of the conversation, the replies coming through the radio, but it's too far away.

'No, no, it's too unstable,' the commanding officer says. 'No more entries.'

He turns to face me, his expression grave, and strides over. His boots crunch against the pavement. The paramedic steps to one side but continues to clean my wound.

'Miss, I have to ask, was she definitely inside the house?'

I nod. The motion feels stiff and robotic. 'She gave me this.'

The officer looks down at the gash in my flesh. His lips press into a thin line. He then turns, heading back to the fire engine.

'You've got thirty seconds and then you'll need to fall back,' he calls through his radio.

Thirty seconds.

Anna has thirty seconds left to be found, if she's even still alive after the cabinet fell on her. Thirty seconds before the firemen will give up and leave her to the mercy of the flames. Thirty seconds before certain death.

I count them in my head, eyes fixed on the front door. Every now and again I think I see them, but each time it ends up being a piece of the house falling or the hoses being angled at a different part of the fire.

Ten seconds.

Every single person here, apart from the paramedic, is staring at the same thing, waiting for the same thing. It's like the entire street has collectively held their breath.

Twenty seconds.

Blood fills my mouth and I realise I've been chewing down on my lips too hard. I swallow hard.

There's a sudden commotion as the three firemen who had gone in after Anna stumble out of the house, their faces streaked with sweat and soot.

Anna isn't with them.

My house burned faster than I thought it would.

And, from the looks of things, it burned fast enough.

# FIFTY

One Year Later

'Watch your step,' Lee says, promptly tripping over the step that he was warning me about.

I chuckle behind the box in my arms. Somehow, I ended up with the books, quite possibly the heaviest box we've packed. I heave it into the house, avoiding the step, and let it down on the carpet with a thud. I lean on it for a few seconds, huffing and puffing.

'You okay?' Lee says, putting his own box down and coming to my side. He wraps his arm around my shoulders and squeezes.

'Yeah, just nearly popped my elbows out of their sockets, that's all.'

I grin at him, and he grins back. The truth is, I am okay. The investigation after our house burned down was intense. There was a lot of questioning, a lot of interviews, a lot of repeating my story over and over. But there was no trial, that's the main thing. Anna was pronounced dead at the scene. Fraser's body was recovered when they eventually got to search through the wreckage and debris, but all they found of Anna was her necklace. The fire was too out of control, the house beyond help.

To be honest, I wish they had found her body. I needed that closure. It took a long time for me to accept that it all really was over, that I didn't need to be afraid anymore. I went back to therapy and this time I actually did what they said. Attended all the sessions. Took the pills. Unlike before, when I could deny that there was anything wrong with me, this time I knew I needed the help. The nightmares alone were enough to tell me I had PTSD.

But now it's a year later and we're moving into our new house, our fresh start, and I'm feeling okay. I'm not back to normal. I'm not sure if I'll ever be fully back to normal. But the nightmares are less frequent now, and I'm looking to the future with a sense of positivity, which, for a long time, I thought would never happen.

Abandoning the box of books, I move into what will soon be our living room. Now there's just a sofa in here. It's not our sofa. That went up in flames along with everything else. This sofa was donated to us via the drive that Priya organised after the disaster. Priya and I never even had to officially make up from our falling-out. We barely spoke about it. She was just so pleased we were all okay, and I was so pleased to have my best friend back. Both she and Lee apologised to me endlessly for everything, and now it's kind of like a nightmare we've all woken up from. Still there, but distant.

It was enough to bring tears even to Lee's eyes when we saw how many people had turned up to Priya's drive to offer us furniture, toys, books, food, everything we would need to start over again. Now, when I close my eyes, I can picture it. Mason drawing at the coffee table. Toys strewn about the place. Movie nights with popcorn, cuddling up under a giant family-sized blanket. This is where our life is going to restart. I collapse into the sofa cushions and arch my back, allowing it to pop and click.

Lee comes to sit beside me. He nudges me with his elbow and nods towards the still open front door. From where we're sitting, we can see the house opposite ours. The family who live there, parents of a whopping five kids, are returning home.

'So, are you going to go and introduce yourself to the new neighbours?' Lee says, smirking.

I roll my eyes at him. He already knows the answer.

'Bit soon for jokes, Lee.'

'Sorry.' He puts his arm around me, and I lean my head on his shoulder. I don't really mind the humour, but it does still feel a little bit raw. Every night when I get undressed, I stand in front of the mirror and look at myself, at the thick scar that serves as a reminder of what happened.

I got an apology from Sergeant Hargreaves, too. That was unexpected, to say the least. He came to visit me in hospital a couple of days after everything went down.

'We've recovered Julia's body,' he said, sitting in the chair beside my bed with his hands clasped in front of him. 'It was in the suitcase, as you said. And we spoke to the receptionist at Orbital Solutions Group, Esme. Her testimony confirmed that she went through a similar situation with Fraser and Anna. She had been paid hush money to keep quiet about it.'

I nodded, absorbing the information. None of it was new or surprising, but it was different coming out of Sergeant Hargreaves' mouth. It was a sort of validation that I craved more deeply than I had realised.

'I wanted to apologise,' he said, his face pinching slightly, as if it pained him to say the words. 'For not taking your concerns more seriously. For not following up on the suitcase theory properly.'

I shook my head, surprising myself. 'You found Anna alive and well. No wonder you thought I was crazy. I even started to think I was.'

Because the truth is, I don't blame Sergeant Hargreaves

anymore. Once I realised what must have happened, that they did indeed visit Anna and determined that my report that something had happened to her was false, I understood. All I had, really, was footage of a man putting a suitcase in his car and driving off. If I were Sergeant Hargreaves, I'd have dismissed it, too.

'Are you thinking about it again?' Lee says now, pulling me back to the present.

I nod slowly. 'I'm never not thinking about it.'

I look up at him, at his sad, concerned face, and smile. I've made it a habit to be honest with him at all times, now. Any concerns I have, any niggling worries, are shared with him straight away. And he's got better at listening. All doubts I had about Lee were quashed with the showdown I had with Anna at our old house, but here, looking at him now, I can't believe I ever suspected he may have had something to do with it.

'But it's okay. It doesn't bother me as much anymore,' I say, nuzzling back into him. 'It just sort of... sits there. You know?'

We sit together for a moment in contented silence, reflecting on everything we've been through. Eventually, one day, maybe I won't be thinking about it all the time. Maybe, as we turn this house into a home and build our lives here, moving into this new chapter, it will fade into one of those distant memories that seems more like another life.

'I'll tell you what.' Lee hauls himself up and moves to one of the boxes, pulling at the brown tape. The noise of it rips through the house. He digs his hand into the box and rummages around before retrieving a small container. 'I'll start by getting this installed, shall I?'

A small smile creeps onto my lips. In his hand is our new video doorbell. We had ummed and ahhed about whether to get one or not. It was actually something we spoke at length about with my therapist: whether it would help or hinder my PTSD. Eventually, it was decided that the security benefits and the sense of safety that it would bring me would make it worth it, but that if ever I started down the path again of spying on the neighbours, and especially if I ever saw something that concerned me, I should talk to both Lee and my therapist straight away. It seemed a good compromise.

I go and fetch another box, a lighter one this time, while Lee faffs with the doorbell. It's a newer model this time, with extra bells and whistles that I'm not sure we really need, so the instruction manual he pulls out is novel-length. He flips through the first few pages, then swears.

'What's up?' I say as I place the box labelled 'cutlery' onto the kitchen counter.

'I'm an idiot,' Lee says.

'Well, we knew that.' I smile as I come to join him on the porch.

'I've got the doorbell itself working, but I need a screwdriver to attach it to the door. I don't suppose you know which box it might be in, do you?'

My eyes pan across the many boxes still piled up in the moving van. 'I have absolutely no idea.'

'I'll tell you what.' He places the doorbell on its side on the brick wall of our porch. 'We wanted to get some milk for tea anyway. I'll go and get some from the shop we passed. I'm sure they'll have a screwdriver.'

I almost tell him not to bother, that we don't need the doorbell installed right this second, but my craving for a good old cup of tea stops me. I watch him drive off down the road, then look again at the doorbell, still lying on its side. It feels like déjà vu as I pull my phone out and navigate to the doorbell app, but this time, when I open it, I'm greeted by a fresh, empty recordings library. I squint at the tome of instructions and follow through step-by-step, setting it up to sync with my app. When it only takes me five minutes to get everything connected, I grin, quietly pleased with myself.

With nothing else to distract me from what I actually need to be doing, I have two choices: carry more boxes from the moving van to the house, or begin to unpack some. My aching back tells me to choose the latter. I start in Mason's bedroom, as that's the room I'm most excited to get sorted. He's staying with Lee's mum while we get ourselves moved in, and I want to make sure his room is perfect for him before he arrives home. Second most important will be ensuring our wine glasses and booze are unpacked, as Priya is visiting for a bit of a housewarming slash catch up slash gossip session tonight.

I busy myself with pulling out *Star Wars* memorabilia and bedding, arranging things carefully, just like Mason would like it. I'm so engrossed in what I'm doing I barely register the knock at the door, but when I do, my stomach tightens.

It's probably just Lee. He'll have forgotten our new set of keys. Or perhaps it will be the neighbours coming to welcome us. I move down the stairs slowly, wanting to prepare myself if it is indeed the neighbours. I'm not really in the right headspace to be chatting to them just yet, but I also don't want them to think I'm rude. Just a quick hello is all that's needed. Simple. Polite.

The smile I've pasted onto my face drops when I open the door. There's no one there. My eyes drop to the front step. There, in a glass vase, is a gorgeous bouquet of flowers. Not the type you'd pick up from the corner shop. It's big and extravagant, the kind you'd see displayed proudly in a florist shop window. I scan the street, looking for any sign of who might have left them, but there's no one around. It must have been one of those flower delivery services, simply dropped off by the postman. I pick the vase up and take them into the house, placing them on the kitchen counter. There's no card.

Maybe whoever left them will have been picked up on the doorbell. It's lying on its side on the porch, so it's not going to have recorded at the best angle, but it might be just enough so that I can see which neighbour I need to thank for the flowers. I go back to the app and click through to the movement detection recordings. There's just the one: today's date, timestamped a few minutes ago. I click into it and wait for it to buffer.

The doorbell is angled too awkwardly to capture any footage of the doorstep itself or who left the flowers. It's pointing towards the street as opposed to the front of our house, and, of course, it's on its side, so I have to tilt my phone to see properly. Annoyingly, it also doesn't seem to have picked up the flower-delivery person coming to the door. What it did capture, however, was the person walking away from the house, retreating down the street.

I suck in a breath.

My eyebrows draw together. I pinch the screen and zoom in. And again.

The person walking away from the house in the footage is a woman.

A woman with long, sleek hair and a lean figure.

A woman who, despite me trying to assure myself that it's all in my head, looks exactly like Anna.

## A LETTER FROM BECCA

Dear Reader,

You made it to the end! You absolute legend. Thank you so much for diving into this book and letting my fictional chaos live rent-free in your brain for a while. I hope it gave you thrills, chills, and at least one moment where you shouted, 'WHAT?!' at the page.

If you're anything like me, you might now be wondering what to do with all your feelings (and theories). May I present an excellent solution: come and join my reader Facebook group! It's where I hang out, spill behind-the-scenes secrets, drop sneaky hints about future books, and chat with lovely readers like you who also enjoy plot twists and slightly unhinged characters.

Here's the link to join the fun: https://bit.ly/BeccaDayReaders

Also, if you'd like to be the first to hear about my new releases, you can sign up to my mailing list using the link below. Your email address will never be shared and you can unsubscribe at any time.

*www.bookouture.com/becca-day*

This book was exceptionally fun for me to write. It was one of those manuscripts where the characters just came to life on the page and led the way. As someone who thinks about *Final Destination* every time I drive on the motorway or get on a plane, I empathise with Miranda. Always seeing the worst-case scenario in every situation and worrying that it might come true can be exhausting. Luckily, I've never had the worst-case scenario actually come true (touch wood) but it does make for excellent book idea generation.

If you enjoyed *The Secret at Number 7* and could spare a moment to leave a review, I'd be so grateful. Thank you again for reading. You're officially my favourite.

Big love and bigger twists,

Becca Day

beccaday.com

facebook.com/authorbeccaday
instagram.com/authorbeccaday
x.com/authorbeccaday

# ACKNOWLEDGEMENTS

First of all, I'd like to thank caffeine. Without you, this book would still be a bullet point in a Google Doc called *Someday, Maybe*.

In all seriousness now, this is the part where I get to thank the people who made this book come to fruition, which is always the most difficult part. Yes, more difficult than writing an entire novel. I'm always so worried I'm going to leave someone out. For the record, I delivered this book AND my edits for this book to my publisher early, but the acknowledgements are being written on the day they're due. Go figure.

Let's start with my publisher, since we're on the topic. The team at Bookouture welcomed me to their ranks last year and, wow, what a journey it's been. I remember when I first got on a call with my editor, Jess Whitlum-Cooper, and she said she was a big Becca Day fan. Well, I'm a big Jess Whitlum-Cooper fan. I have absolutely adored working with Jess every step of the way, and I'm endlessly thankful for her thoughtful edits and encouragement. Of course, there are so many other people at Bookouture working tirelessly behind the scenes to make this book what it is, so thank you to Imogen Allport, Laura Deacon, Hannah Snetsinger, Jane Eastgate, and everyone else who had involvement in this project.

To my wonderful agent Emily Glenister, who is off doing the real heroic work of raising a tiny human but has promised me she will be returning to me once she has finished her maternity leave. I have video evidence of that promise, Em, and I'm not afraid to use it! Also to David Headley, who has stepped in as my agent while Emily is off. Thank you for making the transition so smooth.

To my husband, thank you for tolerating my complete emotional collapse every time I write a novel, and for keeping me sane when the 'business' side of being an author stresses me out. Thank you also for being my top cheerleader. Less thanks for the moment directly after I sent off the manuscript to my publisher when you said, 'But what about the plot hole in Chapter 4?' That was just mean.

To my two daughters, thank you for reminding me to take breaks, usually by sitting on my keyboard or asking me for another snack. Élise – just a few more years and I'll let you read one of my books.

To Mum, Grandad, Dad, Debs, Isaac, Molly, Colette, Jonathan, Grace, Thalia, Elijah, and the rest of my family – thank you for pretending to listen to me rant about fictional people as though they were real.

Thanks to Jasmine, Shelly, Pippa, Ali, Rob, Harrison, and Sandra, for supporting me even though I disappear for months on end into the word vortex. I promise I'll come out and be a normal human with a social life now. Maybe. Also to Lauren North, Graham Bartlett, Eve Ainsworth, Phil Viner, and all the authors I'm lucky enough to call friends.

Massive love to my reader group Becca Day's Psychological Misfits on Facebook, whose enthusiasm for my books keep me going when writer's block rears its ugly head, and to the Psychological Thriller Readers Facebook group, who kept *The Woman in the Cabin* in the top fifty for months on end.

To the amazing people at Jericho Writers – colleagues who I'm pleased to call friends. What other job can you come to a meeting and spend twenty minutes discussing your plot holes? And to the members – as Head of Membership, I am honoured to get the chance to cheer other writers on, which, in turn, reminds me to listen to my own pep talks.

To Anna – before you left Jericho Writers you asked that I use your name in my next novel. I didn't forget!

Finally, to you, dear reader, for picking up this book. I hope your neighbours are nice, sane, normal people with minimal skeletons in closets.

## PUBLISHING TEAM

**Turning a manuscript into a book requires the efforts of many people. The publishing team at Bookouture would like to acknowledge everyone who contributed to this publication.**

### Audio
Alba Proko
Melissa Tran
Sinead O'Connor

### Commercial
Lauren Morrissette
Hannah Richmond
Imogen Allport

### Cover design
The Brewster Project

### Data and analysis
Mark Alder
Mohamed Bussuri

### Editorial
Jess Whitlum-Cooper
Imogen Allport

**Copyeditor**
Jane Eastgate

**Proofreader**
Becca Allen

**Marketing**
Alex Crow
Melanie Price
Occy Carr
Ciara Rosney
Martyna Młynarska

**Operations and distribution**
Marina Valles
Stephanie Straub
Joe Morris

**Production**
Hannah Snetsinger
Mandy Kullar
Ria Clare
Nadia Michael

**Publicity**
Kim Nash
Noelle Holten
Jess Readett
Sarah Hardy

**Rights and contracts**
Peta Nightingale
Richard King
Saidah Graham

**RAISING READERS**
Books Build Bright Futures

Dear Reader,

We'd love your attention for one more page to tell you about the crisis in children's reading, and what we can all do.

Studies have shown that reading for fun is the **single biggest predictor of a child's future life chances** – more than family circumstance, parents' educational background or income. It improves academic results, mental health, wealth, communication skills, ambition and happiness.

The number of children reading for fun is in rapid decline. Young people have a lot of competition for their time, and a worryingly high number do not have a single book at home.

Hachette works extensively with schools, libraries and literacy charities, but here are some ways we can all raise more readers:

- Reading to children for just 10 minutes a day makes a difference
- Don't give up if children aren't regular readers – there will be books for them!

- Visit bookshops and libraries to get recommendations
- Encourage them to listen to audiobooks
- Support school libraries
- Give books as gifts

There's a lot more information about how to encourage children to read on our websites: **www.RaisingReaders.co.uk** and **www.JoinRaisingReaders.com**.

Thank you for reading.

www.ingramcontent.com/pod-product-compliance
Lightning Source LLC
LaVergne TN
LVHW041622060526
838200LV00040B/1387